Honey Flava

ALSO BY ZANE

Dear G-Spot: Straight Talk about Sex and Love

Love Is Never Painless

Afterburn

The Sisters of APF: The Indoctrination of Soror Ride Dick

Nervous

Skyscraper

The Heat Seekers

Gettin' Buck Wild: Sex Chronicles II

The Sex Chronicles: Shattering the Myth

Shame on It All

Addicted

EDITED BY ZANE

Succulent: Chocolate Flava II
The Eroticanoir.com Anthology

Caramel Flava: The Eroticanoir.com Anthology

Chocolate Flava: The Eroticanoir.com Anthology

Breaking the Cycle

Blackgentlemen.com

Sistergirls.com

Purple Panties

ZANE PRESENTS

THE EROTICANOIR.COM ANTHOLOGY

Honey Flava

ATRIA BOOKS

NEW YORK LONDON TORONTO SYDNEY

COPYRIGHT NOTICES

*This book is dedicated to all the people in the world
who do not engage in boundaries when it comes to love,
who realize that passion is universal,
and who recognize that every day is truly a gift.*

CONTENTS

INTRODUCTION

Once again, I have had the immense pleasure of editing a marvelous anthology of erotica. It has been a great experience to be able to showcase the talents of so many others. As with *Caramel Flava,* I decided that it was important to cross the color lines of love and romance and do a collection full of vibrant Asian characters and a kaleidoscope of other races.

Nationality is one of the few things in life we cannot choose, like gender. That is why racism itself is such a foolish thing. Passion, sensuality, and love are truly universal, and life is too short to spend it worrying about things we cannot change. I loved the submissions for *Honey Flava* because it opened me up to another culture. Now I plan to do some traveling, both to the Orient and Latin America. The world is a big place, a huge melting pot of expression.

I hope that you will enjoy this collection of erotica as much as you have enjoyed all the rest. While all of this, editing anthologies, has been a fun experience, I am a novel writer and that is what I plan to go back to.

I appreciate and love all of the contributors and hope that

your being showcased in these national bestsellers has helped your careers. Thanks for sharing your talents with me, and the world.

Most of all, thanks for the love and support shown by my loyal readers. Without you, I could not exist. Over the years, we have bonded through emails, book signings, and letters. I look forward to the next ten years.

If you are not on my email list, please send a blank email to Eroticanoir-subscribe@topica.com to be added immediately. Visit me on www.eroticanoir.com or check out my provocative blog at www.myspace.com/zaneland. Lastly, make sure that you watch *Zane's Sex Chronicles* on Cinemax every week. It will get your juices flowing and warm up your nights; possibly even inspire you to get a little freaky.

Peace and many blessings,
Zane

Honey Flava

The Meaning of Zhuren

JEAN YOUNG

ᘏ

WHEN DIRK ASKED JEAN how to say *master* in Chinese the first time they dated, she answered pleasantly, *"Zhuren."* Little did she know what *zhuren* would mean to her in the coming days.

Dirk was a tall, handsome, thirty-year-old man. His charm and alluring appeal captured Jean's heart from the moment they met. Soon, their romance heated up and became physical within a couple of dates. Three weeks after they met, Jean asked curiously about the ropes Dirk always carried with him in a black duffel bag. "Are they for rock climbing?"

"No, they are not for climbing. They are . . ." He looked at Jean with a teasing smile. "For fucking."

"Oh!" Jean was stunned and intrigued. She remembered seeing pictures of women being tied up and how such images turned her on. "Perhaps," she said, blushing, "we could try it one day."

"Why wait? Let's do it now."

Jean stared at him for a brief moment before she nodded. Her face lit up with excitement while her heart pounded anxiously.

"Good. I'm pleased you'd like to try. Remember," he spoke as he took out the ropes, "don't say no. It doesn't mean anything. If you want me to stop, say a safe word." He looked around the bedroom and pointed to the Chinese painting. "Say *peacock* if you want me to stop the whole thing. And say . . ." He looked up again. "*Crane,* if you want me to skip whatever I am doing. *Crane* is the caution word and *peacock* is the safe word. Got it?"

Jean nodded nervously.

"Don't worry." As if he heard her unspoken words, he assured her, "It seems you are going to be helpless and out of control. But you are in control, with the caution word and safe word. Just don't expect me to stop when you say no. I won't. Oh, call me *zhuren* when you address me, each and every time. If not, you will be punished. Understand?"

Jean was surprised he remembered the Chinese word for "master."

Bang. He spanked her hip with his right hand. "What did I tell you? Address me as *zhuren* every time I talk to you. Understand?"

Jean was shocked. Even though it wasn't too painful, it did hurt. "Yes," she said hurriedly, "yes, *zhuren.*"

"Good. Be a good doll." He took out a black blindfold from his bag. When he looked up, he saw Jean was watching him with wild eyes. "Another thing," he whispered as he put the blindfold over her eyes. "Don't look at me directly. I am your master. Lower your head when you talk to me. Never look at your master in his eyes, unless he asks you to. Understand?"

"Yes, *zhuren.*"

"Good doll. Remember, before I release you, you are my doll and I am your master. Now, take off your clothes. Slowly."

Obediently, Jean followed his instruction. Soon, she stood naked in front of him.

"Now, wiggle your body. In a sexy way. Like a call girl."

She wanted to protest, but knew better not to. Reluctantly, she wiggled her body.

"Good." Dirk sounded pleased. He grabbed her breasts and twisted her nipples in his hands. Jean wiggled more, out of pain.

"Yes, good girl. I like the way you twist your body. You . . ." he whispered, "you turn me on." He pinched her nipples a little harder. Hearing her whimper and watching her struggle, he smiled and said, "It's time to reward my good doll." With these words, he let go of her breasts, scooped her up off her feet, and threw her onto the bed nearby.

Jean cried out. But before she could make another sound, a ball with small holes was stuck into her mouth.

"Say *peacock*."

"Pea . . . cock." She barely made out her own word.

"Say *crane*."

That was even harder to pronounce clearly.

"Okay, I can still hear you." He pinched her left nipple, this time quite hard. Jean cried out with her muffled voice. "You forgot to say *zhuren* again. Remember, every single time you open your mouth, you have to say *zhuren*."

What am I doing? she wondered. But her curiosity kept her going. Well, to be fair, she liked the excitement, just not the pain. She had little tolerance for any pain. How could she allow someone to inflict pain on her deliberately?

Before she answered her own question, she felt a rope being tied on her right wrist. It turned several times around her wrist before being knotted to secure the tie. Then her arm was stretched toward the upper-right corner and was soon securely tied to the rod of the headboard. One by one, all her arms and legs were tied up.

When he finished, Dirk stood at the end of the bed checking his piece of work. In front of him, on the bed, Jean's naked body was tied up—spread-eagled, with only a blindfold and a mouthpiece. He watched for a few seconds, marveled about her beauty and his own work. A satisfied smile curled up his lips. "Now it's time to give my good doll some reward."

He picked up a vibrator from his bag. "When I say it is a punishment, I know I will enjoy it, you won't. But when I say it is a reward, I know both of us will like it. Or at least I think you will like it as well." With his left hand opening the upper part of her vagina, Dirk turned on the bunny-eared vibrator and placed it on Jean's clitoris.

Jean jerked at once. As a normal adult, she had masturbated from time to time. The pleasure of touching herself down there was enormous. When she was a conservative teenager, she thought it was a terrible thing to do. Yet, even then, she couldn't stop pleasing herself that way. Often she did it with shame and regret. Now she knew it was a healthy and normal way to please one's self, but she had still never touched herself with anything other than her finger.

The pleasure was so intense that she thought she couldn't even handle it. She moaned and struggled in her bondage, trying to get away from the vibrator. However, Dirk was prepared for her struggle. He placed his left arm on her stomach and leaned his body on her to stop her movement. Meanwhile, his left hand kept on spreading her vagina, and his right hand pressed the vibrator firmly on her clitoris.

"No! No! No!" Jean cried out through her mouthpiece. Her whole body tensed. Sweat appeared all over her body. Her head tilted backward and swayed from side to side. She wanted to get away from the intense pleasure. It was too much for her. She wanted to put her legs together to reduce the intensity, but obviously it wasn't possible. The bonds he tied were so tight; she couldn't move an inch. She felt so helpless under his weight and with all the bondage. Such helplessness seemed to intensify her experience. The excitement and the pleasure became an unbearable torture. Her cry grew louder as Dirk continuously and mercilessly forced the vibrator on her.

Soon, she felt she was going to explode. Her legs stretched rigidly. Violently her whole body jerked. Her clitoris was red and swollen. Body fluids gushed out of her vagina. She could even hear her own wet noise accompanying the vibrating sound. "Oh, God!" she screamed as she was on the verge of coming.

But then, it stopped! Jean couldn't believe Dirk turned off the vibrator right before she came. "No!" she screamed again. This time she meant for him not to stop the vibrator. She wanted the vibrator placed back on her. She desperately wanted to come. The pressure had built up so much inside her that she needed to let it explode.

At first she thought Dirk probably didn't know she hadn't yet come. "Please!" She was hoping that her plea would give him the right message. But soon she realized she was wrong. Dirk did know. He'd stopped it right before she came, on purpose! Jean felt hot and cold at the same time when she heard him say, "That's all for the reward. As a good doll, you shouldn't come before your master, unless I want you to. Understand?"

Jean was breathless. Her body was burning with desire. She wanted to come, to release the intense pressure inside her, to end her torment. "Please!" she begged, hoping to move him, wishing to receive his mercy.

"Wrong." Dirk lifted up her left hip and spanked her again. "How many times do I have to tell you to address me as *zhuren*?"

Tears welled up in her eyes.

"Now," he said as he moved up, straddled her neck, and set his body weight lightly on her chest. "It's time to give me a reward, for being your good master."

With the blindfold, Jean couldn't see what he was doing, but she guessed from the way he sat on her. "No, please!" She shook her head in protest when Dirk rubbed his penis on her cheeks.

Although she was twenty-five, Jean had never experienced oral sex before. Somehow, it seemed so intimate and intimidating to have a penis in her mouth rather than in her vagina.

She took a deep breath and then shut her lips tightly after Dirk removed the mouthpiece. *Perhaps it is time to use the caution word.* But then her curiosity and her sense of adventure prevented her from saying so. Her fear of the unknown and her concern for discomfort and embarrassment seemed to weigh as much as her curiosity and her willingness to experience new things. She hesitated. The split-second hesitation took away her chance to choose.

While his knees clamped her head in place, Dirk pinched Jean's nose. As she opened her mouth for air, he shoved his large, hardened penis into her mouth decisively and forcefully.

Jean made a muffled noise of "No." But before she could say anything else, Dirk thrust his penis farther, reaching for her throat. It made her gag. Tears seeped out the corners of her eyes. She wished that Dirk would see her tears and then perhaps treat her differently, with care and mercy. But either he didn't see her tears because of the blindfold or he didn't care; Dirk continued taking his pleasure. He pulled his penis out, then thrust it into her mouth again, repeatedly, in a moderate rhythm.

After the initial shock and a few more gags, Jean calmed down a bit. Having a hardened penis thrusting in and out of her mouth seemed extremely erotic and even became enjoyable.

"Suck it," Dirk instructed. Jean followed without any hesitation this time. She was eager to please him. Hearing his groan as she fervently sucked on his penis excited her. She knew she wet the bed even more. How she wished that he would enter her body, now! She was so ready for him.

As if he heard what she thought, Dirk moaned and thrust a couple of more times before he forced himself out. He moved down and knelt between her spread legs.

Oh, please. Give it to me, Jean pleaded loudly in her mind. *I can't stand it anymore. Take me!*

Dirk didn't seem as on fire as Jean. He lifted up her hips and shoved a pillow underneath so that her vagina was more open and easily accessible to him. Then, with one hand opening up her vagina, Dirk placed his penis at the opening, barely touching her.

This is it! Jean wiggled her body, lifting toward him, welcoming him to enter her.

However, Dirk didn't seem to be in any hurry. "Say, 'Fuck me.' " He sounded so calm, but cold.

"No!" Jean whined. She had never used this word in her life. That was one word she'd decided never to use. "Please, *zhuren,*" she said pitifully, "don't make me say it."

"Good. You remembered to address me correctly. For that I will reward you." He massaged her clitoris. "Now, say, 'Fuck me.' Be a good doll."

"No, *zhuren,*" she whimpered again.

"Well, it is your choice." Dirk teased her by moving his penis in a circular motion at the opening of her vagina. "I'm not going to fuck you down here if you don't ask me to. I can fuck your mouth again. I don't mind coming that way. Is that what you want?"

"No!" Tears leaked out from the blindfold.

This time Dirk saw it. "Oh, poor doll." He wiped her tears as he said, "You look so adorable when you cry. So, have you made up your mind? I can't wait for too long. If you want me to fuck you down here, you have to say it. Now! Otherwise it'll be too late. I know you will regret it if I come in your mouth."

Jean knew then that Dirk wouldn't show her any mercy. She had no choice. Not having vaginal sex with Dirk at this point would be a torture to her. She would do anything to avoid that, including saying the word she would never say. She shook her head and smacked her lips briefly before she said, "Fuck me, please, *zhuren.*" Her voice was barely audible.

"Speak up."

"Fuck me, please, *zhuren.*"

"I will be more than happy to fuck you." Dirk grinned in satisfaction. "This is what a good master should do—train his doll to ask for what he wants." He laughed as he spread her vagina with one hand and guided his penis inside her with the other.

Jean cried out in ecstasy. What pleasure! Finally he was deep inside her. *Oh, God. Take me. Move. Thrust. Do it!* she kept on demanding loudly in her mind.

Even then, Dirk wasn't in any hurry. Slowly, he pulled his penis out, leaving Jean breathless for a split second before he inserted it again. Slowly and repeatedly, Dirk took his time to thrust his entire penis deep inside her and then take it all out. But before long, not only Jean was breathless and burning in desire; Dirk was on fire, too. His thrusts became faster, and he no longer pulled his penis entirely out.

As he moved quicker inside her, Jean moaned louder. For the first time since they'd started playing, she felt their bodies in tune with each other. Her moan wasn't because of pain, but because of intense pleasure. A sweet smile radiated on her face as she welcomed every thrust from Dirk.

Dirk saw her sexy smile and wanted to see more, so he removed her blindfold. "Look at me. Look at my eyes. Please!" This time he sounded gentle and warm.

Jean opened her eyes. As she looked into Dirk's downward gaze, she felt she was struck by lightning. She had to close her eyes briefly before she dared to open them again. He looked so different from what she'd imagined all along when they started playing. No longer a cold and demanding master, he smiled at her so warmly and was as out of breath as she was. His gaze was intimate. He seemed utterly pleased and satisfied.

They stared at each other for a few minutes before his smile disappeared. His thrusts became so fast and mighty powerful. All the muscles on his body tensed. Jean could even see the vein on his forehead bulging. His sweat dripped on her face. His face turned serious, even painful. She knew it was time. How she wished she could hold him! After all the teasing and the pain, he did give her the ecstasy and the ultimate high she had never experienced before. But all she could do was lift up her hips a little more to welcome his final thrust and cry out with him when he finally came inside her.

Dirk fell limp on her. They lay there a few minutes, in each other's sweat. Finally, he lifted up his head and kissed her gently on her lips. Hungrily and appreciatively she returned his kiss.

They kissed a couple more minutes before he pushed himself up. One by one, he untied the ropes on her arms and legs and took time to check and massage the bond areas. "You've been a good doll. Just need a little more training."

Jean shivered. She didn't think she could handle any more. Not today.

"Kneel," he commanded, as cold as ice again.

Jean didn't know what to do exactly. She sat up immediately and knelt down on the bed.

Dirk moved to one side of the bed. "When I say *kneel,* you kneel in front of your master."

Jean moved quickly to face him.

"Good. And when I say *present,* you put your hands behind your head and open up your legs to me. Present."

Jean followed. Now that her head was up, she closed her eyes to avoid his gaze.

"Good job." Dirk was pleased. He moved a little closer to Jean and placed his right hand between her legs.

Jean started to moan again as Dirk stroked her vagina.

"You've done well," Dirk whispered. "There is still lots to learn, but for now . . ." He thrust his finger in and out of her a few more times before he kissed her again and whispered in her ear, "I release you."

Jean took a deep breath and launched up to hug him. They embraced for a long while. Then, she let go of him. With a cry of relief, she plopped backward onto the bed. "I had no idea," she commented in between her breaths, "about the meaning of *zhuren,* until today."

Dirk burst into a pleased laugh and went into the bathroom.

Photo Shoot

MITCH

ༀ

THE LIGHTS WERE BRIGHT, like in an operating room, but it was a photo shoot for *Play Thing,* the hottest exotic-modeling magazine on the market. Background and foreground scenery with an Asian motif was moved from place to place in the square, warehouselike room. Technicians were rats racing with cords, lights, and furniture. Camera assistants were setting up cherry pickers and tripods, and checking on film and filters as on a Spielberg set.

It was almost 9:30 a.m. on Friday a week prior to Christmas. Lu Xun, the elderly but brilliant photographer, came into the room, crying in his Chinese accent, "Are we ready on the set?" Randy watched a parade of women moving to the middle of the room from his far right. A willowy female, robed in white, at the center of the procession was directed to a chair. She sat, and the other ladies fussed with her face and hair. "Ladies," intoned Lu impatiently.

Finished, the ensemble moved to the side out of camera range. The figure on the chair stood and shed her robe. She was average in height, curvaceous, and wore a white bathing suit splattered with purple; the top was held in place with narrow straps and swooped to a point near her navel, exposing the insides of large breasts; a thong bottom bypassed her rounded hips and derriere, revealing sculpted legs. Black hair hung loose to her waist. Her smile was dazzling, like that of a Kewpie doll with bow-shaped, mauve-colored lips.

"Fabulous, Mali, you and that suit were made for my cameras; now move to the Chinese lanterns." Lu indicated with his left hand and started taking pictures as she sauntered toward the scene.

Randy stood at the back wall; he was writing an article for *Still Photo Magazine,* and Play Figure management had arranged for him to observe and interview those involved. He was in his late twenties, stood more than six feet tall, had striking facial features, and wore his all-white hair in a neat shoulder-length shag cut. Two silver chains embossed with the yin-yang lay loosely on his hairy chest between the folds of a red, long-sleeved shirt open halfway down his chest. Faded black jeans circled his narrow waist and tucked into dark, ankle-high boots with short, one-inch heels. He stood comfortably near the concrete wall and occasionally wrote a comment in his Mead spiral-bound notebook.

"Fabulous, Mali, you're a jewel to work with. Now change while the set is rearranged. Remember, people, it may be December but this session is for a summer issue. Give me more light and more motion."

Mali's entourage hurried to the dressing room. Randy observed her graceful walk and took additional note of her physical charms; he memorized the details of her body.

During the change the stage director stopped and asked Randy if he had any questions.

"Who selected the model?"

"Play Figure's casting department."

"Who decides what outfits are modeled?"

"Prada, they provide the outfits."

"Who selected the scenery?"

"Prada. It's for a special line for the Asian market."

"Is every shoot as scripted and structured as this?'

"With Lu Xun, yes."

"Are the photos going to be used for other purposes?'

"Probably, they belong to Prada."

"When will the layout be completed and will copies be available for my article?"

"Yes, Prada would like the exposure in *Still Photo Magazine*."

"Thanks for your cooperation. When can I interview the staff and technicians?"

"Anytime there's a break and it doesn't interfere with the shoot."

Mali and her company returned. She was wearing a sleek, black, one-piece suit with a plunging neckline and another thong bottom. A white bandanna around her forehead set off her ivory complexion and her dark brown eyes; her hair was pulled back in a single strand with three white coils separating it into four equal parts. Lu directed her to a scene of the Great Wall, lights were adjusted, a fan whirled, and Mali posed. Pictures were taken from a variety of positions. The scenery was changed to Shangri-la, the lights dimmed, smoke filtered across the scene like an early morning fog, and Lu, moving with the grace of a bird in flight, directed the poses and filled the room with flashes.

* * *

During a break Mali was sitting drinking Gatorade, and staring at the dirty old man who had been lurking, like a barracuda, against the back wall of the studio. However, up close he was not the same, and his effect on her was sexually arousing.

"Mali . . . Mali . . . Mali . . ." Breaking out of her trance, she heard her name. "Mali, I'd like you to met Randy Newsome. He's a freelance writer working on an article for *Still Photo Magazine*. He'd like to speak with you," Jerry said.

"Okay, yeah, sit down, Randy. It is Randy, isn't it?"

"Yes, Randy. God, you're beautiful," he said, taking her hand in his.

"You're not bad yourself," she said, squeezing his hand and ogling his handsome, tanned face, "but you look much older at a distance."

"My hair fools a lot of people," he said, smiling. "I'm gathering material for an article about the shoot, but all I want to do is make love to you."

"Why don't you tell me what you really want?" she asked. "Is your hair natural?"

"Yes, but I really want you to go to bed with me. It started turning when I was eleven, and by the time I got to college, it had changed completely. My nickname is Whitie. When did you start modeling?"

"*Whitie* is appropriate, but I like *Randy* better. I started modeling in high school. This is my first shot at the big time, modeling for *Play Thing*. Is that your aftershave?" she asked, placing her other hand on his.

"Thanks, I prefer *Randy,* too; I'm wearing Old Spice. Why are you modeling?"

"The possibility of becoming a supermodel—you know, fame and fortune."

"Will you sleep with me?" he asked as he covered her second hand with his.

"Will it make me famous?"

"No." He hesitated. "But wait, the article I'm writing could make you famous."

"Okay"—she smiled—"if that's the case, you can take me to lunch."

"Does that mean we can make love?"

"No, it means I need meat after the rigors of a session like this."

"I have meat," he said, smiling.

"Protein, protein, protein as in food." She laughed. "I like your sense of humor."

"Is that all you like?"

"No, but we can talk about that during lunch."

"Great, I'll meet you here at noon. I have interviews the rest of the morning."

Mali and Randy were ushered to their seats at the Elite Epicurean, one of the oldest and best restaurants in Chicago. Its high ceilings, large windows, and early-twentieth-century wooden furniture had a nostalgic look, even in winter. Mali removed her coat, revealing a formfitting brown sweater that would make Pamela Anderson jealous. Randy, who was already horny, took a deep breath and raised his hand for a waiter.

They ordered soup and sandwiches from a tall male server wearing a white apron.

"I see you're wearing yin-yang medallions?"

"Taoism was one of my favorite subjects in college; I'm a convert."

"What practices do you follow?"

"I read the *Tao Te Ching* daily, meditate, belly breathe, and follow traditional sexual practices," he said, staring into her eyes. "I'd like to introduce you to some of them."

She smiled. "I'll have to admit you have tenacity and an unusual approach, but I seldom meet a man who doesn't want to sleep with me."

"Will you?" he asked as their food arrived.

They fell silent and smiled as the waiter expertly arranged their food on the table.

"I haven't thought about anything else since you walked on the set."

"The potato soup is good, although it's too hot," she said.

"My cock is telling me how hot you are."

"I wet my panties when I saw you up close, but that doesn't mean I'm going to sleep with you."

Encouraged, he said, "This article I'm writing about the shoot is going to include your sexiest poses and introduce you to an untapped market. Now will you go to bed with me?"

Lowering her eyes, she reached across the table, placed her hands on his, and flipped her hair to one side. "I have an itch between my big toes. Is there a Taoist solution for such a problem?"

A big smile spread across Randy's face. "I believe there's an old-fashioned remedy for that specific malady," he said excitedly.

"Is it something I can sink my teeth into?" she asked, staring shamelessly at him.

"That's not exactly what I had in mind, but it could be part of the process."

* * *

Randy kept a suite of rooms at the Rubicon, a residential hotel, a short distance from the restaurant. Inside the sitting room they kissed with tongues of fire. Her coat dropped to the floor, and they clutched each other in seeming desperation. Her sweater was over her head and arms when he unfastened her bra and pulled it from beneath her pendulous breasts. He stepped back to admire the ivory beauty of her twin curves before he bent and kissed her pink nipples.

Sweeping her from the floor, he carried her into the bedroom, turning on the lights with his arm. "Are you in a hurry?" she asked, removing the sweater from her arms and hands.

He sat her down and they undressed.

"Damn, you're beautiful and built for pleasure," he said.

"You're as hairy as a bear, and I've been dying to meet a cock like yours."

He sat on the bed holding his bulging, blue-veined erection. "Here's your chance."

Laughing, she dropped to her knees. "I could take a bite, but I won't," she said, looking up at him.

"I'm glad to hear that," he said, stoking himself.

She licked pre-cum from the tip, kissed it, took the head into her mouth, swirled her tongue around it, then licked the length of his shaft. He shuddered when she swallowed as much as she could. Waves of pleasure surged though his body as she plunged up and down his cock with firm lips.

"Did I tell you I have a breast fetish?" he said as he bent over her and stroked, fondled, and manipulated her dangling flesh until her nipples were rigid. The soft, smooth texture and weight of her hanging tits calmed the itching of his palms but further aroused his emotions.

He stood her up, and they kissed with tongues dancing like whirling dervishes. The taste and texture was intoxicating, and their excitement rose. Holding her upright, he buried his head in her cleavage. He kissed and licked between her mounds until she was soaking wet, and then like a kitten he took a nipple and areola into his mouth. Licking, tugging, and sucking one breast, he manipulated the other nipple with his hand.

She uttered a low moan, swaying to and fro to increase and decrease the tension on her nipple. "Oh, you've got a wonderful mouth."

When he changed breasts, he toyed with her moist labia, which were spreading as she was stimulated. He inserted his finger into her pussy, searching for her G-spot. She arched her back and moaned when he found it.

"Oh, Randy, that's wonderful."

He changed positions and plunged his finger into and out of her canal. Her juices were flowing, her breathing was fast and shallow, and her nipples were aflame with passion.

His finger sought her clitoris. When he found her mound of pleasure, he gently manipulated it in all directions. She went rigid and cried, "Yes, yes, yes," as she climaxed. He continued to finger her and suck on her breast until she pulled back and said, "Oh God, oh God, oh God, the feeling's fantastic, but I'm ready for bigger and better things. I've never had this many orgasms."

He sat her on the edge of the bed, spread her legs, and dropped between them. Picking up her legs, he placed them over his shoulders and nuzzled her pubic hair.

"What are you doing?" She said nothing further as his tongue was like a snake searching for its prey. She moaned as he lifted her ass from the bed, pulled her toward him, and used his tongue as a rapier to dart back and forth around her clit. She squirmed in delight, and her cries of pleasure increased until a loud scream coincided with another orgasm. He continued to drill her clit until she pushed his head back and said, "Stop, stop, stop, that feels so good it hurts. Now I want your cock. You promised to soothe the itch between my big toes."

Smiling, he took her by the ankles, spread her legs, and placed his dripping cock onto her pubic hair. Hesitating for a moment, he stared at her pleasure-contorted face, and heaving, perspiring breasts. He leaned forward and slipped the head of his cock into her pussy. He could feel her vaginal walls separate as he entered because of the tight fit. She gasped as he stretched her to new widths. "Oh, I've never been this full," she said with widened eyes.

That first moment of encasement for him was sacred; he lingered in its glory. Widening her legs, he stroked her moist, pulsating haven. She squealed in delight. Occasionally he stopped to survey her elegant expression and bountiful breasts. Her eyes closed as she concentrated on her physical and emotional ardor. He brought her legs together and placed them on his chest with her feet beside his head. She tightened around him, and their stimulations increased. Guttural sounds escaped her as she climaxed. Using his legs, he pumped into and out of her. He was on fire, his cock throbbing as he pulled and pushed over and over.

His Taoist discipline enabled him to delay his climax by belly breathing and concentrating on his mantra, *Searl-sie*. He varied his thrusting motions from slow to fast, short to long, rhythmic to random, pumping her while massaging and gorging on her nipples. She climaxed with moans of pleasure. She experienced orgasms, howling in bliss, as he kneaded her clitoris and rammed

her with abandon. He kept her in an almost continuous orgasmic state.

She responded to his every touch and action. She arched her
back to meet his thrusts, moved her pelvis in small and large
circles, and wiggled her hips from side to side. She grabbed his
hands, massaged his arms, ran her fingers over his face and neck,
and rubbed the hair on his chest. This was a new experience for
Randy; he was used to passive partners.

As he ground into her, she countered in kind. Looking down
on her incredible form, he realized he was approaching en-
lightenment. He felt an electric charge of passion surge from his
scrotum through his penis. Accelerating his movements he jack-
hammered her until with a cry of ecstasy—"Aaaagh"—he exploded and filled her with fluid.

"Ooooh, ooooh, ooooh," she cried as he spurted into her
over and over. His continuous spasms brought them to tears. He
stood belly breathing, knees shaking, fatigued and satisfied with
his earth-shattering release and her response. Amazed, he stared
at the slowly disappearing aura surrounding her head.

When he was flaccid, they dried themselves with a towel.
They lay facing each other in the middle of the bed covered with
a sheet. When their breathing returned to normal, she asked,
"Can we talk? Did we just experience some form of magic?"

"Yes," he said, "the world moved for me. That was the most
awesome orgasm I've ever experienced."

"Thank God you said that because I lost count of my orgasms."

Randy woke before Mali. After he showered, he put on a robe
and went to his laptop and composed his story for *Still Photo*.

After printing a copy of the conclusion in a size 20 font, he taped it to the mirror in the bathroom.

CONCLUSION

Prada's Asian summer fashion line is stunning, but clothing details will be found in other sources, because the objective of this article was the filming process. The management of Play Figure provided the best camera equipment and personnel available. The four-hour session was designed to produce the highest-quality still photographs possible. The organization and planning of the process was choreographed like a Broadway musical. The chief photographer and set director, along with a wide variety of technicians, worked as effectively and efficiently as an automated assembly line. However, the star of the day, the figure that added spice to the photographs and clothing line, was the lovely, voluptuous Mali Chun. Prada's exotic Asian styles may sweep the summer fashion market, but they have also propelled a young lady toward the top of the list of supermodels.

Calling room service, he ordered fruit, club sandwiches, coffee, and chocolate mousse. Sitting on the couch, he watched the muted TV while thinking about his life and the gorgeous female lying in his bed. He was living the good life: good pay; traveling the world; mixing with the economic, social, and political elites; and having access to some of the best-looking females in the world. He was having his brains fucked out regularly. However, he knew he had found something with Mali. He was now aware that he wasn't so sure he was living the good life.

He heard the water running in the bathroom and waited with anticipation. Soft footfalls approached the back of the couch.

"Randy," he heard his name called in a sweet singsong voice, "when did you write this?"

"While you were sleeping."

"It's wonderful. I can't believe the last two sentences."

"They're true."

Mali walked to the front of the couch. She was wearing his bathrobe. It was open in the front. She allowed it to drop, revealing her magnificence.

"You're trying to make me famous," she said, bending to kiss him.

Her melons dangled provocatively in front of him. As he accepted her lips, his hands cupped the flesh that calmed the itching of his palms; he was instantly hard. "I was planning on this being a one-night stand," he said, "but I've changed my mind."

"Am I worth two nights?" she asked, smiling as she straddled his legs and pushed her breasts into his face.

"I'm being serious here."

"So am I," she said as she rose, guiding his cock into her.

He groaned at the pleasure of her formfitting flesh sliding over him. Holding her upright, he stared into her face. Before he could speak, she placed her finger over his lips and said, "You were wonderful this afternoon. I've never had an experience like that. Can we do it again?"

"On one condition."

"What?"

"You move in with me."

Wickedly, she smiled at him and said, "This is my answer." She lifted a nipple to his mouth, and using her haunches, she pummeled him.

He suckled on the rosebud of her nipple and arched his back to elevate himself farther into her. Switching sides, he helped her move with his hands on her hips.

"Ooom, you're good," she sighed, "keep that up."

As she moved relentlessly on his cock, he said, "I'm serious. I've only known you a few hours, but I don't want to give you up. I don't want to think about other guys being with you. I want you for myself."

"You've got me spindled. What else can I say?" she said with rapid, shallow breaths.

"Say yes."

"Only if you give it to me right now."

"I can't in this position."

"Let's change then."

He pushed her off, turned her around, and entered her from behind. "Hold on to the couch," he said as he rammed into her fast and hard. He was lost in the sensations of the friction between them, and wave after wave of pleasure moved from his scrotum through his cock.

Mali was moaning and pushing her pussy at him. "Randy, Randy, Randy, give it to me, give it to me," she groaned.

Holding her by the hips, he plunged into and out of her as rapidly as he could. Over and over, he thrust; he could feel the heat rising in his body.

"I'm cumming!" she screamed, "I can't wait any longer, fuck me!"

Like NASCAR at the starting line, he accelerated his strokes until he passed his point of no return. Normally, he would delay, delay, delay, but her command and the ecstasy was too much for him, and he exploded like a blown engine. He ejected hot sperm in a torrid flow of fluid and passion and was rewarded by Mali's scream: "Oh God, oh God, oh God, Randy, you fuck like a Chinese god. Yes, yes, yes, I'll move in with you!"

Emma's Cricket Lesson

ANNA BLACK

ॐ

HE WAS THE HANDSOMEST man sitting at the hotel bar.

Emma frowned. Scratch that. He was the *only* man sitting at the hotel bar. But that did not undo how fine he was. But it wasn't his gorgeous face or his sexy body Emma was interested in.

She frowned. Scratch that. She *was* interested in his gorgeous face and sexy body. Very much so. But not right now.

What had her attention was that he was avidly watching the bar's television, and on the screen, men were playing cricket. Or at least she assumed they were playing cricket. Emma knew as much about cricket as she knew about thermonuclear physics. But, between now and tomorrow morning, she needed to learn about the game or risk blowing her career as a talent agent before it even got started.

She rose from her seat and walked over to the handsome, cricket-watching man. His eyes were glued to the television.

Emma glanced at the screen. All she knew about cricket was that it was as popular in India as baseball was in the United States.

She cleared her throat. "Excuse me?"

He didn't turn around. Emma reached over to touch his shoulder, but he suddenly turned and looked at her. From a distance his eyes had looked hazel, but she saw now that not only were they hazel but green and what looked like gold. Never in her life had she seen such striking eyes.

"Sorry about that." His Indian accent was lighter than that of most of the people she had encountered since arriving in Bangalore. "Didn't mean to be rude."

Emma smiled. "I'm the one who should be apologizing. I didn't mean to interrupt the game." She shook her head. "Scratch that. I did mean to interrupt."

His smiled widened. "How may I assist you, Ms. . . . ?" He raised a brow inquiringly.

"Emma. Emma Edwards."

He inclined his head. "Sanjay Kumar."

She gestured at the empty seat next to his. "May I?"

He nodded and Emma sat down.

"Now, what can I do for you, Ms. Edwards?"

She looked up at the television screen. "I was wondering if you could teach me about cricket." She glanced nervously at Sanjay. "That is cricket, right?"

He laughed. "Yes, it's cricket. Why do you want me to teach you about it?"

"I'm a talent agent. From America."

"America? Really? I never would have guessed."

Emma ignored his teasing. "I've been sent here to sign . . . to try and sign Harjit Patel."

"Sign him? You mean as a client?"

Emma nodded.

"Why?" Sanjay asked. "Cricket isn't very big in America."

"Are you familiar with *The Golden Lotus*?"

"The novel by Lalima Bhanjee? Of course. She may not be as big a celebrity here in India as Harjit, but she's very well known."

"All the major Hollywood studios are involved in a bidding war to option her book into a movie. My boss believes Harjit would be perfect in the lead role. He wants me to sign him so we can have him on board once the book is sold."

Sanjay slowly nodded. "And you want to learn about cricket in order to establish some common ground before you begin negotiations."

"Yes."

"Well, Ms. Edwards, I will be more than happy to teach you about cricket." He hesistated. "But, in return, you must do something for me."

"And what is that, Mr. Kumar?"

"Go to bed with me, of course," he said, smiling. "I've wanted to go to bed with you since I saw you walk into the bar."

Emma didn't know whether to believe him; especially the part about his having seen her walk into the bar. His eyes had been glued to the television from the moment she entered.

She did, however, believe the part about his wanting to go to bed with her. Not that she was vain, but Emma had had enough men pay her compliments about her voluptuous body, her smooth caramel skin, and her large black eyes to know she seemed to have what most men wanted.

Even Indian men, it appeared.

She shrugged and tried to act nonchalant, but a sharp current of lust arced through her. Sanjay folded his long, slender fingers. The fingers Emma had, in spite of herself, been imagining stroking deep inside her pussy.

"So we are agreed, then?" he said.

"Only if you promise to teach me enough about cricket that I won't make a fool of myself with Harjit."

The corner of Sanjay's mouth curled up. "I can't guarantee you won't make a fool of yourself, Ms. Edwards. However, I doubt that will be so."

He rose from his chair and offered her his hand. She liked the way his hand felt. Warm and smooth. She could well imagine what the rest of his body would feel like. Just as warm. Just as smooth.

He guided her hand to the crook of his arm and rested it there. Lord, this was too much. Emma giggled.

He looked over at her. "What is it that you find humorous?"

"Look at you. Taking my arm like we were on our way to a dance instead of . . ." She stopped. "Where are we going exactly? You're staying here at the hotel?"

He nodded. "I'm here for a business conference. But why don't we go to your room."

"Fine with me. Anyway, as I was saying, you're acting like we're going to a ball instead of to my room to . . ."

He grinned. "Teach you about cricket?"

She smiled. "That's one way of describing it, I guess."

They entered the lobby and made their way to her room.

Emma took her room's key card out of her purse. However, before she could slide it through the magnetic reader, Sanjay put his hand over hers.

"Allow me."

He slid the card through the reader, opened the door, and gestured for her to enter. Once inside, he pulled her to him so that her back was pressed against his chest. He moved his hands over her silk blouse and kneaded her breasts.

Emma's breath hitched in her throat. Well, he certainly wasted no time. She didn't usually allow potential bedmates to move so quickly to first base but she wasn't about to tell him to stop.

"Hmmm, that feels good. You know just how to touch a woman's breasts."

He molded them between his hands. "I've had some experience."

"Speaking of experience, don't forget you're supposed to be teaching me about cricket. That is what we came up here for."

He pressed his groin against her buttocks, his erection sliding along the crevice. "You still want to learn about cricket? When all I want to do is fuck this delicious derriere of yours?"

Delighted by his words, Emma couldn't help but wriggle her butt against his cock. "Of course I want to learn about cricket. My meeting with Harjit is tomorrow."

Sanjay moved his hands to the buttons on her blouse. He slowly undid them as he skimmed his lips along the side of her neck. Once her blouse was open, he slid his hands inside it and cupped her breasts again. He squeezed her nipples where they swelled beneath her bra.

Emma sighed. She loved it when a man took the time to play with her breasts before fucking her.

"Cricket," she gasped as she felt her pussy growing wetter. "Tell me about cricket."

He nibbled her neck. "There are two teams. Eleven players each."

"Isn't it . . ." Emma shuddered as Sanjay sucked hard at the spot between her shoulder and neck. "Isn't it . . . oh, God, that feels so good . . . isn't it something like baseball?"

"Yes," he murmured. "It is something like baseball. But not quite."

He rubbed his cock in the crease of her buttocks. Gripping the top of her bra, he pushed it down. He grasped her bare breasts and rolled her tightening nipples between his fingers.

"Oh, yes, yes. Don't stop, don't stop."

Sanjay took off her blouse and threw it on the floor. He unhooked her bra and tossed that on the floor also. He turned her around, leaned over, and wrapped his mouth around one of her breasts. Sucking hard at her nipple, he lapped it steadily with his tongue.

Lord, but his mouth was so hot and wet, his tongue so long and agile, and he was sucking at her breasts as skillfully as he had played with them.

He unzipped her skirt, pushing it down her hips. He grabbed her buttocks and squeezed them as he continued to suck hungrily at her breast. Emma stepped away from her skirt and moved back toward the bed.

Sanjay followed, his lips still sucking at her nipple. When Emma felt the back of the bed bump her thighs, she gently pushed him away. He looked at her, his eyes hot.

"Don't forget about cricket," she said.

He grinned. "I've already forgotten."

Damn him! "This meeting tomorrow with Harjit is very important to my career."

Sanjay grabbed her buttocks and caressed them while he nuzzled the side of her neck. "But can you not, at least for tonight, forget about your career?"

Forget about her career? Was he crazy?

But as he continued to caress and kiss her, Emma's skin grew hot and her body tight. He nibbled at the tender skin along her neck, and his fingers stroked the dampness of her panties. If he kept doing what he was doing, she might very well do as he suggested. She moaned, grinding herself along his chest, groin, and thighs.

Sanjay eased her panties down and guided her to the bed. He moved his body over hers and eagerly caressed her naked body.

All Emma wanted was for him to fuck her, but she had not been joking about his teaching her about cricket. In her mind, her whole future as an agent hinged on whether she was successful in getting Harjit to sign with the agency.

"Sanjay."

"Hmmm?" His face was burrowed between her breasts, his fingers pulling steadily at her stiff nipples.

"Tell me more about cricket."

Sanjay lifted his head and grinned at her. "I'd much rather eat you. Your cunt smells so ripe. My mouth is tingling from wanting to lick it."

She'd much rather he'd eat her, too. But if his mouth was full of her pussy, he'd be unable to talk, and if he wasn't able to talk, he couldn't tell her about cricket.

"How about I go down on you first?"

His eyes lit up. "You are a very generous woman."

Emma raised a finger. "But while I'm doing that, you'll have to tell me about cricket."

"You expect me to talk about cricket while you are sucking my cock?"

She looked up at him from under her lashes. "Consider it a challenge."

He grinned, rose off the bed, and took off his shirt and pants. His cock strained against his underwear. Emma got on her knees on the bed. She pulled Sanjay's underwear down and, once his cock was free, leaned over and wrapped her mouth around the thick, bulbous head. Sanjay rocked his groin against her face, his cock sliding between her lips.

Emma didn't consider herself a connoisseur of the cock. It wasn't because she had any problems with sucking cock. She didn't. It was just that she'd be the first to admit she was rather selfish when it came to sex. She preferred to be the recipient of oral sex, as opposed to its provider.

However, as she moved her mouth up and down Sanjay's cock, she had to admit that sucking his cock was quite enjoyable.

"Umm, Emma. Yes, suck it. Suck it."

Emma quickly pulled her mouth away and looked up at Sanjay. "Cricket."

He drew in a deep breath, his flat, muscled stomach rippling. "Very well."

He gently guided her mouth back to his cock. And as Emma sucked it, in between Sanjay's moans and groans, his gasps and cries, he relayed to her the fundamentals of the game of cricket.

Or at least he tried to.

As for Emma, she was really getting into sucking Sanjay's cock, and a lot of what he said sounded like gibberish. The only thing that registered with her was that cricket sounded about as exciting as baseball.

Sanjay grunted, and his hands, which were still tangled in her hair, tightened about her head. His groin snapped hard against her face, bumping her nose.

"I'm going to come, Emma. Do you . . ." He moaned throatily. "Do you want me to pull out?"

Emma shook her head and closed her eyes. Sanjay's cock throbbed in her mouth as his semen slid thickly down her throat. He let out a long, low groan as he climaxed.

Once he was done, Emma pulled away and looked up at him. He stroked her jaw and lips.

"That was wonderfully done."

Emma's cheeks warmed. "Thank you."

Sanjay pushed her down onto the bed. "Now I will return the favor." He moved down until his head was between her thighs. Then he looked up at her. "Unless you want me to tell you more about cricket."

"Have you told me enough so that I won't look like an idiot at my meeting tomorrow?"

He grinned slyly at her. "As I told you before, whether or not you look like an idiot is entirely up to you. But there are a few other things I can tell you about cricket, and specifically about Harjit, that may help you."

He gently parted her thighs, exposing her moist and ready sex. "But I will tell you these things only after I have dined."

He lowered his head and slid his lips along her swollen pussy lips. Emma threw her head back and moaned. He lapped at her with his long tongue, the tip of it easing among her dewy nether lips. He was as skilled down there as he had been sucking on her breasts. He ate her so skillfully that Emma quickly climaxed. And she came again and again and again until finally she had to beg him to stop.

Sanjay moved up her body, and Emma felt his cock, which was once again thick and hard, sliding against her. He kissed her, thoroughly and deeply, and she tasted herself on his lips and his tongue.

Emma pulled away from his mouth. "My purse."

Sanjay kissed her neck. "It's on the floor."

Emma rolled away from him and, leaning over the bed, picked up her purse. Sanjay showered kisses on her back and buttocks as she did so. She took out a packet of condoms and turned back to him.

"Were you planning this?" he asked as he took the packet, tore it open, and slid the condom on.

"Of course not. But you know what they say. Better to have a condom and not need it than to need one and not have it."

She moved back into Sanjay's arms. He slid his cock inside her. Emma moaned and the bed rocked beneath them as he thrust hard and deep and fast inside her. Gasping, she wrenched her mouth away from his. He buried his face in her neck, his lean hips driving his cock deep into her shuddering body.

"Sanjay," she panted. "Don't forget . . . Oh, sweet Lord! . . . Fuck me. Fuck me. The rest . . . you promised."

Sanjay didn't answer her. He just kept fucking. It wasn't that Emma didn't want him to fuck her. God knows, he knew how to move his hips in just the right way to stimulate her clit, and she felt her orgasm rising, but it was getting late, and her meeting with Harjit was early in the morning. She couldn't forget about it. Even if she was getting fucked so hard and so good.

Despite his having her pinned to the bed, Emma was finally able to twist her body around until he was on his back and she on top. He stopped moving and looked up at her.

"You wish to fuck me?" He grinned at her. "Excellent. For I can now see your beautiful breasts."

Emma smiled and, leaning over, rubbed her breasts all over

his face. Sanjay tried to snare them with his mouth. She quickly pulled away and lifted her hips off his groin. He groaned and wrapped his arms around her waist to pull her back on top of him.

"You can suck my tits and I'll be more than happy to fuck you," she said, "but first you must promise you'll tell me what else I need to know about cricket for my meeting tomorrow."

"Are we still in negotiations? I thought we had concluded those."

"One thing my boss taught me is that you're never done with negotiations. It's an ongoing process."

Sanjay smiled and slowly rubbed his hands over her hips. "Very well. Now, come here."

Emma lowered herself back onto him. She moved her hips and began fucking him in earnest. Sanjay lifted his head and licked her dangling breasts. Heat flooded Emma's body. She was tempted to let him keep sucking her breasts, but that was not part of the deal.

"Sanjay," she said in a warning tone.

"I have not forgotten." He sucked hard on one breast then pulled away. "One thing you should keep in mind about Harjit is that he's considered one of the greatest batsman ever. However, he has been criticized for playing for the record books first and his team second."

Sanjay thrusts his hips up, driving his cock hard into her. "Now, what does that tell you about him?"

Emma moaned, then gripped his shoulders as she rode him. "That he . . . oh, God . . . that he wants to make his mark on the world."

"Indeed." Sanjay grabbed her buttocks with one hand. With the other he reached down and stroked her clit.

"What else . . . ? " Emma let out a long, slow hiss. "Oh, sweet Jesus . . . What else do I need to . . . know . . . oh . . . *oh!*"

Emma sharply arched her back as her orgasm gripped her. Then she threw herself onto Sanjay, her body undulating hard from the force of her climax. She felt Sanjay throbbing inside her as he also came. She slowly lowered her body onto his.

"Are we done?" he asked, his breath as ragged as hers.

She raised her head and looked at him. "Done?" she gasped. "With what?"

"With the cricket lesson." He smiled. "Not with the fucking. I would like to do more of that."

Emma stroked his lips. "So would I. But I don't see why you can't squeeze a few more lessons in between our"—she gripped his cock where it still lay inside her swollen pussy—"extracurricular activities."

"Indeed."

Emma lowered her head and claimed his mouth as completely as he claimed hers.

"It's beautiful." Emma ran her hand over the red and gold sari.

"That's why I chose it," Sanjay said. "To match your loveliness."

"You've no need to flatter me any longer, Sanjay. Our negotiations are officially at an end."

"It's not flattery. And I thought you said that negotiations were ongoing."

Emma smiled. "They are. But since I was successful in signing Harjit, our deal is concluded. And if I hadn't spent that night with you, I would have been so stressed meeting Harjit, I probably would not have succeeded."

Sanjay stroked her cheek. "You would have. You are a very determined woman."

Emma glanced around the hotel lobby. Her taxi was due to arrive soon. She hesitated to say what was on her mind, but she knew she didn't have much time.

"Will we see each other again?"

"Do you want to see me again?" Sanjay asked.

Emma thought about that. The last thing she needed to complicate her life was a long-distance relationship. "Yes, I do."

He smiled. "Then we shall. Though I doubt that you will have occasion to return to India anytime soon."

Emma nodded. "Harjit is coming to Los Angeles to finalize the deal. He's very eager to visit California."

"Actually, I plan to visit L.A. in the near future."

A sudden happiness leaped within Emma. "Really?"

Sanjay nodded, his eyes glittering. "Perhaps we can get together and negotiate a new deal."

"A new deal?"

"Why not? Except this time around you will teach me about baseball."

"I don't know that much about baseball."

Sanjay leaned over and kissed her. He whispered against her lips, "And I couldn't care less about baseball."

Emma smiled. Then she heard a taxi horn blaring outside the hotel. "That's for me."

Sanjay picked up her bags and escorted her outside. Once she and her bags were inside the taxi, he took her hand and brushed his lips across the palm.

"Till then."

She smiled. "Till then."

Pins and Needles

IAN FREY

I wanted to support Miki. She'd done a lot for me in the year we'd been together. For example, she'd backed me up when I wanted to return to school, even though it meant sacrificing the overtime pay I'd been using to treat her to the occasional fancy restaurant—so I knew that giving her the same kind of consideration was the least I could do. She didn't say a word against the weekly poker nights with my friends, the first long-term girlfriend who'd given me that space; and even when I came home a loser from those games, she just shook her head and told me to do better next time.

She was also the most beautiful woman I'd ever been with. Her small stature and heart-shaped face would have given her an innocent air if it weren't for the leather skirts and high-heeled boots she favored, or the plunging necklines of the sweaters that showed off her surprisingly generous curves. I was lucky to be with her and I knew it . . . but I still couldn't bring myself to be a practice dummy for her new dream job as an acupuncturist.

"Come on, David," she said, leaning over my prone form. "I need to be able to practice when I get off work, and the school closes by seven every night. I can't get all the hours I need for certification without some help at home."

"Hon, I'm sure it's therapeutic, but I just can't. Those needles give me the creeps."

"You got your ear pierced," she said accusingly.

"That was when I was in high school, and I hated every second of it. I only did it because everyone else was."

"Everyone else is doing acupuncture, too! God, even professional athletes are getting it done these days, you know that."

The arguments went back and forth, but always came down to the same result: I wasn't about to let her, or anybody, stick a needle in me. After the fourth time we'd discussed it, she gave an exasperated sigh and rolled her eyes at me. "Okay, fine. I'll make do with what I can get in class. It'll just take a few months longer than I expected."

I thought that would be the end of it. Was I ever wrong.

For the next several days she got in so late at night that she'd skip dinner and go right to sleep, her eyes closing the minute her head hit the pillow. I'll admit that I felt a little guilty, but I just couldn't get over the idea that the needles were going to hurt or draw blood. All I could do was ensure there was food in the refrigerator that she could take for dinner at the school and let her sleep as much as she needed to. Of course, that meant going without anything more than a good-night kiss—and even though we'd been together a long time, we hadn't ever gone a full week without at least a good session of mutual masturbation. I could have gone it alone, of course, but somehow even that seemed like it would be unfair when she was going without just as long as I was.

That Friday I came home to find Miki in the bedroom doorway, wearing nothing but a pair of exercise pants. With a grin I came to kiss her hello, lifting my hands to cup her warm, golden, heavy breasts—but after a few seconds of my kneading her nipples, she pulled away slowly.

"David." She kept her lips close to mine. "I'd love to have your cock in me, but I've got to get to school if I'm going to make my practice time. Maybe when I get home . . ." She took my lower lip in her teeth and bit down softly, running her little hand along the tent in front of my pants.

"Miki, it's been over a week . . ."

"I know," she breathed into my ear. "I know it has, and believe me, I want it, too."

"I don't just want it," I growled, "I need it, Miki, please. My balls are turning blue."

"Oh, really?" She raised an eyebrow and sank to her knees. She toyed with my zipper for a moment, then opened it, reaching in to pull my hard cock and swollen balls out of their boxer briefs. Curling one hand around my shaft and slowly pumping, she hefted my balls with the other and let them roll around on her palm a second before giving them a squeeze.

"God, Miki, please." I let my head roll back when she moved her face close to my crotch. I could feel her hot breath on the sensitive skin beneath my balls.

"Oh, I don't know," she said, still pumping slowly. "I don't think you could seriously call these blue. There's a lot backed up there, but a few hours more shouldn't hurt."

"Miki, please." I reached a hand to cup the back of her head, wanting to pull her lips onto me, but she backed away and removed her hand from my shaft, still cupping my balls in her other hand and squeezing them gently in time with my rapidly increasing heartbeat.

"Then again, blue balls are a serious medical condition for young men, aren't they? I think I could help you with these, but it's going to require some real therapy." She moved back in and ran the pointed tip of her tongue along the vein beneath my cock, curling it under at the base of the head. "Are you willing to be a good boy and take your medicine?"

"Oh, yes. I want my medicine," I groaned, inching my hips toward her face. "I want it now."

She leaned in and took my cock in her mouth, moving slowly until its entire length was buried in her throat and her cute little snub nose was resting against my pubic bone. I gasped aloud and reached back to steady myself on the doorjamb as she pulled away, increasing the suction so I could feel the sweet, warm smoothness of her mouth along the sides of my shaft, sucking harder until the head left her mouth with an audible pop.

"Get on the bed," she said, her face all sweet innocence despite the thin string of saliva running from my cock head to her lips. "And I'll give you your medicine."

I scrambled out of my pants and onto the bed while she got off her knees and moved toward the closet. When she turned around, she was holding a thin, black vase inscribed with a yellow diamond and a red *kanji* character. Sticking out of the top of the vase was a set of acupuncture needles.

"No," I said, shaking my head, and Miki smiled with a glint in her eye that said she had me right where she wanted me.

"If you won't take your medicine like you promised, like a good boy, then I guess there's nothing I can do about your symptoms." She ran a fingernail up the seam of my scrotum, ending the trail just short of my cock. "It's such a dangerous condition, though. I bet you could just pop right now." With that, she rolled my sack in her palm and squeezed again.

"God . . ." I hissed. "You're a wicked bitch."

"And you're a bad patient, David. I only want to help," she cooed. "Why don't you let Dr. Miki help you?"

Her voice was playful, and the look in her eyes was the same, but I knew she was dead serious. Strangely enough, I didn't really feel cheated or taken advantage of. Sure, she'd played a trick to get what she wanted, but she'd done it well, and I could respect that. It was the same as a good bluff in a poker game.

"Okay," I groaned. The pressure in my balls, that sweet voice, and the thin sheen of her lipstick on the sides of my cock finally overcame my fears. "You win. Please, Dr. Miki, I want to take my medicine." I tried to put the same playfulness in my own voice, though I was sure it sounded more like desperation.

She put the vase of needles on the nightstand. "Just relax," she said, "it'll all be worth it. Trust me." I closed my eyes and felt the weight of her body as she straddled my calves and lower legs, then let out a deep moan as she took me in her mouth again; not as deeply as when she was teasing me, but with the gentle pressure I always enjoyed at the beginning of a blow job.

When she took me in fully, I felt a tiny pinch on my right side, but the sensation of her breath in my trimmed pubic hair and the moist warmth of her mouth around my cock more than made up for that. In fact, it didn't hurt at all; like I said, just a tiny pinch. I knew it was the first needle, but I still kept my eyes closed, focusing all my attention on her willing mouth. She came up slow and moved her hand into action, pumping my shaft rhythmically while her lips and tongue played around the head. With her other hand I could tell she was going for another needle, and this time when her mouth came down, I barely even felt the pinch on my left hip.

Miki kept it up, going from gentle suction while she retrieved needles to a full deep-throating when she slid the needles into me. After the sixth pinch I opened my eyes and saw her looking up at me, her beautiful almond eyes peering through a phalanx of tiny silver trees rooted in my flesh. I was amazed at how it felt. It wasn't just my cock anymore; my entire lower body was beginning to respond to her steady sucking. She'd talked about the way acupuncture could work, the way it unfroze rigid muscles and brought about a feeling of freedom, but I'd still bet it had less to do with those needles and more to do with her hot little mouth.

Her eyes locked on my own; she brought both hands up and slowly withdrew the needles from my body one by one, placing them back on the nightstand (though not in the vase) as I watched. I guessed the training session was officially over when Miki took hold of my hips and lifted herself into a push-up position, letting me grab her waistband and pull the sweatpants down her beautiful legs. She hadn't been wearing any panties, and I knew she'd had no intention of going to practice at school at all. This had been a setup from the beginning.

I hardly cared. She moved her body to hover over my face, letting me see how wet and ready she was, her clit thrusting out from between her slick folds like the head of a tiny pin. I lifted my head and barely took it between my own lips, running my tongue along its sensitive tip.

Miki growled and ground herself down as she took me deep into her mouth. She wasn't teasing anymore and she needed to come in my arms. I ran my tongue up her slit and began lapping with broad, slow strokes, and her hands tightened on my thighs.

She accelerated her own speed as I kept mine steady, making little animal noises in the back of her throat, which sent a new thrill up my shaft.

I didn't want to be the first to lose it, though. While my pride wasn't hurt from the trick she'd pulled, I wanted to be sure she knew I had a few up my sleeve as well. I lifted my hands to her ass, swiping my tongue along my thumb before I let it trail up the cleft between her cheeks. The noises in the back of her throat stilled for a moment. She wasn't sure what was coming and held my cock rigid and immobile in the warmth of her mouth.

The moist pad of my thumb moved along her perineum, sliding along its exposed flesh before lifting to separate her cheeks. I started rubbing circles into the delicate flesh just along her rear entrance, and as my hand moved back to cup her right cheek, I lifted my tongue to gently probe at her musky asshole.

"God!" She lifted her head from my cock, grabbing at it with her hand and pumping slowly as I tongued her sweet ass. "Do it, do it right there." My chin was already wet from her slick pussy lips, rubbing against my lower face as my tongue danced around the edges of her cheeks. I squeezed the golden globes of her ass together around my tongue, then pried them apart and brought my head up to start really working into her.

Miki put the crown of her head against my thigh, and I imagined her eyes were squeezed shut, as she bit her lip with the sheer pleasure I was bringing her ass. She kept pumping my cock, adding a twisting action as she came to the base and returned to the top. I groaned into her, loving the imaginary vision before me as much as I loved the taste of her. When I felt the tip of her tongue return to the slit in my crown, I popped my index finger into my mouth and replaced my tongue with a gently probing finger.

She was whimpering now, and I'm pretty sure I was, too. I

moved my head back down to nibble on her lips and thrust my
tongue back into her pussy, keeping the first knuckle of my index
finger crooked in her ass. Her whimpers turned into full-fledged
little cries, and as she ground against my face, she popped the tip
of my cock back into her mouth, sucking frantically at the sensitive head while gripping the base tight. She was coming hard
against my mouth, and it took everything I had to keep from
shooting into her own.

When she finally stopped roiling against my chin, I took my
finger from her ass, wrapped my arms around her, and rolled her
over onto her back. Her legs were spread wide and I lifted off
her, panting and covered in sweat, looking down at that perfect
little body.

"Fuck me," she growled, "fuck me, fuck me, fuck me,
David." My cock was already dripping with pre-cum as I lined
up and buried myself in her with a single stroke, pressing my lips
hard against hers. She returned the kiss with equal ferocity, still
making the same sharp noises, then broke her face away to look
into my eyes.

"Did you like your medicine?" She ran her tongue along my
lips, grinning from ear to ear underneath me.

I could only growl in response. Words were gone now, and I
needed to come. Miki seemed to understand but she wasn't going
to let me get away quite that easily.

"We're not quite finished yet, are we?" Her hips were bucking up into my own, rolling on the tide that every couple knows,
slick with our saliva and with her orgasm. "You've still got those
terrible symptoms . . ." With that I felt her little hand slide between us and gently squeeze my balls.

That did it—I couldn't take another second. With a shout I
pinned her fully to the mattress, stopped pumping my hips, and

let myself go completely. I flooded her with my cum as she bit down on one earlobe and rolled my sensitive balls between her palm and thumb, milking every last drop out of them. Even when I collapsed on top of her, she was still cradling them, whispering gently in my ear.

"So what do you think? Are you going to be able to let me practice medicine on you?"

I caught my breath and rolled onto my side, carrying her with me. "Miki, by the time we're through," I promised, "you'll be top of the class."

Double Ten

LISA G. RILEY

ॐ

"WONG'S HAPPY EMPORIUM."

Trisha Logan felt heat curl in her belly. He hadn't said his name, but she knew it was Brett Wong answering the phone in his parents' store. She hadn't expected this. He never came to Chinatown. The last time she'd seen him, she'd been in his lap and he'd had his hand in her panties while she'd ridden his fingers and screamed into his mouth. She took a deep breath. "Hello, Brett."

"Rissy."

Biting back a moan, she closed her eyes. He'd said her name exactly that way the night they'd gone beyond the bonds of their longtime friendship. What had started as a kiss had ended with her splayed wantonly in his lap. It had happened in a private booth in a nightclub. She remembered how he'd sucked her nipple through her clothes, tonguing it hard on the roof of his mouth, and she had to clench her pussy muscles to stem the flow of arousal. "Um. How are you?"

"Why haven't you called me back?"

Abort, abort! "Can I speak to your mom?"

"I've been out of town; otherwise, I'd have settled this by now."

Don't you know what abort means? Get off the phone, stupid! "I've gotta go." She hung up the phone. At the nightclub, she'd scrambled off his lap and hurried out. What they'd done had changed everything, and she'd known that immediately.

Brett thought about Trisha as he drove to Chinatown for the second time that week. When she'd hung up on him four days before, his first instinct had been to call her back, but he'd decided not to. His dark eyes narrowed as he thought about when he'd last seen her. He remembered how her slick opening had quickly closed around his fingers and she'd moaned deep in her throat. She'd worried about what they were doing, even as she'd lifted her silk-covered breast and fed him her nipple.

Her hips had been pumping, her thighs had been squeezing, and he'd had to struggle not to pull his dick out of his pants and plunge it into her hungry body. He regretted that he hadn't because she'd been avoiding him ever since.

"Should have known the little chicken would run," he said. She'd been running since she was a kid and had moved to Chinatown; a lone African-American face in a sea of Chinese ones. Then, as now, she was running from a past she didn't know and trying to create a new history.

Even as he thought it, Brett knew that many believed he was running, too. As soon as he was able, he'd left Chinatown, a place so steeped in the past and history that it was sometimes hard to distinguish the here and now from the then and gone. "I didn't run, I left," he mumbled.

As he drove along Wentworth Avenue, his eyes caught by the high, green and red pagoda-covered structure called the Chinese Gateway, his cell rang. He put his earpiece in and checked the caller ID. "Hello, Mary," he said to his twin sister.

"Hey! Are you at the store?"

"No."

"I wish I could be there."

"So do I. Then maybe I wouldn't have to go."

"It's the Double Ten Parade, and *you've* even been invited to tonight's reception. Number One Son has to be there," she teased.

In Chinese culture, male children were favored over female, and the oldest male child was the favorite of all. A lot was expected of him. Brett had always felt pressure because he was the only son and the eldest by three minutes.

It used to bother him when Mary had felt slighted. However, as an adult, she practically reveled in their parents' concentration on him because it lessened the pressure on her. "*Qin wode pigu,*" he said, telling her to kiss his ass in Mandarin.

"Shame," she chided gleefully. "You kiss your mother with that mouth? Just suck it up."

"Said the woman who's tucked away in Idaho."

"Hey, you're lucky. Ever try finding a place to celebrate Chinese independence in middle Idaho?"

"Poor Mary. You're going to miss out on the antiquated pomp and circumstance of a Chinese celebration," he said sarcastically.

"Well, maybe if you'd stuck to the sciences, you'd have found yourself in the wilds of Idaho, too. Who are you taking to the reception?"

"Nobody." He turned onto his parents' packed street.

"How about taking Trisha?"

"She's avoiding me."

"Are you teasing her about her job choices again? We're not kids anymore, Brett."

Rissy had been a fixture at the Wong apartment from the time she'd moved to Chinatown. She'd been a smart, beautiful, curious girl who'd gotten under his skin. Nothing had changed. "She's wasting her intelligence and her degrees in those jobs."

"They're just a means to an end. She hasn't caught a break with her jewelry designs."

Brett saw a car maneuvering out of a spot and pulled closer. "Her designs aren't putting food on the table. She's as flighty as a fairy. She dresses like a hippie and jingles so much from all that jewelry she wears that I can't hear myself think," he finished. What he left unsaid was that he wanted her, jewelry and all, and had since high school.

"You're just mad because you're attracted to her, Mr. Buttoned-Down Architect. Just make a move and stop being a wuss," Mary baited him.

"Guess Rissy doesn't tell you everything," Brett crowed softly.

"Listen—wait. What did you say?"

Brett was silent.

"Come on, Brett, tell me," Mary wheedled.

Silence.

"You know," she began conversationally, "sometimes, I can't stand you."

Laughter.

"Fine. Be that way. Whatever you do, don't hurt Trisha. I mean, I know you wouldn't intentionally," Mary hurried to say because she knew she'd insulted him. Despite his teasing, he'd always had a soft spot for Trisha, and next to herself, she'd be the last person he'd hurt. "You know what I mean. Trisha's special."

"Yeah," he agreed. "I'm at the store. I'll talk to you later." After his visit with his parents, he'd corner Rissy in her apartment and make her face what they'd done and hopefully get her to do it again.

Trisha fixed the items in the display case/counter at Wong's Happy Emporium, the graceful bend and sway of her body betraying years of dance and yoga. She straightened and looked around to see if anything else needed fixing. It was a slow day, and her cinnamon-colored eyes took in every inch of the small, empty store. She'd been working at the store for three days because she'd lost her job at Pitter-Patter Daycare the week before.

Her pretty, full mouth turned down in self-disgust. It had been the second job in six months. Lost in thought, she took her fingers through her short, curly Afro. For the most part, she loved her life. She lived in a great neighborhood with people with a rich culture and history that she didn't think she'd find anywhere else. Sometimes she envied them because she had nothing even close to it, but she was grateful that her adoptive mother had chosen Chinatown to move to all those years ago.

She worked jobs that helped pay her bills and gave her the freedom she needed to work on her designs. The downside was that the money she made was almost always only enough to take care of essentials with little left for more. She didn't mind that so much, except she was always needing supplies to make her jewelry.

She didn't have any savings and had little in checking. Her mother had died three years before, leaving her some money. Trisha had spent it all trying to start a jewelry design business, which had eventually failed. Still, she didn't regret it. At least she'd tried, and she'd try again someday.

She sighed, and for the umpteenth time her thoughts turned to Brett. She knew he was angry because she knew *him,* but she couldn't help avoiding him. She was attracted to him and was even in love with him, but she'd learned to hold those feelings back because she knew nothing could come of them. As much as his parents cared for her, they wouldn't approve of a relationship between them. They would want him to have a traditional wife. She chose to concentrate on their friendship instead. He was almost as much her best friend as Mary was. "And now I've even blown that," she mumbled forlornly.

Brett stood in the doorway, staring at Rissy. He was not at all surprised to see her there. His eyes took in her small, lithe body, dark skin, and dream-filled eyes. As usual, the sexy, little dreamer's mind was in the clouds.

"Let me guess: You lost your job at Pitter-Patter."

Trisha jumped at the deep, smooth timbre of Brett's voice. Her breath caught as she stared at him. He was gorgeous with his deep-set, dark eyes and black hair. Tall, thin, and muscular, he simply oozed sexuality. Every step he made, every breath he took, was a mating call to her hungry body, which became embarrassingly hypersensitive when he was around. She walked around the counter and into his arms. She hadn't seen him in the two months since that night in the club and she'd missed him.

She said nothing as he lifted her and held her closely. She wrapped her arms around him, buried her face in his neck, and breathed him in. The sexy, wholly *maleness* of him made her weak, her nipples beading and her mound tightening greedily in anticipation. When it became difficult to resist wrapping her legs around his hips and dry-humping his dick into oblivion, she released him, signaling that he should put her down.

"Hi." She stepped back. "I haven't seen you in a while."

"Gee, I wonder why," he said drily.

"I'm sorry I've been avoiding you."

"Then why have you?"

"Because it would never work," she said as she moved back toward the counter, the split of her sarong skirt flashing open to give a peek of her thigh. His intense stare made her feel jittery, and she resisted looking down at herself. She didn't *think* anything had popped out of the scooped neck of her long-sleeved leotard.

"That's what I used to think, too. Even though I've wanted you more than I've wanted to breathe, I didn't believe it would work because you've got the Chinatown mind-set and I'm trying to move forward. But now that I've gotten a taste of you," he said as he moved closer, "there's no way in hell I'm not getting more."

Trisha felt stalked and her eyes widened. She willed herself to stand her ground and tried to ignore the shiver his words sent down her spine. "I don't have a 'Chinatown mind-set,' whatever that means."

"You never leave," he reminded her.

"I do," she insisted. "I just haven't moved out."

"Why?"

"It's what I know. I'm inspired here."

"True artists find inspiration anywhere, and you're a true artist. It's like you've cloistered yourself here. I know the fact that you're adopted bothers you because you don't know who your family was—"

"Stop it." Trisha wanted to scream. She hated not knowing and didn't like to be reminded of it. She tried to move around him.

Brett blocked her. "You fulfill your need to have roots by staying in Chinatown. But you know that the clannish nature of Chinese culture won't really allow you to have roots here," he finished angrily. It had always pissed him off that she was never fully accepted because she wasn't Chinese.

"People here are very good to me," she said stubbornly. "Chinatown means family." She ignored the voice that reminded her that just because Chinatown was where she'd felt the most accepted didn't mean that she'd truly been accepted.

"You have family—real family—in other parts of the city. Stop being scared of rejection and go find them."

"I'm not afraid."

"Then look up your mother's sister who used to visit when we were kids. Maybe she could tell you about your biological family."

"I haven't seen Aunt Pearl in twenty years. Why do you care, anyway?" Trisha asked defensively. "Just because you hate Chinatown doesn't mean I should."

"I don't hate Chinatown, and I care because I care about you. You're stifling yourself here."

"I don't agree," she said weakly, her heart pounding furiously. "You must hate Chinatown, otherwise you wouldn't down it so much."

He could see how upset she was and ran a gentle finger down her cheek. "I just want something different and I wish people wouldn't dwell so much in the past—rich as it is, I prefer to live in the present."

"You don't know how lucky you are to be able to trace your ancestors back thousands of years," she said, her voice wistful. "To know who you are and where you came from."

"I know what I have, sweetheart, but that's not to say that I have to revel in it." He pressed a kiss to her trembling lips. She just looked so scared and lost. "It's okay. We don't have to talk about it." He kissed her again. "Come to the reception with me?"

It took Trisha a second to catch up. "Really?"

"Yes, and after, you'll come home with me. Agreed?" A pinch to her nipple made sure that she knew all that coming home with him would involve.

As her heart raced, Trisha could only nod.

"You look gorgeous."

"Fifth time," Trisha said as they walked toward his town house a few blocks away from the downtown hotel where the reception had been.

"I know I keep saying it, but you'll just have to get used to it." Brett grinned when she chuckled shyly. "I can't believe you wanted to walk."

"It's a beautiful, warm night."

"I wasn't worried about the weather so much as I was about your feet in those stilettos. They must be at least four inches."

"How do you know?"

Brett herded her toward his front door and trapped her against it. "I know because you fit my body better, and it's easier to do this." He bent his head and hungrily took her lips with his, his tongue sneaking out to cut a wide path through her mouth.

Trisha whimpered in the back of her throat and sucked him in hard. Her arms went around his neck and she lifted a leg to wrap around his waist.

He pushed against her, slamming her hard against the door while he ate at her mouth, using tongue and teeth. He felt the sultry heat of her pussy as she rubbed against him, begging for fulfillment, and lifting her other leg, he wrapped it around his waist so that she was straddling him fully, her heat encompassing him now. Her vagina was drenched and leaking its juices to wet her panties, tantalizing him enough to caress and finger her through the satin.

"Oh, God, Brett," Trisha panted. It felt so good. "Let's go insi—oh, oh, ohhhh!" He'd slid two fingers beneath her panties and into her slick opening. Her muscles clenched around them, making greedy, wet, suckling sounds as she rode the fingers furiously, pumping her hips and tightening her muscles to keep them inside. "Please, Brett, I ache," she sobbed out.

"Hold on tight," he told her as he pulled his fingers out. "Hush, baby," he soothed, and kissed her lips when she mewled her disappointment. He unzipped his pants and, bracing himself with a hand against the door, ripped her panties away.

The cool air against her hot flesh sent shivers coursing through Trisha's body, making her tighten her legs and arms even more. "Here, Brett? What about your neighbors?"

"It's one in the morning. If someone's watching, fuck them," he groaned just before he plunged inside.

Trisha screamed, the sound bouncing through the night air as she threw her head back. He pounded into her, his thick penis gliding easily in and out and stretching her almost to pain. Each time he thrust into her, slamming her back against the door, a cry of pure joy escaped her mouth.

She dug her nails into his shoulders trying to gain some semblance of control over the heat, the pleasure . . . her mind. The sheer ferocity of the pleasure blew through her, making her lose her grip on her sanity. The faster he thrust, the more she wanted. "Yes, Brett, yes!" She couldn't take it anymore and pressed her mouth into his shoulder to muffle her screams right before she exploded around him.

Brett's strokes were bruising as he rushed toward his own orgasm, pounding her repeatedly against the door. Trisha loved the animalistic side of him and reveled in a new wave of arousal. She pulled her bodice down to feed him a nipple. "Bite it, Brett." The pinprick of pain went straight to her clit, and she closed her eyes at the renewed pleasure.

"Fuck me, baby," she begged when he began to yell out his release and push more forcefully into her. "Fuck me!" She reached between them to finger her clit and squeeze his dick, her hand slippery with their combined cum as it slid from her to drip onto his thighs.

Hours later in his bed, Trisha moaned in her sleep, the tongue working at her clit bringing her forcefully out of her dreams. She lifted up to see Brett's head buried between her thighs. Her hands went to the back of his head and she pushed at it, simultaneously grinding her pussy into his face.

Brett bit lightly at her clitoris and lapped up the salty juices that gushed from her body. Needing more, he put his hands beneath her ass, lifted her to his face, and fed. She shrieked, her shaking thighs tightening around his head. He lay on top of her and drove his cock into her streaming labia just as the first wave of her orgasm rocketed through her.

* * *

"Behave, Brett," Trisha whispered. She stood in front of him watching the Double Ten Parade. He'd just slipped a hand under her short skirt to caress her butt. "People will see." Even so, she wantonly ground her behind against the erection in his jeans.

"No one's paying attention," he teased in her ear, chuckling when the thunderous applause for the lion dancers made her jump guiltily. "But you said you wanted to talk, so let's find some privacy."

They walked away from the crowd. "I've called Aunt Pearl," Trisha told him.

"Really?" Brett said in surprise. "And why would you do that?"

"You just have to make me say it, don't you?" she accused, and tried not to smile when he grinned unrepentantly. "You were right about my being afraid of rejection. But I realize now that I have to try to find my biological family."

"And what about moving?"

Trisha groaned. "One step at a time, Brett."

"Okay. Wanna celebrate this momentous occasion?"

She cocked her head. "What'd you have in mind?"

He cupped a breast. "I was thinking . . ." His fingers pinched her nipple.

"Brett!"

He ignored her halfhearted protest and continued, ". . . that I could take you to my parents' party later."

"The parade *and* the party? What gives?"

He shrugged. "I decided that I could appreciate my culture without getting lost in it."

"Really? Good f-for you . . ." Trisha barely got it out. His hand was under her skirt again, tracing circles on her inner thigh.

Brett reluctantly removed his hand. He'd actually felt her heat and hadn't even touched the hot spot yet. "Let's hope this will make you as happy as my sudden realization has." He gave her a small cardboard box.

Surprised, and more than a little horny, Trisha pulled off the lid. "It's beautiful." It was a small, gold globe. "Oh, Brett, you're giving me the world," she choked out as realization dawned.

"Let's see it together."

Trisha was stunned. "But what about your parents? What will they—?"

"Don't worry about them. I've never been traditional, and they know it."

She launched herself at him.

He caught her, laughing when she buried her face in his neck. "Should I take that as a yes?" He nuzzled the top of her head when she nodded. "Are you wearing panties?"

Rendered mute by happiness, and so wet that she was practically dripping, Trisha shook her head no.

"No?" His hand slid beneath her leotard. "God, baby," he growled as his fingers slid across her slick wetness. "Is this all for me?"

She helplessly burrowed closer, licking his neck. "*Wo yuan yi cheng gui da diao,*" she purred.

Brett lifted a brow at the dirty talk. "Ah . . . so size really does matter, huh?" He pushed a finger into her opening and swirled it around. "And we have another yes," he teased when she cried out.

Prince of Roses

S. J. FROST

HIDEKI GLARED DOWN AT the polished dark-wood bar and took a sip of his water, hoping it would help cool his annoyance. As Club Platinum's number one host, he had yet to engage any of the female clientele since one of his regulars had contacted him earlier saying she would be in and not to get occupied with anyone else. Seeing that it was now one o'clock, and she normally arrived by midnight, it looked like he had wasted his time waiting for her, which could have been spent earning the club money and boosting his commission. This was the exact reason he laughed whenever anyone said how lucky he was to be such a popular host. He knew what it was like to be at the bottom of the host-club food chain, scrubbing the toilets, catering to the top hosts, pounding the streets in all weather trying to coerce women to come into the club. Hard work, brains, and tenacity had gotten him where he was, not luck.

A pair of arms wrapped around his shoulders and a forlorn sigh wisped past his ear.

"Let another one get away, eh, Eiji-kun?" Hideki said.

The younger host laid his head against the back of Hideki's. "I tried to use your trick of pouring her champagne while whispering sweet things in her ear, but I overpoured and some dribbled on her leg. She got irritated and left."

"As she should. She shouldn't have to waste her time and money on so clumsy a host."

Eiji plopped down on the barstool next to him. "You're so mean to me, Ouji-sama."

Hideki smiled at him. Eiji always addressed him by a shorter version of his full nickname, Bara no Ouji-sama. *Bara* for the white rose he always wore on his suit jacket, *Ouji-sama* for his princelike charm and sophistication.

Eiji nudged Hideki and pointed toward the door. "Why can't I get a client that looks like that?"

Hideki followed Eiji's finger to the two stunning women speaking with his manager, his eyes locking on the one who had her long hair dyed deep mahogany and styled with a slight wave. He moved his gaze to her high-heeled, black leather boots hugging her calves, then to her thighs, which were less than half-covered by the black miniskirt. His vision graced higher to her slender hips, and he couldn't help but think of what beautifully formed handholds they would be if he were to take her from behind.

Hideki chuckled inside. It had been a long time since he had thought about a woman like that, and he wasn't even done scrutinizing her yet. He continued his visual trek up to her torso, clothed in a black mesh blouse over a black silken camisole that stretched across her small, round breasts. His eyes floated up her throat to her delicate jaw, lingering for two breaths on her lips. As he looked higher, his eyes locked with hers, and he realized that as he had been studying her, she had been doing the same to him. He smiled and inclined his head in acknowledgment.

Before she could respond, her companion tapped her arm.

"Onee-chan, pay attention. The manager is asking if we'd like to see the available hosts."

Natsumi broke her stare with the gorgeous man at the bar and looked to her sister. "I don't know what I find more disconcerting: that my little sister knows more about host clubs these days than I do, or that this isn't her first visit to Kabukicho."

Keiko giggled and shrugged. "I grew up in the time you were gone."

Natsumi gazed at her. It was true. This young woman preparing to enter college in the spring looked so different from the schoolgirl Keiko had been when Natsumi saw her last, but she was no longer the same person either. Her time in the States had changed her. Seven years, all devoted to education, work, and the man she believed had been her soul mate, but she had been proven wrong by Michael's admittance of his affair with another woman. Now she had returned home to Tokyo carrying the burden of a significant divorce settlement that she didn't want, and what better way to get rid of it than by blowing it on the company of a beautiful man.

Natsumi faced the manager. "I'll take your number one if he's available."

"Nishikawa-san will be pleased to entertain you this evening," the manager said, and moved to get a lineup of the other unoccupied hosts.

Natsumi watched as Keiko selected an energetic young host named Eiji, his black hair dyed blond at the tips and sticking out at wild angles. Her attention shifted from them to the exquisite man walking with measured grace toward her.

His black hair was layered, falling to the bottom of his neck in back and parted slightly to the right with a silken cluster of bangs falling close to his left eye. His elegant cheekbones swept high, revealing his refined bone structure, which had features soft and captivating. She caught sight of the white rose on the left breast of his black jacket, which he wore over a white dress shirt, the top few buttons of the shirt undone to show a hint of smooth, defined chest. Her eyes drifted lower, taking in his narrow hips, the thought passing through her mind that they were a perfect fit for her body. She raised her eyes, meeting his with an unwavering stare.

Hideki bowed to her. "I'm Nishikawa Hideki. It's a pleasure to be able to share the evening with you."

Natsumi bowed slightly deeper, absorbing his rich baritone, which sent a surge of warmth through her. "And with you, Nishikawa-san. I'm Tanaka Natsumi."

"Please, call me Hideki," he said, guiding her to a burgundy leather sofa tucked back in a corner.

He sat down beside her, making sure to not crowd her, but staying close enough that she'd be able to feel his body warmth and smell his cologne. Keiko took a seat on Natsumi's other side, and Eiji beside her. Hideki noted the enthusiasm with which the two were talking and hoped Eiji had finally found a customer who thought his hyper ways endearing rather than wearisome. He brought his eyes back to Natsumi, flashed his most charming smile, and handed her a menu of drinks.

She glanced over the menu, turned to the waiter, and ordered a bottle of expensive chardonnay.

Hideki watched her with an amused grin. "You're a very confident and bold woman, aren't you Natsumi-san?"

Natsumi looked at him. "No, not at all."

"Then, forgive me if this sounds rude, but I always strive for honesty; perhaps you're a bit uptight?"

Natsumi let out an indignant snort. "I didn't think honesty was a prevalent quality in your line of work with how hosts spin lies to flatter women, Hideki-san."

"That's how some hosts work, but not me. There are more ways to flatter people than being deceitful." Hideki chuckled softly. "And for me, lying is too challenging because I'm very forgetful, so it's safer to be honest."

Natsumi stared at him, amazed at the juxtaposition of seduction and innocence he balanced. Her eyes lingered on the bit of his exposed chest, her heartbeat quickening. She slowly lifted her stare to his penetrating gaze, which caused a warm throb to pulse between her legs.

A waiter stepped forward to deliver the bottle of wine.

Hideki took the bottle and poured, keeping his eyes on hers, timing it in his head as he spoke to know when to stop. "Are you married, have a boyfriend, a lesbian lover?"

Natsumi laughed and took the glass he offered. "None. I just got divorced and returned home from living in the States. I moved there when I was twenty for college."

Hideki's mind lit at the information. That would explain her tense air. Well, she might not be ready to release whatever restrictions she had put on herself, but he knew he could break them down. He reclined one arm across the back of the couch behind her.

"It's my dream to move to America someday. English was my

major in college, though I dropped out. I've thought about going back, but I think I'm too old now."

Natsumi shot him a doubtful look. "How old are you?"

"I just turned twenty-four." He grinned at her. "You look surprised."

"No, but I don't usually date younger men."

Hideki's innocent smile shifted to sly. "I didn't realize we were dating."

Natsumi clenched her glass, fixing him with a sharp glare. "Listen, pretty boy, I can see why you're such a good host, but I'm not a fool, so spare me the delusion that you'd make an ideal boyfriend. I don't want a relationship, and we both know that you're no prince, so let's keep things professional."

Hideki laughed under his breath. "That's fine. But you're the one who said we were dating, not me."

Natsumi looked away, embarrassment heating her cheeks. "I'm sorry. I'm not very good at this sort of thing yet."

"Then leave everything to me." He leaned close to her ear, taking a strand of her hair and wrapping it loosely around his index finger. "But, I will have to behave very unprofessionally."

Natsumi swallowed hard, her heart pounding faster than she could breathe. A voice in the back of her head reminded her that Keiko was sitting beside her and she shouldn't be acting like this in front of her. She pulled her hair out of his hand and stood, tapping Keiko on the arm. "We're leaving."

Keiko looked up at her, confused. "What? Why?"

"Because I promised Ryota we'd visit him at his club. Remember?"

Keiko sighed and nodded, reluctantly rising to her feet.

Hideki stepped to Natsumi's side. "I'm jealous that you leave me so soon." He walked her to the door, gave the club a discreet glance, and slipped his business card into her hand. "Perhaps after you visit your friend, you'd like to meet me away from the club. Feel free to call my personal cell."

Natsumi didn't acknowledge his suggestive tone and walked away with Keiko.

Eiji tossed his arm around Hideki's shoulders. "Did you secure yourself another regular?"

Hideki smiled and shook his head. "This one is not client material."

Natsumi took in a shaking breath. She hadn't been in a love hotel since she was seventeen and couldn't believe she was in one now. She knocked softly on the hotel room door, and as she lowered her hand, it opened. At the sight of a shirtless Hideki, her desire pushed her nervousness into nothingness.

Hideki stepped back to let her in. "I'm glad you called."

Natsumi walked in and removed her boots. "I'm glad you wanted me to."

She stepped into the room. Hideki grabbed her around the waist and pulled her to him, covering her mouth in a rough kiss. He swept her up, carried her to the bed, and dropped her down, bringing himself down on top of her.

Natsumi drew in a fast breath, trying to catch what she'd lost from Hideki's intense passion, only to have it stolen as he delivered another deep kiss. He slid his hand over her breasts to the bottom of her shirt, slipping underneath and rubbing across her stomach. Natsumi broke the kiss with a soft gasp, arching up toward his heated touch.

Hideki flicked his head toward the flat-screen TV hanging on the wall. "There's lots of interesting porn, if you like that. Or maybe you'd like to get something to play with." He pointed to a small vending machine near the bathroom filled with assorted sex toys.

Natsumi shook her head. "I've got a feeling you're all I need. However, if you're a ten-minutes-and-out type, I'll make you buy me the most expensive thing in there."

Hideki chuckled. "Then it's good I've worked my stamina up to eleven minutes."

Natsumi giggled and pulled him back down to her lips, her heart pounding faster as his fingers tickled up and down her inner thigh. She could feel his erection pressed against her other leg and gave it a taunting bump with her thigh.

Hideki moved his hand up, rubbing his thumb over the outside of her drenched thong. He drew back, smirking down at her. "Has it been a while?"

Natsumi opened her eyes, blinking rapidly for a second before her brain could compute his words. She blushed and glanced away. "Um . . . yes."

Hideki grazed his lips over hers. "You don't have to be shy. It's been a long time since I've been with a woman, too."

She gave him a suspicious look. "What do you mean, *with a woman?*"

Hideki shrugged nonchalantly. "Normally, when I want sex, I call my lover. But he's been so busy lately that he never has time to see me. Don't worry. He doesn't care if I take other lovers, as long as they're not men. He's married with two daughters himself."

Natsumi smiled up at him. "I should have known. You're too beautiful to restrict yourself to one gender."

Hideki laughed. "Thank you, but I don't really think about

things like gender when it comes to sex. The only thing that's important about sex is that it feels good."

"I think there are more important things than just that," Natsumi grumbled. "You should care, at least a little bit, about the other person."

"You think so? I've had sex with people I don't even like, and it still felt good." Hideki nuzzled against her neck. "You're very romantic. If that's what you believe, then you must care about me; even if it's just a little bit. Eh, Natsumi-chan?"

Natsumi lifted her lips to him, deciding to answer him with a sensual kiss.

Hideki moved the saturated fabric of her thong aside and smeared her wetness over her swollen clit with his index and middle fingers. He massaged it, in gentle circular motions, then slid the same fingers down and pushed them deep inside her. Natsumi moaned at having his touch enter her and thrust down on his hand. Hideki pressed his thumb to her clit, rubbing it while he pumped his two fingers in and out of her. With his free hand, he unfastened her bra and pushed up her camisole. He lowered his head to her breasts, setting his tongue and teeth to work on one erect nipple.

Natsumi writhed under his lust-filled assault, his skill, his confidence, his aggressiveness, making her forget her own inhibitions. She wanted him to make her come. She wanted him to take her, pound into her, leave her weak and shaking.

Hideki felt her muscles beginning to tighten, her thrusts on his soaked fingers becoming more desperate, causing his cock to leak anxious drops inside his pants.

Natsumi snapped her hand down, clenching his biceps with a high, loud cry as she climaxed, the electric pleasure taking control of her, leaving her panting on the bed until the last of it pulsed away.

Hideki hovered his lips over hers, enjoying the moment of her ecstasy, before easing his fingers out and climbing off the bed.

Natsumi opened her eyes, seeing him pushing his black pants down to reveal his cock, long with an elegant curve, its head glistening with eagerness. She scrolled up to his toned abdomen, his lithe body letting her know that he wasn't one to tire easily.

Hideki paused in tearing open a condom and smirked. "Is it good?"

Natsumi brushed her fingertips up the silken-soft skin of his length. "Perfect."

"Thanks. I like it a lot, too." Hideki laughed and set to rolling on the condom. Before he had it on, Natsumi had thrown her camisole over her head and wiggled out of her skirt. He stepped toward her, running his fingers through her hair. "How would you like to start?"

Natsumi met his eyes. "From behind."

Hideki gave her a wink and a thumbs-up. "Nice choice."

Natsumi smiled, wondering how anyone could look so sexy and adorable at the same time.

Hideki put his lips to hers and crawled on the bed. Natsumi went down on her back, breaking the kiss to roll onto her stomach. Hideki brushed her hair to the side and grazed his lips across the back of her neck. He drifted his lips lower, kissing her shoulder blades. He moved to the center of her back, sliding his tongue down her spine to her tailbone, kissing over her cheeks and nibbling at the soft skin where her leg met her body. He slipped lower, licking down her right leg and coming back up her left.

Natsumi felt his knee nudging her thighs farther apart and shifted onto her hands and knees. At the feel of his wrapped head pushing against her entrance, she moaned softly. In one firm thrust, he dived inside her, the force of it driving the breath from her.

Hideki clutched her hips. The tight, drenched, heated confines of her seemed intense enough to melt the condom. He pushed deeper, pulling her back by her hips while moving his forward, inching in until he was buried to his base inside her. He moved in short, easy thrusts, stretching and opening her to him.

Natsumi rocked back on her knees, grinding in rhythm with him. Just as she began to get used to the steady motion, his next thrust came harder, his fingers biting into her hips. She grabbed the headboard with both hands and slammed back toward him.

Hideki grinned, yanking her back as he rammed forward. He scratched the short fingernails of one hand down her back, pounding hard and steady, making her groan and gasp with each thrust. He brought his upper body over her and pulled her right hand away from the headboard, moving it down between her legs. He eased his thrusts to rhythmic, deep pumping and placed her hand so she could feel him gliding in and out of her.

He put his lips to her ear, his voice coming soft and throaty. "Feels incredible, doesn't it?"

The surge of heat from his words and feeling them connected together gave her a dizzying rush so all she could do was choke out a stuttering "Y-yes."

Hideki brushed his fingers over her clit. Natsumi pressed his hand in place. At her bold demand, Hideki felt the first hint of his burgeoning climax and matched the stroking of his fingers to the thrusting of his hips. He nipped at the back of her neck; a groan that sounded more like a growl rumbled in his throat. He licked down the side of her neck, gave the curve a light bite, and thrust harder. A high, choked gasp came from her, with her muscles clamping around his already sensitive cock.

Natsumi's head swam with the euphoria of his ardent thrusts, the firm massaging of his fingers on her clit, his groans getting louder with each thrust. Her climax began growing, her body trembling as it started to take control. She cried out, bucking back hard against him as she came. Hideki slammed deep with a yell, his own climax breaking free.

He lingered inside her, taking a moment to catch his breath before slowly easing his length out and climbing off the bed. Natsumi collapsed under the blankets, her arms and legs feeling too weak to hold her. She looked toward the bathroom as Hideki walked out, seeing he had a fresh condom package in his hand and realizing this had just been a precursor.

Hideki slipped under the covers and lay on his back, pulling her close to him with one arm. "Natsumi-chan, would it be okay if I asked a favor of you?"

Natsumi draped her arm across his chest. "Of course."

"Would you not come to the club after tonight? I'd rather you not be one of my regular customers. I wouldn't feel right earning commission off my lover's money."

Natsumi sat up, trying to get her stunned mind to function. "Lover?"

Hideki nodded. "Yes, unless you don't want to see me after this. I'd understand, since I keep other women company. And there's my other lover, of course."

Natsumi looked into his eyes. "I would love to see you after this. I won't make any complaints about your life, but you have to do the same for me. Right now, my life is for me, not for starting a relationship. I'm sorry if that sounds cold."

Hideki twisted a strand of her hair around his index finger. "It's not cold. We'll take each day as it comes. Agreed?"

Natsumi nodded and slid up his body, giving him a passionate kiss.

Hideki tangled his fingers deeper in her hair, wondering what each day would bring them.

Dragon's Breath
ANNE ELIZABETH

HANDS BRUSHED THE SUDS, gently rubbing them with caressing strokes from her skin. She was being dried, tended, and her brown eyes drifted shut. He fondled her, and it was her job to take it, to accept each indulgent touch and every decadent whim. The decision was his, because tonight she gave him his greatest desire: the gift of her, to do with as he pleased.

"Ginger, girl, open wide." His voice was mild as he waited for her to comply. His Zen-like roots were well hidden in the blandness of his request. "Be good, my geisha girl, and don't make me raise my voice."

A smile danced on her lips before she parted the cherubic, plum-shaped form and performed as bid. Her tongue lay flat, and her teeth showed behind the tease of a smile.

Candy—crystallized ginger—was placed inside. She held it in

the center, cupped it with the sides of her tongue, and waited for his next words.

"Indulge, my sweet. Enjoy the fire."

Rolling the treat on her tongue, she pushed it to her teeth and bit down. Succulent heat filled her mouth, and she breathed in—to draw the dragon's breath. It filled her senses: the smell of citrus, the bite of heat, and the score of fire. Out it flew to encompass her sensory perception until it was pulled reflexively, with a breath, down her throat. Like the dimensional creature that traversed between the spirit and physical planes, it took her back and forth, and she felt as if she traveled on wings.

They reached for her then, those hands of his, and picked her up. Took her from the bathhouse toward the temple. She lay over his shoulder, but the burn of ginger preoccupied her, made her too consumed to be thoughtful of jostling against him, until it was too late and the ginger was gone.

But when it was gone, she became hyperaware of everything.

Feet touched cold, as she was placed—righted—onto the center of the dais. Air chilled her skin and gooseflesh rose. There was something eerie in the familiarity, and yet she knew she had never been to this place before.

He moved around the room and paced around the dais.

She watched him, intrigued.

The look he gave her said she shouldn't take notice.

She bowed her head and looked away. Couldn't ask what he was doing. She didn't dare believe what he might want or even contemplate what he planned to do. Images ran through her mind from ancient rites of ceremonial thunder, from naming and ownership to battle and celebration. No others were here to witness this event, and nothing she could see would mark this day on her flesh. Yet, here she stood, naked, clean of cosmetics and clothes. No mask of makeup distracted her, no shawl wrapped over her breasts with their perpetually hard nipples and draped down to her small hips. Nothing could conceal her figure or distract from this moment.

"You excite me." His voice was low, raspy.

Blood rushed her cheeks, and she could feel them redden. Emotion seemed a strange cover and yet she felt warmed by it.

"Spread your legs." The order was loud and it filled the room.

She took a step, widened her legs by a foot. A mixture of defiance and excitement made her push her hips toward him.

"More."

Legs moved, and she lifted her arms to wrap them around her waist.

"No. Arms at your side. So charming."

She nodded and made them be still next to her. Her eyes darted from him to the floor, then began to search the room for clues. She was too nervous to push him for answers, as if he would explain the chain of events—what might come—now that he was in control. She felt truly vulnerable and exposed.

The design of the room slowly sank in. Jade was laid from floor to ceiling with two pillars on the dais next to her and six more on each side of the room. Symbols graced the four corners. A temple room—what she would have done with it, she did not know—the place, the room, even the man before her, held such immeasurable power she felt humble before it. He was a rarity, a former Keeper of the Temple Ways, and he still carried that spiritual deepness in his handsome, finely honed skin.

Clap.

The sharp sound made her jump and brought her eyes immediately to him.

He rubbed his hands together, as if the smack of flesh on flesh had been pleasing to him. Brown eyes held her own; except his were sharper like a bright light—a color that changed depending on his mood.

She watched, wide-eyed, unwilling to take her eyes from him, trying not to blink, trying not to let her imagination run away with her: needing to focus on him and her.

Here she stood, naked in a room filled with jade; filled with him.

The torches on the walls flickered, and one spat out sparks.

"Arms up."

Like a butterfly opening her wings, she dramatically lifted her arms. In all things, in all ways, she wanted to communicate: her beauty, her ability to rise to the occasion, and the fragile nature of form. She gave him a heart-filling grin.

"Lovely." The appreciation in his voice was strong. "Such thoughtfulness. I will truly enjoy the gift of this eve."

A smile was not just an expression when it came from that secret place. It was the lingering evidence of lust and languorous emotions, the one that took compliments of beauty and wrapped them in silk to be examined and enjoyed further, another day, in another time, when such gifts may be unwound, savored, and prized.

"I prefer it when you smile. You are so beautiful."

His preference mattered to her. The significance of her smile was treasured, the gift of this response so cherishingly shared. "Thank you . . ."

"Master." His tone was firm.

"Thank you, master." Those words felt too good to her.

An indulgent smile filled his features, and for a moment lips and cheeks looked so sweet—almost boyish—before they melted like sugar dissolving in water. The blaze in his eyes became so intense and hot, as if he could morph her form, draw it away, and make it into another. Perhaps she would be able to travel through dimensions like the dragons.

In two steps he took the platform and stood beside on her the dais. From his waist, he drew a long golden rope.

With deft fingers, he began at the shoulder and wove the rope—over and around, tucked, pulled, then over and around again—until it reached her wrist. The series of H loops covering her made her flesh plump slightly over the sides, and she watched as he made an intricate series of knots and loops to cover her hand before attaching the rope to a metal ring on the side of the pillar. He moved to the other side and repeated the procedure. His fingers were elegant and swift as he made the loops into a golden crochet pattern over her skin.

After he had secured that hand to the opposite pillar, he moved behind her and gathered her waist-length jet hair. Fingers combed through the heavy silk, and she dropped her head back to enjoy the gift of his play. Moving the strands here and there, he touched the nape of her neck and massaged the tender flesh there.

She sighed.

A very male chuckle came from behind her, and the hair was brushed back from her ear. "Tell me how you feel."

"Happy."

Fingers trailed down her side. "Yes, soft and precious." Over her hip and down her buttocks, they moved. "But this is about what I want. Concentrate on this." They slid between her thighs and cupped her.

A moan escaped from her lips.

"Hmmm, do you like that my pretty, my Ginger girl?"

The fiery candy had long been swallowed, and the breath—that distinct heat of the dragon—was gone, but she could almost swear it pulsed its fire into her veins.

The presence of his hand drew that dragon magic to him, until it was all she could do to fight herself, to not rock into his heat.

"When you fight this, you fight me." He squeezed again.

She cried out and rocked herself forward onto him.

Fingers moved, shaped to her, so her clit had something to catch, to make its wish come on, to bloom into fullness. The other hand snaked around the side of her and caressed her breast, teasing the skin, until the nipple drew tight. Those talented fingers drew her nipple out and plumped it, before reverently holding her in his hand.

The dual sensations made her body whimper its pleasure as she made small moans of delight.

"Yes, my sweet Ginger, bring your crystal-covered pearls for me."

Her body rocked to his command and spasmed in a rush of need.

"That's my sweet. Thank you for answering my call."

He came to stand in front of her. With one hand, he dropped the robe that had covered him. This handsome former monk brought a hand to his mouth and tasted her.

She arched toward him, as if her lips might be where that hand had been.

His lips gleamed with her cum. His tongue licked the length of that succulent mouth and he smiled, one of those rare boyish grins. "Sweet. Like my Ginger, all sugary with a bite of fire at the end." Lowering the hand to his cock, he rubbed the rest of her wet against him.

Her dark gaze locked to that gorgeous cock. It bounced in delight and she licked her mouth reflexively in want.

He tilted her chin up to him. "Soon, my darling, it will come. For now, you will do as I wish."

She nodded and lowered her eyes.

Fingers squeezed her chin. Her gaze snapped automatically to his. "It is not subservience I want or seek, it is your intelligence, wisdom, and grace. Only a strong woman—one who is the mistress of her own destiny—might make a gift such as this so precious. Nothing less than the gift of your best is welcome here. So bring me the heat of your passion, the fullness of your desire, and the most exuberant of your need and then let me slake of my own desire."

The beat of her heart was racing. Never had a man wanted so much, and more. Her body arched toward his as her gaze gave him everything she was.

"Yes. That is my Ginger; full of spirit and fire. Give me it all." He stepped behind the pillar to his right and came back with more ropes and a box. He set the box gently on the ground and began to unwind another gold length.

Her body was roped from center to collarbone and down each leg. She hadn't noticed the rings in the floor until she was secured in this spread-eagle position.

He stepped back from her, seemed to admire his workmanship, before he took the dais again. He leaned down and took the box from the floor. Inside was a small jar full of powder and a delightful pink puff. Blotting the strands in the fine grains, he shook the excess off. Ever so slowly, he approached her and teased the tips of her nipples, brushed the powder over her belly and again between her thighs.

Heat bloomed almost instantly and she strained forward toward him.

"What . . ." she began before her breath was taken away.

He moved in and whispered in her ear, "Ginger."

Heat bloomed into heat and the dragon's breath took form. She arched in titillation and almost pain, as a hand gently loosened the grains.

Moans escaped from her mouth, one after another. He drew himself against her and rubbed his body into the fire. His flesh joined hers and cock entered cunt. Together, they became joined as his body moved with hers.

She was on fire with the heat of the powdered ginger and him, and as his body rubbed, it drew the dragon onto him. Together, they shared the fire, and her gaze steadied into his, her body grabbed his cock and milked his seed from him. As she cried out her sheer pleasure, she climaxed on him and the dragon. But still she grabbed him, her body seeking more, needing more than heat.

"My hungry lady of fire, I see that want in your eyes. Do you trust me to bring you more than desire?"

"Yes, master." The words tumbled from her lips fast and tight.

His lips caught hers and rewarded her bravery, her truth, and her desire.

He pulled out and clapped his hands in a short burst of sound.

She didn't jump this time, only looked around.

Men streamed from the doors, young and old alike. They

stood reverently in the center as if she were a goddess to be praised and was already so adorned. Then they bowed down, and something in her mind and between her legs gave. Perhaps it was the appearance of being so vulnerable, rawly displayed—her emotions on her face and her body open—but the men bowing to her made her body begin to tighten and moisten, making wet drip down her leg.

Breath caught in her throat as he—the master—took to the stand. With boldness, his hands stroked over her, owned this moment in front of them.

She raised her head and stared above all the heads. It declared her power with the force of her stance. This was a testimony to her strength, her prowess, and her ability to be as she was.

He nodded his head in agreement, approving of her steeled spine and calm face. Winked at her, before he moved behind, reaching hands around and down between her legs.

She convulsed at his touch. Her senses wringing rapture from her mouth, her cunt wet in its decadent display, she performed the command—his, hers, and both of theirs as one.

He stepped away and clapped his hands again. The men disappeared as quickly and quietly as they had once come in.

Alone again, she stared into his eyes, feeling stronger, yet unsure.

As if reading her mind, he laughed. "Don't you know my greatest pleasure is pleasing you. Every time an orgasm slides from your throat, I am renewed." He reached to the floor and drew a small knife from his robe. "I feed on passion, like air streaming against the dragon's wings and energy through spirit's eye. You are my burst of breath, and I have a thousand ways I wish to raise and feed both of our desires."

The knife slid against rope and ring, freeing first hands, then feet, until released, she was free of pillar and floor.

Gently, he lowered her bound form to the ground.

Her breathed whooshed out in a soft huff. Cold jade touched heated flesh, shocking, then easing the places where the blood was held, where the rope had plumped her skin higher.

He put the knife away and slowly began to unwind the rope. First one, then another, working his way up. He freed her torso, then removed the ropes from her arms. Hands rubbed continually in light or heavy strokes as needed. She couldn't articulate anything, just felt the surge of rushing blood.

He was hovering over her, pushing his cock in, sliding on the wet warmth and fitting so tightly, caught in her wedge.

She felt him bumping to the top of her cervix, a darling and heated kiss. Again and again, he hit that spot, making her arms grab for him. The sensations were so overwhelming, blood pumping so hard and him inside, that by the time her limbs obeyed her, all they could do was grab him and hold on for the ride.

Nails sank into his shoulders, and she heard a noise of protest, but he didn't adjust or move her, just pushed deeper.

The pulse in her womb joined the pulse in her veins, and her body tightened hard. She screamed on the near-pain sensation. Orgasm spilled through her, her pussy catching his cock and squeezing tight. It gripped him as if this were their last second on earth and their climaxes took them apart.

His cries echoed hers, as he was trapped with ferocity in her sheath. Muscles bulged on his arms, and his seed spurted deep.

The heat of the dragon held them, let them pulse in each other's arms, cascades of orgasms bringing sighs in equal parts. She hardly dared close her eyes for fear of missing a moment of the pleasure on his face. This was the man she had vowed to love, and it rekindled the newness of the lovers' embrace. "Will every time be like this?" The words came before she could stop their exit. Too dear had been the moment, and she didn't want it to be spoiled.

His grin was that of the boy, and for now it stayed on his face. A gleam of inquiry hinted at the corners, though his will was seated firmly and indelibly in place. "What is it you seek, my sweet Ginger? You only wished me master for a day."

"Perhaps I should examine the idea more closely." She blushed. "I feel the best of me rising. There is more of me now than there was earlier today. I feel strength where there was trepidation."

He rolled them over, so she lay on top and his heated skin touched the cool of the jade. Hands rubbed along her flesh. "You've already taken the first step to be taught, if you believe it is so. Tell me what you desire."

"Bring me to the dragon and let me breathe his fire." This time the words felt right and she knew exactly what she sought. "I want you, and the best of me. I can't define it and I won't. But I know what released in me: the touch of great power."

The curiosity behind his question drained from his eyes. "Yes, a goddess who encompasses warrior energy. My sweet Ginger welcomes desire." Hands squeezed her shoulders. He laid his lips to hers. Against her mouth he vowed, "Always, I protect what I treasure, the sweetness of my Ginger, and the pleasure of her fire."

May I Ask a Favor of You?
Onegai-shite-mo iidesu-ka

M. LAVONNE JACKSON

I DREW THE BLINDS so that just a hue of light shone through. I had to create a certain ambience for myself that allowed me to escape the walls of my exquisitely furnished office suit and journey to the realms that only Wang could take me. I know it must sound silly to name an inanimate object, but I liked to have a personal relationship with anything and everyone that I had such intimacy with. Wang and I had been through so many difficult times together. He was there during my first two breakups, my divorce, and the passing of my best friend. He was also there for the good times. He was with me during my first promotion, we celebrated my thirtieth birthday together, and he sang for me and my last assistant when she found out her husband was cheating on her.

Her name was Sakura. She was actually with the company prior to my coming on board. She captivated me the moment I met her. She wasn't the timid Asian woman that was often portrayed on television. She had style, class, and confidence. She introduced me to the world of Jimmy Choo and Manolo Blahnik.

Sakura wasn't the average height for an Asian woman. I was five feet six inches, and without her heels she still towered over me. When you'd see her, the first thing that came to mind was *model* in every sense of the word. Her ebony hair was a beautiful contrast to her flawless, light skin. She wasn't skinny but had natural curves, and even her 36D bosom didn't look out of place on her size 4 frame.

Over the next few months, many employees came and went, which opened doors in higher ranks for Sakura. She and I had become fast friends, and I felt guilty for my previous thoughts about her. She was not the bitch that I'd presumed her to be. She was warm and genuinely *shinsetsu,* kind.

Sakura confided in me that she thought Garver was cheating on her. I, too, sensed that he was probably having an affair, although he never approached me other than as a total professional. His travels became more frequent while Sakura stayed at home.

Garver was *bisheinen,* handsome and suave. He tried to hide his Asian ancestry behind blond hair and blue contacts. I always had a thing for Asian men. They exuded intelligence, confidence, arrogance, and, more times than not, money. Other than for his almond eyes and tanned skin, one wouldn't have known that Garver, who I later found out was birth-named Takahiro, was Asian at all. There was no coincidence that my favorite play pal was aptly named Wang.

It was late one evening when I received a call from Sakura. I could tell she had been crying so I invited her over to talk. Truthfully, she was the only friend I had made at the company. The other women in our department were so damned phony that I didn't bother trying to make them part of my circle. They weren't worthy of my friendship or the company perks that came along with it.

An hour or so had passed when the slamming of the front door startled me. I was silent as Sakura pounded on my floor screaming with such pain that I felt it in my very soul. *Bastard . . . son of a bitch . . . ass . . .* all yelled in her native tongue. I knew her worst fears had come true.

I clung to her every word as she spewed the details of seeing Garver with another woman. I felt bad for my friend, but I was getting turned on as I listened to all the details. I decided to make us some tea to help calm her nerves. While I was in the kitchen, I heard my CD player come on. I opted for wine and grabbed two bottles of my favorite sake, Ozeki, from the wine rack. Sakura was swaying to the mellow tune with her eyes closed trying to drift away.

I sat both glasses on the table, which brought her out of her trance. We sat on the love seat and finished the first bottle in less than thirty minutes. I began to get a little loose and bopped to the music as well. I commented on her sensual selections and she started sobbing once more. Through the sobs, she told me it was a CD for Garver. Suddenly she hopped off the couch and retrieved her bag from the table. She handed me a pink Victoria's Secret bag and instructed me to open it while she poured us glasses from the newly opened bottle of wine. I held up the tiny garment.

"This is what he is missing." She continued, "Wanna see what it looks like?"

She disappeared into the bathroom and returned moments

later. The moonlight shone on something so beautiful that not even Harunobu himself could have captured its detail. Sakura was *utsukushii,* beautiful. Her long tresses were pinned up, her makeup was flawless, and the silk kimono was absolutely beautiful. She stood there for a moment with a little sassiness as she switched from side to side.

"*Nani?* What? You like?" she asked.

"*Zettaini sou desu.* Absolutely." I nodded.

"Wait." She slowly let the kimono fall to the floor.

I watched as she slowly walked toward me. I tried desperately not to stare at her breasts bulging from the bra. I noticed an opening in the bra that allowed her bronze nipples to wink at me. She twirled around and I almost salivated when I saw the thin thread of her thong disappear between her smooth ass cheeks.

"You like?" she asked once more.

I nodded. At least, I think I did.

Sakura sat on the love seat and patted the space beside her. I tried to maintain my composure and not let on how much I wanted to reach out to pinch her nipples and my own. She shivered slightly as she scooted back on the cool leather. Even in the dim light, I could see the cool air teasing her flesh, making her strain against her already tight bra.

Sakura propped her newly pedicured feet across my lap. She wiggled her toes, which indicated she wanted me to rub her feet. Her voice coolly guided my hands farther and farther up her thigh. I held my breath when I reached the folds of her sex. I didn't have the nerve to tread farther, so massaged back down her leg and rested it on my right thigh. I went through the same process with her other leg, but this time I allowed my index finger to glide ever so slightly down the crevice of her cunt as a moan escaped her *aka,* red-glossed lips.

"Now I do you," she said as she swung her feet to the floor.

I attempted to prop my feet across her lap as she had done mine, but she stopped them in midair.

"No, I show you what I learn. *Kinasai,* come," she instructed as she pulled me from my seat and led me to the guest room I had prepared for her.

"You take clothes off and lie on bed." She sounded forceful but graceful in her orders.

I took off my shirt and proudly showed off my blessed bosom. I hesitated with taking my bottoms off. This was one moment that I wished I had worn underwear.

"All off. Now!" Her words cut through the overly lit room.

On instinct, I dropped my sweats to the floor and stood there naked. I prayed that she didn't notice the glistening trail my juices coated my inner thighs with.

"Lie down on back," she said as she grasped my shoulders and eased me to the edge of the bed.

The chill in the air kissed my body with its cruel lips, lingering more on my nipples than any other area. I looked at Sakura as her eyes burned into my flesh.

"*Miryoku-teki.* You are attractive woman, but we have problem," she said, reaching into the bag.

"You lie still. *Ochitsuite,* relax." Her words eased my worries.

I closed my eyes tightly. I felt something cold and hard traipse down my chest. The metal against my body caused me to flinch and heightened my senses. It stopped at my mound, then I heard the shears open and close. With each movement I felt my pubic hair being cut away like overgrown hedges. I had never thought about shaving myself until I'd noticed Sakura's smooth mound while I rubbed her feet. Then, I heard the buzzing of the clippers. I felt a skillful hand, starting at the top, sweep down first the outer areas and then the middle. Sakura's soft hands followed each newly smoothed area.

Suddenly I felt the clippers move closer to my clit. The vibrations sent waves of ecstasy through me, and I knew Sakura could see the dampness between my legs. I felt a warmed washcloth wipe away the remaining traces of hair. I let out a long, deep sigh.

For a long moment, nothing happened. I peeped around and Sakura was nowhere in sight. Disappointed, I left the guest room and heard Sakura faintly sobbing on the love seat. I went into my bedroom, slid between my black satin sheets, and tried to relax. As much as I fought the urges, I reached into my nightstand, and Wang was right there ready as usual to never judge, but always satisfy. I hesitated because I knew he could be a little loud at times. After much debate, I didn't care.

I let Wang explore my freshly shaved sex, and he approved so much that he brought me to my first orgasm in seconds. I was so involved with Wang whispering beneath my blanket that I didn't notice that Sakura was sitting across from me on my chaise lounge. I stopped abruptly and turned off my vibrator.

"Don't stop. I enjoy." Sakura continued, "Move blanket. I want to see."

I slowly removed the blanket, then the sheet underneath. I massaged Wang and finally he was turned on. The sensual sound of his humming always relaxed me and prepared me for whatever destination he desired to drift me away to.

I watched Sakura as she watched me. We moaned in unison as she sucked her fingers and mimicked my motions. I imagined it was my fingers swirling around her tongue one at a time. I closed my eyes as my cunt throbbed with excitement.

My eyes rolled into the back of my head as I glided Wang to my hot spot. I glimpsed Sakura and noticed her head back and her eyes closed as well. I realized that she was furiously rubbing her sex, but she didn't seem to be getting any relief.

I watched her head sway side to side as her hips pumped against her hand in no particular rhythm. She fought with herself, trying to reach the euphoria that came with satisfaction. I saw the frowning and the anxiety and then finally the tears as she tried unsuccessfully to release her tension. I walked toward her.

Wang had never touched any woman's body other than my own. I could practically hear him begging me to allow him to caress, tease, and please Sakura the way he pleased me. My heart was beating so fast and loud that I was almost certain that I would disturb her or embarrass her if I stood too close. I conjured up the nerve to stroke her right cheek with the back of my hand. She slowed her rhythm and rubbed her face against my hand. I felt the dampness that her tears left behind.

Wang grew impatient with me. He wanted Sakura that very moment. I tried to calm his urges, but his voice roared louder with rebellion the moment I allowed him to kiss her lips. I watched as she parted her mouth and allowed him to enter. I couldn't help but touch myself as I watched Wang make love to Sakura's mouth. The deeper she sucked him in, the farther her legs spread apart.

I don't know what came over me, but I was getting jealous of Wang having all the fun. The next thing I knew, I latched my mouth around the one nipple that had managed to escape from her sexy bra. I suckled her like a newborn baby. I played with her between my teeth as she stroked my hair.

"*Hai*, yes . . . *Onegai*, please . . . ohh . . ." She moaned deeply as her body created an erotic dance that Wang enjoyed. He hummed all the way down her body. He caressed her sides. He teased the insides of her thighs. He whispered just above her clit. I knew Wang loved to take his time as he nuzzled his head around the clit to make certain the passage was dripping wet before diving right in.

Sakura was now completely lying down with one leg thrown across the back of the chaise and the other dangling to the floor. Her mouth was parted while her fingers busied themselves pinching her nipples. My own breast ached to be touched, but I was focusing more on my friend.

I could see why she thought I had a problem. There was no sign that hair had ever existed on her mound. It was as smooth as a baby's bottom and as fragrant as a rose. I had never smelled another woman's sex, but she had the sweetest aroma and I yearned to get a stronger whiff.

I closed my eyes and ever so slowly inched closer to Sakura. If anybody had ever told me that I would be touching another woman's breast, let alone tasting her sex, I would have had him or her committed.

Sakura opened her eyes the moment my tongue flicked across her clit. My body was in an awkward position, but I didn't care. She tasted as sweet as she smelled. Wang moved lower down her slit so that I could fully take her clit between my teeth. I felt her body gyrating beneath me and caught her rhythm. I sucked and licked, teased and pleased. I was encouraged more the moment I felt her hand on the back of my head.

"*Onegai,* please. Tease no more. Fuck me now." Sakura uttered the last real words spoken between us.

Wang seemed to awaken at her command. His force in my hand was relentless. He stroked Sakura to four, maybe five, orgasms. He couldn't decide if he wanted to be buried in her sex or to tease the outer realms. Sakura decided for him and plunged him deep inside her cunt, then her ass. I watched as my fingers plowed deeply within my own sex. We became a trio roaring our sexual song through the night. The song ended all too soon. By the time I awakened the next morning, Sakura was already gone. I wondered if we'd crossed the bounds of friendship, but I didn't regret it.

A few months had passed since I'd last heard from my friend. I reminisced about the times we shared and conversations we had. I then remembered that was also the last time I saw Wang. I missed him and needed him to comfort me. I was about to search for him, but I was interrupted when the doorbell rang.

"I have a package, Ms. Lee," said the weak voice.

It was from Sakura. The postmark was Tokyo and I knew she must have left Garver and returned home. I was as giddy as a child on Christmas morning. I immediately plopped on the love seat to open my package. It was a fairly large box and I couldn't imagine what it contained. My birthday was several months away, so I figured it was something she'd borrowed and wanted to return.

The large box contained a note and four other packages. Since it had been so long, I wanted to read the note. She had taught me a little Japanese and I was able to make out a few words. I read:

Dear *Tomodachi* [Friend],
   Ogenki desu ka? [Are you well?] I will see you soon.
Be happy. Live happy. *Ai shiteru* [I love you]—Sakura

The first item was a CD of her favorite jazz tunes. This one was different from the first. Instead of melodies of love, it contained melodies of lust and sexual desires against backgrounds of waterfalls and tropical sounds. On the front of the CD she wrote, "*Junbi dekita,* ready?" My interest was piqued as I opened the next package while the music played in the background. It was a replica of the lingerie she'd worn the last time I saw her. This one was *shiro,* white. The note attached read, "*Oishii,* delicious." I licked my lips as memories trailed back to the last time I'd seen her. My clit twitched. I imagined Sakura smiling at me as I blushed. I immediately took off my clothes and put on the lingerie. I felt sexy, sensual, and desirable. I pulled out another package. I gasped after opening it. It was massive. I admired the sleekness, the curves, and the details. The note read, "*Doozo yoroshiku,* pleased to meet you." I stared in awe at the beautiful gift Sakura had sent me. He was double the size of Wang and I saw the word GODZILLA etched in his base. Godzilla had a detached unit that contained batteries and an AC adapter.

Kochira koso, the pleasure is mine, I thought to myself.

I couldn't wait to let him explore the regions of my flesh, the depths of my loins, and the passions of my passages. I knew he would take me to places Wang had only dreamed of.

I finally got to the last package in the box. Godzilla sat beside me and waited patiently as I read the final note from my friend: "I want to see." I didn't understand the note until I turned the package upside down. It contained what had to be the world's smallest digital camera. Never in a million years could I get up the nerve to do what Sakura was asking me to do. We did cross the bounds of friendship, and I knew there was no turning back.

A flat envelope was taped to the very bottom of the box. I carefully lifted and opened it. It contained several photos of Sakura and Wang. I couldn't believe he'd betrayed me and left me for my friend. He looked happy exploring the depths of her innermost regions.

Before long, I was setting the camera up on the far arm of the love seat. The music had stopped playing, but the mellow tunes continued in my mind. I turned the camera on. It was set up to flash about every five seconds. The flashes seemed to come more and more frequently as I explored my body. My head swirled with visions of Wang and Sakura. I heard Godzilla whispering that he wanted me to turn him on. The power of the vibrations made my body crave his touch. Like Wang, Godzilla was impatient. He wasted no time finding his way to my sex. My eyes were closed, but I could feel and hear the camera snapping. I opened my eyes just long enough to see one of Sakura's photos with Wang making love to her on her white featherbed. Godzilla could sense I was ready for him. He dipped the tip of his head into my cunt. I was ready to cum. I imagined it was Sakura gliding him around and teasing me. Godzilla was turned to maximum power. His song became a thunderous roar. My eyes rolled to the back of my head as wave after wave after wave swept through me. The fury of Godzilla was relentless as he caused me to fall from the love seat to the floor as I tried to prove that I was a worthy opponent. I was on my right side, then my stomach, then my left, then my back, as I thrashed around while my body lost control. I pinched my nipples; I bit my lip; my hips moved at warp speed as I tried to keep up. Godzilla was victorious on our first encounter.

My body had never experienced the pains and the pleasures that I had just been through. Not even during my best and wildest sexual encounter had I felt the complete satisfaction I felt at that moment. I looked under the table and noticed a small folded piece of paper. It must have fallen out of one of the packages. I opened it.

It read, "I see you soon. We have fun."

I couldn't wait.

Gimme Some Yang

LARISSA LYONS

I SAUNTERED UP THE Zen-scaped path, heading to the entrance with anticipation flaring in my loins. Today was the day I indulged myself—or made every attempt to.

When it comes to things I love, I tend to *overindulge*. (Chocolate, sex, margaritas . . . did I mention chocolate?) To better myself, I'd devoted this year to finding balance.

I wrapped my fingers around the tail of the metal dragon that doubled as a handle and opened the door of the sanctuary I'd discovered seven weeks ago. Crossing from the humid outdoors into the cool, inviting interior, I was reminded of how I'd learned to balance chocolate brownies with chocolate fudge and strawberry margaritas with coconut-lime ones.

The sex? Unfortunately, it's easy to abstain when no one of your acquaintance has the spark to fire your engines. I'd gone almost the entire year balancing hand jobs with vibrator usage, but everything had changed the day I discovered the White Dragon Center for Healing Arts, run by the delectable Yang brothers.

One look at the muscular, dark-haired studs and I knew— they could be the yang to my yin anytime.

As always, my poor clit was instantly on alert the second I entered the sprawling building that housed the wide variety of services available at the White Dragon. I still hadn't determined exactly how many sexy siblings there were or taken advantage of everything their center offered, but what I had tried so far (Beginner's Yoga, under the expert tutelage of the fine Taek Dae Yang) was definitely working . . . working me into one sex-starved—but limber—thirtysomething ready to indulge.

Bells chimed as I walked down the long hallway leading to the yoga studio. Never before had I arrived early enough to hear them. The melodic tones echoed around me, striking just the right note and causing subtle vibrations throughout my body. In the resulting stillness, I thought of how I'd balanced my lack of sex with an abundance of fantasies—all spun around the tall, chiseled Korean who looked better in a black T-shirt and exercise shorts than any man had a right to.

For almost two months now, in an attempt not to seem like an overeager yoga groupie, I'd been careful not to arrive excessively early, not to throw my back out trying to impress Taek, and not to step on my tongue—which I considered my greatest feat of all, considering how it hung out of my mouth as I drooled weekly over his hard body.

But today, I was going in with a new plan, determined to get what I wanted . . . which was Taek's well-proportioned cock sliding between my thighs (those tight shorts left little to the imagination). I reached the end of the hallway and stepped through the curtain of hanging bamboo strands.

Taek was the only one in the mirrored room, and I blurted out the first thing that came to my mind. "Do you think I'm flexible enough to take your intermediate class?"

He released the yoga blocks he'd been stacking and stood. Our eyes locked; his were glowing, dark slits.

"Ah . . ." He blinked. "I've been watching the way you move." His statement was as loaded as my clit. "Your technique needs a little work, but I agree, your body seems primed for more advanced asanas, perhaps even vinyasa work."

Asanas were poses, I knew, but . . . "Vinyasa . . . performing select moves in a certain order to bring about a desired end result? Usually heat in the body. Is that right?" I questioned my understanding of the term, knowing exactly which select moves and desired end result I wanted with him.

Taek's eyes flashed to my hips, then rose, catching mine again. His high cheekbones lifted when he smiled. "That is one way to word it, although we could improve upon your interpretation. Stay after class," he suggested, fisting his hands and placing them on his waist, drawing my attention downward. I saw the erection growing beneath his black trunks. "I'll direct you through a few moves, make sure you are prepared for my intermediate class."

The scent of sex suddenly permeated the air between us. Could he smell my arousal? I swallowed and attempted to balance my eagerness to fuck him with my need to appear in control. "I'll be happy to stay and learn any moves you want to share, Mr. Yang." I pulled my bottom lip down with one finger, staring at him in invitation. "You can count on it."

"I will." Boldly, he reached into his shorts and adjusted himself, his eyes never leaving mine. "And call me Taek."

The next hour was fraught with tension.

As yogi wannabes filed into the workout room, sexual excitement percolated through my every muscle. Surprisingly, Taek avoided making eye contact with me during the entire class, but he did put his hands on me every chance he got.

When everyone practiced the Downward-Facing Dog, Taek took the opportunity to trail his fingertips along my spine, causing me to hum with pleasure.

When the other students had their heads averted, holding the Triangle pose, Taek corrected my posture by easing his hands between my upper thighs and separating them farther apart. I barely bit back a moan.

Near the end of class, Taek led us through several relaxation asanas, ending with Mountain pose, which he instructed us to do with our eyes closed, while he talked about the importance of proper breathing. And familiarized himself with every nuance of my ass.

Could one hyperventilate while practicing yoga?

By the time the last student exited through the bamboo-curtained doorway, leaving us alone in the spacious room, my crotch felt so swollen, I could hardly stand.

"We could go to my office," Taek offered, his hand on the red velvet fabric he'd just allowed to drop in front of the waving bamboo strands. "Or I could demonstrate here."

"Here is fine," I eked out through a throat thick with unfulfilled desire. I needed my exercise clothes *off* and his cock *in* before I imploded.

"Someone might come by." He walked toward me, stacking the leftover yoga mats he passed. "We don't want to be interrupted." He straightened and pulled his shirt over his head, mussing his thick hair. Once his shirt was gone (thank God), I noticed his tattoo. Centered on his back, directly between his shoulder blades, black slashes etched an awesome-looking Chinese symbol into his skin. As I started to ask what it meant, the look on his face made the thought evaporate.

He was staring at me like *I* was a plate of triple-chocolate brownies with a side order of margaritas. I decided I was past caring if we were interrupted. "Trust me, I can be quick."

"I want you all to myself, my quietly alluring student." His gaze pinned me in place as he stalked forward. "As a great philosopher once said, 'Beauty is the bait which with delight allures man to enlarge his kind.'"

So, was I the beauty or the bait? Did it even matter? I glanced at the bulge in his shorts. "I don't think you could get any larger."

He reached me and cupped one shoulder. His other hand went to my waist and he hauled me against his erection. I ground against him and cream flooded the apex of my thighs. I was so ready for this. "Was that Confucius?"

"If we go too quickly," Taek said, releasing my shoulder to skim his hand down my chest, "you may not receive the full benefits from every posture." The pad of one finger tapped my protruding nipple. "Will you still come back next week, my silent beauty? I've been waiting for you to speak since you joined my class."

I reached for his erection, slipping my hand past his waistband to touch the hardness beneath. "Next week and every week after that," I promised, pulling his cock free. My thumb edged over the tip, teasing the tiny slit at the top and spreading the single drop of fluid over the impressive head. "I was playing hard to get. Bad idea." He thrust his thick penis within the circle of my fingers. "It seems I have a lot to learn."

"Then we'll get started. And that was Socrates, not Confucius." He peeled off my leotard, tugging the straps from my shoulders and pushing the snug fabric past my hips. I stepped free and tore off my black leggings. I wasn't wearing anything underneath and—

Wait. Was I getting naked in the middle of a yoga studio?

No, my mind corrected, in the middle of a healing-arts center. *Fine line,* I thought.

"Fine ass," I told Taek, seeing that he'd stripped. And it was . . . tight and curved, the color of an amaretto latte . . . and *dayum,* did I need a taste.

He smiled, white teeth gleaming. "Lesson one. Always use your yoga mat." Taek lifted me off the hardwood floor and slammed my back against the pile of mats he'd positioned in the center of the room. The sharp slap of vinyl stung, stimulating deliciously. I reached for him, but he stepped back. "Relax first. Proper breathing is essential for full benefit of any vinyasa sequences."

"Sequence away," I said airily, enjoying the view. His erection, stretched taut beneath skin of polished maple, looked heavy, powerful. I craved his cock inside me. "But the longer you make me wait, the longer I'll keep you right here." I pointed between my legs, where I knew I was flushed with wanting.

"Lesson two. Take time to arrange your limbs correctly for every posture." Taek bent my knees, placing my feet on the mat near my bottom, and spread my legs wide. Then he curved both of my hands beneath my breasts so that I was cupping the undersides. I thumbed my nipples, wishing he'd get on with it. Months of "balancing" no sex with no sex had me wanting to scream, *Screw the lessons, Taek! Screw me!*

But I waited, aching. I pinched my nipples. Better. I licked my lips, wanting to run my tongue along his muscled thigh.

He gazed down at me, still not touching, surveying his handiwork as he knelt at the base of the mats. "A good yogi knows how to hold the proper posture."

"Am I proper enough yet?"

"Bridge pose, Setu Bandhasana," he commanded.

I lifted my butt off the mats, bringing my pelvis even with my knees. The position brought my drenched folds within inches of his face. I felt sex juice leak from my opening and trickle down the crevice toward my ass. Feeling the slick glide made me impatient. I'd learned one thing today: balance was overrated. If he didn't quit toying with me and fuck me soon, I was going to karate-chop his dick off.

"Pranayama."

He wanted me to focus on my breathing? Ha! I noticed his respiration was smooth and even; his absolute control was a turn-on. Calming the frantic motions of my fingers on my breasts, I did as he instructed and took a deep breath and held it, then slowly released the air in a controlled exhale. The anticipation between my legs skyrocketed.

I breathed in again and Taek nodded. He swooped down, his mouth covering my clit in one quick motion, sucking hard. He licked over my outer and inner lips, drinking in the liquid passion dripping from my body, devouring me. I moaned, starting to come undone beneath the expert ministrations of his tongue.

He held my thighs wide apart, the tips of his fingers edging from my furred mons downward, past where he drank, to explore the receptive flesh leading to my ass. I abandoned my breasts and clawed at his shoulders. My hips flailed, rocking my pussy against his mouth. His tongue drove me higher.

I panted, gyrated, then let go and shoved my knuckles against my lips to keep from screaming when my entire abdomen clenched and spasmed as a powerful orgasm shuddered through me.

My thighs shook, the muscles straining, barely able to hold me aloft. I heard a noise and glanced at the doorway. No one was there. Had someone been watching? The thought fired my excitement.

The walls of my pussy were still shaking. I felt light-headed. *Again.* I wanted him to touch me. *Again and again.*

"Breathe," he whispered, pulling away and licking his lips. They glistened with my juices.

He pushed three fingers of one hand inside my vagina and swirled them around, capturing more liquid. My rippling muscles gripped his fingers, holding him tightly. I whimpered when he pulled out and watched, dazed, as he brought his wet hand to his erection and stroked himself, moistening every splendid inch.

"Taste. I want a taste."

"Next time, you may choose the poses, the actions. This is my day to educate. Lesson three: Always obey your instructor."

I pointed toward his dampened penis. "Do I get that next?"

"Roll over and lift your hips."

"That's not an answer," I grumbled, ordering my weak limbs to obey. I positioned myself as he'd directed, placing my hands and knees on the mats, stretching my spine and angling my butt high in the air, hoping he'd take the hint. I heard a muffled cough. Taek? Or someone else witnessing my descent into decadent debauchery?

God, I was turned on by the thought. I ignored the doorway and looked toward the mirrored wall, focusing on our reflections. The sight of Taek standing behind me, stroking his erection as he admired the view of my ass, made my eyes widen. " 'Chaotic action is preferable to orderly inaction,' " I said to our reversed images.

He playfully slapped his cock on my rump. "Confucius?"

I flicked my hips, seeking the tip of his rod with my wet mound. "Will Rogers. Another great—" I gasped when he knelt behind me and circled my entrance, teasing me, taunting me. "Philosopher! God, will you get on with it?"

I tried to lower myself against the head of his cock, but he moved, keeping out of reach. Keeping me dancing to his tune. "Where's the tequila when I need it?"

Taek leaned forward, blanketing my back with his hard chest, and intertwined his left hand with mine, tangling our fingers. His erection nudged between my thighs. I held still this time and gritted my teeth, praying he'd reward my patience.

"To prolong the anticipation is to prolong the pleasure," he whispered hotly against my ear.

My lower body hummed so fiercely, my heart beat so ferociously, I feared he was right. "Confucius?"

"No, that's all Taek Dae Yang and so is *this*." Taek rammed in to the hilt, filling me completely, indulging my self-indulgent side better than any vibrator on the market.

"Smart man—that—Yang." My words came out in staccato spurts as he methodically pounded inside me, driving so deep I almost slipped off the edge of the mats.

I rocked my hips, bucking against his groin, hoping to encourage him to speed up, but he only slowed the long, controlled—did I say long?—rhythmic glides of his penis. He continued thrusting in and out of my sheath with excruciating stamina. I arched into him, practically purring. "I need you to go faster," I panted, feeling another orgasm hovering, just out of reach. "But, oh, God—*don't stop* what you're doing." My insides fluttered, twitched, clasped around his plunging dick like it was a lifeline. "It's incredible . . . my lips are going numb . . . can't feel . . . my toes . . ."

And I just kept undulating beneath the forceful, penetrating thrusts whose speed he never varied.

Taek's right hand slid up my stomach, past my collarbone and neck, and he lifted my chin until I was staring at him in the mirror. I trembled, seeing my reflection. Was that me?

The female with the wide, uncertain eyes, face flushed with passion, entire body quivering . . . kneeling in an unfamiliar position of submission, under the direction and control of the soft-spoken Asian who quoted Socrates and wielded his erect member as if it should be insured by Lloyd's of London?

"Last and final lesson of the day. 'It does not matter how slowly you go, so long as you do not stop.' "

"Oh, God, don't stop."

He tilted my face until we were staring at each other, no longer using the mirror as a buffer. Twin rivulets of sweat dripped from his temples and edged alongside his nose. His full lips touched mine, then retreated. "I won't, if you won't. And *that* was Confucius."

And then his mouth took mine. Grinding my lips against my teeth, he pushed his tongue inside and I gorged myself on it, loving the spicy flavor . . . my first taste of him. He groaned low in his throat and his hips jerked, forcing his cock even higher inside me. I bit down on his tongue and reared against him, my thighs trembling with the need to straighten. Both my hands went between my legs, where I touched myself, feeling his cock as it slid in and out of my body. My fingers tangled around my clit and I screamed, coming so hard I saw spots—white spots that whirled before my eyes.

His tongue slid from my mouth, scraping against my top teeth. He smiled at me and drove higher, straightening his back and legs and literally lifting me off the mat with his arms wrapped beneath my breasts. I felt the rush of his release as it bathed the areas he'd so recently pummeled.

My arms fell to my sides. I stared again at the mirror, gazing at the exotic man who held me. Now I really needed that drink.

"No worries, you are definitely ready for my intermediate class." His words were a bit unsteady, I was pleased to note. "But I'd rather tutor you in private."

My mind was slow on the uptake, but his meaning finally penetrated. "Private lessons? Won't that be expensive?"

"I'm sure we can agree upon a trade; perhaps my instruction in exchange for your willingness to learn?" He stood and slipped from between my legs, then turned me to face him. I gripped his shoulders, trying to ignore the throbbing in my loins and formulate an answer.

Was I willing to trade my body for yoga lessons? It sounded good to me, but I did have some pride. "Is that an offer you make to all of your students?"

"Only the ones whose eyes follow me for seven long weeks before they ever say a word." He traced my eyebrow with his index finger. "Only the ones who quote philosophers and have the courage to get naked in the studio, where anyone could walk in."

"And how many have there been? That do all of that?"

"Counting you?" He slid his hand down my back and teased my bare bottom. "Only two."

"Two?" Hmm, that was better than I'd expected. "And what happened to the other?"

He flipped me around, until I was once again staring at the mirror. "You're looking at her."

His broad palms covered my breasts. "The woman in that mirror has haunted me since I first saw her Cobra pose and imagined how she, *you*"—he gave my breasts a squeeze—"would look doing the Bhujangasana while nude, riding me."

I started to sweat from the inside out. "Shall we find out?"

Suddenly, the strands of bamboo clacked together. Taek whipped me behind his naked body, where I stood on my toes and investigated his intriguing tattoo with my tongue.

"I'm loathe to interrupt, but I've had three complaints already. Maybe you two should get dressed before we lose any more clients."

I snuck a peek over Taek's shoulder and saw a handsome Asian poking his head through the velvet drape. Another Yang brother, I realized, seeing the same tattoo I'd been exploring adorning this man's neck. My fingers tightened on Taek's waist. "Your tattoos, what are they?"

"Smells like a damn orgy in here." The newcomer pushed through the curtain. "Forgive me, but my tai chi class starts in twelve minutes. I've got to light some incense, try and disperse the stench."

Grinning widely, Taek handed me his shirt, which I quickly slipped over my head. He drew on his shorts and pulled me to his side. "Chae's just jealous. His girlfriend's out of town."

Chae gave us a dark look, got the incense smoking, and left.

Stifling laughter, Taek hauled me to him and gripped both sides of my bare ass. Desire hit me again. I covered the smooth swells of his pecs with my hands and leaned forward, nipping the tight muscles with my lips. "The tattoo?"

"They stand for balance. We all have one."

Indulgence is mine, I thought.

"Dinner tonight?" he asked, his fingers teasing the humid crevice between my legs.

"You bet." I wiggled, positioning one finger just where I wanted it. "I'll bring the margaritas."

Past Reclaimed

RENÉE MANLEY

ॐ

AFTER LAST YEAR'S SPRING holiday in Tobuan, Pangasinan, a two-week period of Catholic mysticism and erotic voluptuousness in Joaquin Madrid's company, I decided to go for broke. When schedules were posted for the new academic year, I bit the bullet and marked my calendar for Christmas. It was the most expensive season for Philippine travel, thereby negating any other vacation possibilities for the rest of the year. I convinced myself that those week- to two-week-long breaks between school terms could be better spent cleaning my apartment while my checking account remained untouched for a little while longer.

For a part-time lecturer who spent more of his time driving between three different campuses than teaching, traveling during the holidays could be seen as a means of self-punishment, crammed in coach class with homebound natives and globe-

trotting tourists for a fourteen-hour flight. But I wanted to go—
needed to go—felt the compulsion. My head swam. My cock
stirred under the influence of an endless stream of delicious pros-
pects.

"So what's going on?" Cyndi asked. We marched out of our
shared office, arms piled high with student essays.

"I'm flying back home for Christmas."

"You managed to squeeze in the time unlike last year?"

I grinned and shrugged, heat creeping up my cheeks. "I have
to. Taking an entire term off just to fly home for Holy Week
really screwed me over financially."

"As if this is going to be any better."

"I'm not taking time off from work. Making up for the gap-
ing hole in my checking account won't be as traumatic as last
year."

We'd reached the staff lot by this time. It was a chilly evening, and I took in several deep breaths to revel in the crisp au-
tumn scents, wondering how Christmas would smell in the
Philippines. It had been several years since I celebrated the holidays back home. For all the visual memories that sprang to mind
when I made an effort to remember, no olfactory connections
could be made. I hoped to rectify that this time around, expecting Joaquin to be a huge part of my experience. A familiar heat
stirred in my jeans at the remembrance of Joaquin's scents—
skin, sweat, heat, semen, all commingling deliciously with the
calm and somber atmosphere of Holy Week, undefiled beaches,
nipa huts, and faceless flagellants.

"Are you seeing your school friend again?"

I looked at Cyndi. She'd gotten into her car without my being
aware of it, and she'd rolled down her window to lean out, a

mischievous grin creasing her features. Even her freckles seemed to smile with her. I chuckled, shifting my burden in my arms.

"I am, yeah. I'll be spending time with his family, too, which will be an interesting way of spending my time—some of it, anyway."

"Ah, let me guess—you're about to reclaim your Catholic roots and participate in all sorts of Christmas-related goodness."

"The whole shebang."

Cyndi turned the ignition, clucking, "My dear, sweet, atheist Matt Esperanza's rediscovering his roots—and all for *him*. You really must be in love."

"God forbid, Cyn, God forbid." I laughed as I stepped away. My friend and colleague slowly pulled out of her parking space, waved at me through her murky windows, and drove off. God forbid. Oh, sure. For a moment, I wondered whether I was fooling her or myself with such a glib, adolescent quasi-denial.

The age of travel, AD 9/11, meant overcompensating for delays, and that was what I did, which left me with little energy and even less good humor by the time the plane touched down at Ninoy Aquino International Airport before sunrise. I felt gutted. Between the homesick and half-senile grandmother on my right side and the young Filipina with blond highlights and blue contacts on my left, I had little peace. One seemed desperate to hold my attention as though talking incessantly to me about her grandchildren and dead husband cemented her firmly to her past, where she wished to remain. She also kept calling me Freddie.

The younger one flirted with remarkable brazenness. She admitted to being so shy with strangers till she went to America and learned to behave as American girls behaved—with an openness and confidence that could easily be mistaken for forwardness (or worse) in other cultures. She didn't care, even making significant physical contact with our arms and shoulders and, yes, our knees. In thickly accented English, she told me I looked like a movie star. I nearly blew Coke out of my nose and into her face. Both women were able to catch some sleep. I never did.

Joaquin picked me up at five thirty in the morning, unnaturally chipper for the time.

"I had to skip out of *misa de gallo* early to get here," he said as he stuffed my luggage in his car's trunk. I stood and watched in a daze, expending whatever energy was left in me to keep myself from falling over in a faint. The temperatures were cooler than I expected but still a hundred times warmer than California. As it always happened when I stepped out into the open Manila air, my lungs felt like lead. The air seemed so thick and heavy even in the early morning hours, and I hoped that I wouldn't fall sick the way I usually did when I flew home.

"You're kidding. What time did it start?"

"Four in the morning."

"I didn't know you went for that," I replied as I fumbled my way to the passenger door and crawled inside. Joaquin jumped behind the wheel with alacrity. I shrugged off my denim jacket and flung it onto the backseat, sagging in relief once the thought settled in my brain that I was finally, *finally* here.

"Oh, I do. All nine days till *Noche buena.*"

"You're so Catholic."

"And you're still fuckable."

I grinned, chuckling weakly, and he leaned close for a kiss. I welcomed it with as much eagerness and hunger as he gave it. In that brief moment of lips pressing against lips, months of separation swirled and coalesced and simply dissipated into nothingness. Philippine Holy Week of 2005 seemed to happen just a few days shy of Philippine Christmas season of 2006. Even with my exhaustion and dizziness, I chased after Joaquin's taste, reacquainting myself with the faint remains of that morning's Mass and the silky texture of his tongue against mine. Blessed wine and wafer, toothpaste, and his unique flavor filled my senses. I was suddenly aware of his hands fumbling with my pants and raised my hips to allow him sufficient purchase as he unbuttoned and unzipped. He pulled my pants and briefs down with some difficulty, then took my cock in his hand and stroked it with rough urgency.

My exhaustion suddenly forgotten, I didn't give a damn that we were in a parking lot by the airport in the dark morning hours. I simply held him more tightly, my hands fisting his shirt, my breaths turning to muffled groans as he jerked me off, my cock thick and hot and dripping with every hurried stroke. Release came quickly. I stiffened and arched against him, my groans turning to stifled cries as I drenched his hand with cum.

"God, I missed you," he murmured against my mouth after a little while. All I could do was nod, my breathing still erratic. I kissed him back—a wet, clumsy, openmouthed kiss—utterly spent and grateful.

He smiled as he pulled back, thumbing some moisture from my lower lip.

* * *

Jet lag took good care of my first two days. I stayed in Joaquin's house in the Commonwealth area, sleeping and struggling with physical and mental acclimation by turns. In the meantime, he was busy with tradition. He got up at three in the morning for *misa de gallo* and didn't come home till nearly two hours afterward, carrying two bags of freshly baked *pan de sal* for breakfast. Those bread rolls instantly became my favorite. Since moving to California, I'd gotten used to lighter fare in the morning as opposed to my mother's more indulgent offerings of eggs, fried *bangus* or *longaniza,* and garlic fried rice when I was growing up in Loyola Heights.

I was hauled off for some shopping afterward. Joaquin frequented the "people's markets," which were open-air markets or a cluster of sidewalk vendors who sold all sorts of things for obscenely cheap prices (yet they were *still* open to haggling). We picked through Christmas decorations, most notably exquisitely made *parol* or star lanterns.

"Pickpockets are everywhere," Joaquin warned me before we left the car. "Don't get too carried away with the goods, or your ass is theirs." He paused as he caught himself, then added, "That old-world ass of yours is mine, and I don't care to share it with anyone else."

"My, my. Possessive, aren't we?"

"Don't be sassy. I only see you once a year. I earned my possessiveness."

We picked our way through the crowd, color, sound, and smell overcoming my senses. Hope and beauty all captured in elaborate and painstakingly made Christmas and house decorations bore down on me. Along with those came the drearier sights of grimy streets and run-down buildings, of filthy, stagnant pools of water, of impoverished people selling their wares, sitting and staring out from behind weathered masks that spoke of resignation and battered pride.

I felt some discomfort at the curious, appraising looks I received from vendors and customers alike. I tried my best to be blasé about it all, but I couldn't help but wonder if I were being targeted for a deftly executed pilfering. In the crowd, I felt at least three people brush up against me. My money remained safe, but it was still touch and go.

Joaquin and I presently stopped at a stall that offered nothing but star lanterns.

"Do you have some kind of theme in mind?" I asked, carefully regarding an elaborate piece made of colored tissue cut into a delicate lace motif. It reminded me of a psychedelic snowflake.

"No, I don't. I just want my house bursting at the seams with these things." He grinned and held up one that was made entirely of *capiz* shells, which tinkled lightly in the breeze. "What do you think?"

"I love it. This will make the perfect nonpartner for yours." I showed him the lacy one I'd been admiring.

Joaquin bought just about everything I fancied, almost childlike when we got into the car. He'd stuffed the trunk with newspaper-wrapped lanterns. His eyes, dark and sultry with their almond shape and long, thick lashes, twinkled. His mouth, beautifully thick and pliant, was almost always curved in a smile. I told him that he looked like a kid who'd just feasted on candy, and he merely laughed me off before proving his age with an emphatic squeeze of my crotch.

He'd grown his hair out a little since I'd last seen him, allowing it to graze his shoulders in thick black waves. Behind closed doors, stripped naked, he looked so primal and raw. His brown skin was firm and lightly dusted with hair, inviting me to drag my tongue over it, tasting and bathing him.

"You'll never get tanned, Matteo," he noted on my third night, when he was assured that I'd gotten over jet lag well enough for a much anticipated fuck. Thank God he only kept one maid, and she slept in a little room on the bottom floor near the kitchen.

He laid atop me, his cock rigid and hot as he stretched me open. I didn't have to do anything because he liked being in control. I discovered that quickly enough, too, and was more than happy to bottom for him. He had his methods. He knew my body well enough to know what to do with it. His way of driving me crazy was to move slowly, giving me a taste of his impressive control. Looking up at him as he hovered above me, I took in the sight of Joaquin's flushed and sweaty features, his hair hanging loose around his face, his eyes darker and stormier as hunger gnawed away at him, and he fought it off. I moved my hands over his damp chest and toyed with his nipples as I struggled with my own excitement in a desperate hope of keeping up with him.

I sometimes wondered how much of my insides he could feel, with his dick so tightly swaddled by my muscles, squeezed and caressed and, in time, milked dry.

"I've gotten tanned in the summer," I corrected him. My words were barely a gasp as pleasure arced through me, and I pushed myself against his hips, my body swallowing every inch of his cock.

"I like you as you are—*mestizo*. I look at you, and I see history."

"You see colonists, you mean."

"I see a colonist worth fucking."

"Be glad that I'm not too fond of the sun . . ." My words trailed off in a low moan as he ground himself in me, and my eyes fluttered closed.

He pressed down and kissed my chin before trailing his lips over my jaw, his tongue flicking against my ear once he reached it. Another wave of heat swept through me, and I was gasping into the night air, his lazy, thorough thrusting picking away at the frayed edges of my control.

"I want the whole package intact," he murmured with a mild chuckle against my throat. "I fell in love with an Esperanza, and I aim to keep him untouched."

My Spanish heritage again—I never felt comfortable with the attraction I had as one of the lighter-skinned Filipinos. I'd experienced some notoriety back in high school, but it was dispersed, for our old Jesuit academy attracted several boys from old-world families. I wasn't the only *mestizo* in school.

"And what does it feel like to fuck an Esperanza?" I stammered, my damp skin prickling.

Joaquin's rhythm increased. "This isn't a good time for ego-stroking," he groaned back. His head dropped as he closed his eyes, and all focus, all energy, was directed at his cock as he plowed my ass. The bed's creaking grew louder and louder, more and more frantic, just as the sounds of skin slapping skin increased in ferocity. Our voices mingled with the rest of the sounds, groans and whimpers dissolving into a spiraling montage till we came, one after the other—Joaquin's outburst a guttural series of curses while I cried out into the dim light, my stomach tensing as my cock spurted in my fist.

He never liked to pull out right away and kept his dick in me even after he'd emptied himself. I always thought it a damned sexy thing—that thorough claiming of someone else, ensuring that every second of every moment would be stretched out to its limits, whether by that lazy rhythm of thrusts or that long wait inside my body, cocooned in spunk-drenched warmth. In the meantime, Joaquin would be kissing me with an energy that never diminished even after his orgasm. He'd force my mouth wide-open with his, our tongues slick, restless, and sometimes semen-flavored. The demanding attention with which he showered me guaranteed a renewal of my energy and a stirring of my cock within moments of our orgasm.

We visited our respective families a week after my arrival. My cousins, aunts, and uncles simply treated Joaquin like a dear (yet less privileged) childhood friend of mine. His parents and siblings were welcoming, though without the stiffness and ostentation that had always been the mark of Esperanza pride.

"You live in California now?" Mrs. Madrid asked, ignoring her son as he took her hand and pressed her knuckles against his forehead. It was almost odd watching that gesture of respect again after so many months of casual, egalitarian interactions with my mother, who'd also moved to the United States.

"Yes, ma'am, I do."

"You like it there?"

"I do—the diversity, especially. The culture . . ."

She nodded in a vague sort of way as she beckoned me over to the dining room, where a veritable feast likely awaited me as their guest. "Not in San Francisco? Your home, I mean."

"I live in the East Bay—Albany, near the Berkeley border."

Joaquin nudged me with his elbow. "She won't know where that is."

"Ah, good then," Mrs. Madrid called back over her shoulder as she stepped through the dining room door, her voice rising in volume as though she were attempting to talk to a deaf man. "San Francisco's diseased—too many drugs and too many gays." She stood by a large *narra* table that nearly sagged under the weight of so much food. "Come, eat! These are good! All ingredients were bought at the market this morning." She pressed a plump hand against her chest in emphasis, her chin lifted. "I chose them myself. Never the maids. They always get the wrong things and—how do you say it in America?—fuck up the cooking."

And she was right. The meal was fantastic.

The frenzied blur of the next several days was a thrill ride. Little by little, as though thick cobwebs were slowly being blown off my memories, ghosts from the past emerged—dulled and faded by time but potent in their effects. The smell of freshly baked *bibingka,* pervasive and defining as one of those scents of Christmas, dogged me day after day from sidewalk stalls or a corner eatery, luring me back from my American path to weed-choked trails of childhood. Without fail, I'd pull out my wallet and spend more money on a little stack of those sweet rice cakes to take home and to gorge myself sick with, much to Joaquin's disgust.

"You're not pregnant, are you?" he asked, watching me with a look both horrified and sickened.

"It's been too long," I said between mouthfuls. "I can't help it. Want some?"

He shook his head and pointedly turned away, raising his coffee mug to his lips. "That's okay. I think I'll be off that stuff for a while."

I tried a few times to get up at three in the morning to experience *misa de gallo* at least once, but I'd never been a morning person, and it proved to be a nightmare in the end. Joaquin didn't care, though he made sure to call me a "shaggable atheist" for the hundredth time since I arrived. Not that I minded, either.

Fresh from Mass, confidence and spirits raised as they always were when he returned home from church, Joaquin took care to wake me up for breakfast. There were no words to describe such an erotic transition. That shift from dreams of childhood and my youth, of long-forgotten faces and voices, all rising from the ashes of my past to swaddle me in familiarity and comfort—to the very real, very visceral experience of Joaquin settled between my spread legs, one brown hand rough and firm against my thigh, the other fucking me with two oiled fingers, his mouth soft and wet around my cock. Dreams would fade as they inevitably did under his handling, and I'd become an adult in a breath—naked and aroused, helpless under my lover's weight, my senses drowning under the sights, sounds, and smells of smog, star lanterns, rice cakes, beggars, crowded churches, and indefatigable hope.

I made it to church once—for *misa de aguinaldo* on Christmas Eve. We didn't drive to either of our families for *Noche buena* afterward. Arriving home after midnight Mass on Christmas Day allowed us another opportunity to celebrate our rare time together. With Joaquin's maid gone home to her parents for Christmas, we had the house to ourselves. Like a Wildean decadent, Joaquin ate naked on his back in the living room before the Christmas tree while I sat astride his hips. His dick fixed me against him as I alternately fed him and sampled dessert off his chest, demonstrating my approbation by grinding my hips, groaning at the luxurious feel of being owned yet again. I hoped that he felt every inch of my body around him, and that he listened to it—the pliant heat a wordless reassurance that, yes, I'd always been his.

Samaya

FRANCES JONES

ॐ

JUST AFTER THE SUN crested the pines, Chokyi took six withered walnuts from beneath the tree in the monastery garden. He peeled back the dried flesh and set them on the stone wall, tapping their shells lightly, beckoningly. Soon a squirrel drifted down on its fleshy wings, chittering as it landed. Chokyi held the nuts in his hand, teasing the squirrel, which sat on its woolly haunches, scolding him and swishing its tail.

They played this game each morning; always it was a struggle for Chokyi to stay quiet, to resist the laughter that gathered in his belly and tickled up his chest. Just when he was ready to burst, he would open his hand and let the squirrel have its pick of the nuts. It would clutch one in its tiny paws and bound along the wall, away from the monastery and into the deep shade of the pine forest.

The game was one of the only things that entertained Chokyi

after so many years living and working in the monastery. When
it was full of monks, Chokyi often wished it were empty, as it
was now. The others had left a week ago to perform a blessing
ceremony in the village of Yangpachen. Chokyi's task was to
stay behind and look after the temple and grounds, a task they
rotated once each season.

But when he was alone, Chokyi found himself longing for the
slap of the monks' bare feet in the halls, the drone of their chants
drifting from the temple windows, the clatter of their chopsticks
when they ate. Even a monk can only contemplate so much silence, so much emptiness. Now, it would be some days before
they returned, dusty and solemn-faced and ready for tea.

By noon dark clouds had stormed the landscape. Chokyi
paused from his bowl of rice to watch the rain pour through
the canopy of conifers outside the window. The steel-gray water
fell in sheets, soaking the hillsides and drumming against the
walls.

Its music was a welcome change from the silence of the Hi-
malayan foothills, but with guilt Chokyi dreaded the tasks it
brought: finding and patching leaks in the roof, placing bowls
under the dripping ceiling, clearing leaf litter from the gutters.
He longed to sit in the sun, to drowse, to feel the Buddha's hand
brush the top of his head with invisible fingertips. He reminded
himself to stop longing.

Chokyi finished his midday meal and retrieved a large basin
of rainwater from the porch, using it to rinse his empty clay
bowl. He set handfuls of richly flavored vegetable rinds to sim-
mer in a deep pan of water over the hearth. From the kitchen he
gathered a handful of bowls, knowing that as the rain pounded
the temple, water would breach the roof.

He dashed from the main building across the deck to the temple, feeling the cold rain sluice across his bare head and sneak its way beneath the folds of his saffron robe. He paused at the entrance to the temple, bowing low to the large golden Buddha who sat in the center of the room. The Buddha's expression never changed; he gazed serenely down at Chokyi, one hand raised and the other touching the floor, unperturbed by the storm that had settled over the land.

Chokyi tracked the sound of dripping water and placed bowls in four locations in the temple chamber to catch the drips. He then returned to his place before the Buddha to make sure the offerings of blossoms, oranges, and water were still adequate, though he had checked them that morning. Bowing low once more, he lit several sticks of incense, folded his legs into lotus position, and let his mind drift into stillness.

The sound of water drips almost merged with the constant susurrus of the rain as it fell everywhere, everywhere, everywhere. Although Chokyi had had plenty of practice with his meditations, he still struggled to find that empty place. Today, the water dripping into those wooden bowls crowded his ears, distracting him.

He imagined himself as a silver fish, thrashing with all his might against the current, just to reach the stillness of a mountain pond. With a sudden and deep breath he plunged into it, his thoughts as dark and sheer as a mirror reflecting midnight.

In the dream he was seven years old again, sitting with his mother as she read to him from a book about the railways of China. Trains, those massive steel structures clattering down miles of track at exhilirating speeds. As she read, he closed his eyes and imagined he was riding on the caboose, watching the landscape vanish rapidly into the distance, feeling the wind across his scalp. There were no trains in Tibet when he was a boy, so he had to dream them.

He longed to do the simplest thing: to purchase a paper ticket and step up onto the car, to feel the jolt as the train pulled loose and boosted its speed. He could go anywhere, become anybody. But in the dream, just as he stepped up to the ticket counter, everything was lost in mists and darkness and the dripping of the leaky roof into brimming bowls of water.

When Chokyi opened his eyes, dusk had fallen over the hills. The rain was unceasing. He returned to the main building and took up a broom to sweep the floors before the light vanished completely. With each sweep of the bristles he chanted, forcing himself to stay present within the words and their rhythm as he cleaned: *"Om amoga-shila sambara sambara, bara bara maha shuddha sattva pema, bibu shitabuntsa, dhara dhara samanta avalokite, hung pe soha."*

As the rain thundered in the growing darkness, his chanting grew louder. Both sounds competed for the Buddha's ears. But as he paused to take breath, he heard the sound of bells chiming at the gate. Someone was asking for shelter.

Chokyi tucked the broom away and quickly lit a lantern, raising it above his head as he went to the doorway of the monastery. There, standing on the footpath in the downpour, was a small figure whose face was obscured by the darkness. Chokyi waved his hand, beckoning the stranger inside.

As the pilgrim came closer, he saw it was a girl—no, a woman, small and slender, her clothes and travel pack drenched and dripping. *"Bhikshu,"* she said softly to him as she stepped onto the porch, bowing low in greeting. "Many blessings. I was caught in the storm and have been searching for shelter."

"Please, come inside," Chokyi said. He led her into the kitchen and gestured her to a large stone bench by the hearth, where a small fire continued to burn. "Warm yourself. I am Chokyi."

When she set down her pack, Chokyi noticed that a long, sheathed dagger jutted out the top. A ragged hank of fringe tied to its handle caught the firelight, shimmering dully. Looking away from the weapon, he bowed to the woman and gestured for her to sit by the hearth. Then he fetched a bowl and filled it from the kettle of broth that was stewing over the fire. He offered this to her.

The woman pushed her long hair away from her face and took the bowl into her small, perfectly formed hands. "*Bhikshu.* I am Pasang," she said, blowing air across the surface of the salty, hot broth so that she could drink it.

Chokyi returned to his sweeping, not wanting to intrude on the stranger's meal. It had been months—no, more than a year—since he had seen a woman, and never one within the monastery grounds. This high in the foothills, the monks rarely received travelers.

When he looked up to check on her, he found that she had emptied the bowl and removed her rough jacket and tunic, which she was spreading on the hearthstone to dry. When Pasang saw that he was watching her, she covered her small breasts with her arms. But just as she lowered her eyes modestly, she raised them again, looking directly at the monk, letting the edges of her full mouth curl into the hint of a smile.

"Forgive me. Do you have any dry clothes I could wear?" she said.

Chokyi smiled apologetically. "Only monk's robes, and we do not keep many spares. But come, let me see what I can find."

He led Pasang to the cabinet where they kept the linens, across from his sleeping quarters.

As he selected a russet-colored shawl from among the textiles, Pasang peered into the darkness of his room, turning back quickly when he handed her the garment. Pasang wrapped the shawl around her shoulders and breasts. Chokyi scolded himself for lingering over the way the deep red of the fabric lay against the milky brown of Pasang's arms, over which her black hair hung like a fringe.

"Have the others already gone to sleep?" Pasang nodded toward the row of sleeping quarters.

"No, they are away, in Yangpachen."

"So you are alone?" Mirth played in her eyes. "It must be peaceful to have the monastery all to yourself. How long have you lived here?"

"Seventeen summers, since I reached manhood. And it is peaceful. It's also dull, but do not tell the Buddha I said that." He chuckled. "Where did you come from?"

"Ngari, far to the west." Pasang leaned against the wall and folded her tawny arms across her chest.

"You climbed all the way up to these mountains?"

"It isn't such a feat," she teased. "Your oldest monks do it."

"They do it because they have to. Few others come this way. Either they travel the lowlands, or they climb the mountain. We are too in-between."

"Soon, only the foolhardy will take the journey on foot at all."

"Why do you say that?"

"Because now the train comes all the way to Lhasa." As Pasang spoke, Chokyi's eyes grew wide. "You didn't know? It goes over the northern mountains. It is so steep that the trains provide oxygen tanks for the passengers, otherwise they get sick." She pantomimed putting an oxygen mask over her nose and mouth.

Chokyi could hardly believe her words. "All the way to Lhasa? But that is not even as far as Yangpachen. So close. Have you ridden it?"

"Not yet. It has not been running long." Her dark eyes studied him. "But I can see you would like to."

"Yes." Chokyi blushed and covered his smile with his hand.

Pasang stifled a yawn, hugging the shawl closer around her tiny shoulders.

Chokyi apologized, "You must be exhausted. Please, choose any of the rooms you like. I do not think this rain will dissipate tonight." As if to prove his point, thunder rolled across the sky, shaking the beams of the monastery roof.

"*Bhikshu,* Chokyi," Pasang said, pressing her hands together and bowing. As she rose, she locked her eyes with his, the dark line of her lashes scooping the air like a bird's wings. This time she did not smile.

Chokyi let Pasang take the lantern, then shuffled to his bedchamber, which was so familiar that he could pick his way onto his sleeping roll in the darkness. He lay down and closed his eyes, chanting, "*Om mani padme hung,*" softly as he drifted to sleep.

Pasang lingered at the end of the hall, lowering the lantern's flame until it guttered and nearly went out. Silently she waited until she heard the soft sound of Chokyi's snores before tiptoeing down the hall to the doorway of his bedchamber. She hesitated there, savoring his breathing, letting him dream.

Calmly she stripped away her damp stockings and trousers

and the red shawl so dark it was nearly black. Then she crept into Chokyi's room, crawling on hands and knees until she was kneeling at his sleeping side.

She lay a finger on his breast, feeling it rise and fall, and began to sing. Hers was a keening melody, wild and low in the night, waking him like a vision.

With both hands Pasang smoothed the cloth of Chokyi's robe away from his chest, baring his flesh. She ran her flat palms across it, raising gooseflesh and nipples. Lightning flashed, illuminating her face for the briefest moment with silver-blue light. Her eyes were heavy as her mouth formed the vowels of her wordless song. Chokyi, half-asleep, did not think to stop her.

Still singing, Pasang lifted Chokyi's hands to her breasts. She made him cup them in his work-worn palms, letting his calluses catch on her smooth skin. She knew he had probably not touched a woman's breasts since his mother weaned him. Chokyi's breath grew deeper and louder as he held her. Pasang's song died away into stillness.

She pressed her mouth to his, seeking his tongue. Pasang was surprised that Chokyi did not resist, did not clench his teeth against her. With one hand she untied the cord that held his robe and pulled the fabric away, exposing the lower half of his body.

Pasang sought his organ and found it firm, the tip still sheathed. In a slow motion she drew back the foreskin, then dipped down to take the head between her lips and suckle it, first gently, then firmly. She smiled as she heard Chokyi's breathing change again, this time to a broken staccato. His fingertips kissed her cheeks, her hair, her shoulders. Pasang resumed her song, vibrating the jewel of Chokyi's flesh as she rolled it across her tongue.

Pasang pulled back and raised Chokyi into a lotus position

on the mat. She lowered herself slowly onto his organ and folded her legs around his waist, wrapping her arms behind his shoulders. "Hold me," she said. His arms locked around her like a harness. She sat motionless, working only the muscles of her lotus, rippling up and down the length of Chokyi's jade stalk. Still he was silent.

"I was no passing traveler tonight, my Chokyi," Pasang whispered. "I have watched you for many months from my perch in the trees near the monastery. I have spied on you as you swept floors, cooked rice, drunk tea, and laid flowers before the Buddha. I know the flying squirrel who comes to you for nuts each day, and I know how you love to sneak fruits into your mouth when the other monks aren't looking. I have listened in the nighttime as you whispered your *samaya,* your secret name. I have longed for you, sung for you, wept for you, dreamed of your body in my body. Like this." She reached down and stroked the place where his treasure entered hers.

She let herself move against him now, a slow undulation spreading from her hips to her shoulders. Chokyi moved, too, first timidly, then with increasing grace and ardor.

Pasang kissed him again, touching their tongues to complete the circuit of energy. She thought of the statues she had studied in other lands. Shakti and Shiva locked in embrace, their stone limbs conjoined for eternity, their lovemaking witnessed by millions of curious eyes. As the storm howled outside, Pasang wondered if the lightning would strike her for seducing this young monk. Perhaps, as punishment, they would both turn to stone. She hoped so.

They remained in *yab-yum* as the night deepened. The rain tapered off. In its wake the low breeze of their breathing stirred the chimes that hung at the corners of the temple. Pasang returned to her melody. This time Chokyi joined her, his low tones anchoring her wailing voice. She climbed the ladder of his chant and clung to his body as a vine wraps itself around a tree, twining her way higher into his branches as his ecstasy rolled across the sky.

Pleasure took them both. It pulsed in slow waves from the place where Chokyi and Pasang were joined and rippled across the floor of the monastery, through the walls, along the rooftops. It shook the trees, the mountains, the valleys. It summoned the wind, which swept the storm clouds from the heavens, leaving only glittering black sky in its wake.

Just before dawn, Pasang rose, fetched her satchel, and packed a bag for Chokyi. She woke him with a kiss. "Come now. Come away with me."

"Where are we going?" Chokyi rubbed his sleepy eyes.

"To Lhasa." Mischief returned to her smile. "Let's go."

Chokyi could not believe how fast the train sped across the grassy Tibetan plain while he sat in a cushioned seat with Pasang curled by his side. He looked out the window at the steep mountains all around them, a landscape he had not seen in many years, never at this speed.

Warily he looked around at the other travelers, wondering if he was conspicuous in his loose gray trousers decorated with a confusion of zippers, his puffy black sneakers, or his bright orange anorak. Pasang had picked them out in a too bright, noisy store in Lhasa. The clothes felt strange to him, but nobody else took notice of the monk in new street clothes.

On the journey to Lhasa, Chokyi had told Pasang about his life, his family, his childhood fascination with railways. Now,

Pasang laid her head on his shoulder and pulled a large fleece blanket over them. Chokyi startled when she tugged at his zipper and reached inside, then cupped his lingam in her small hand.

"In all your dreams, did you ever dream of making love on a train?" Pasang whispered.

Chokyi grinned. This time he did not hide his smile.

The Mistress Charisma Treatment

JOCELYN BRINGAS

❦

AFTER APPLYING HER RED lipstick, Shirley looked at herself in the mirror one last time and smiled. It fascinated her that a curly black wig and a few layers of makeup could transform her from boring Shirley Villanueva to tantalizing Mistress Charisma.

When she was satisfied, Shirley said a farewell to her fellow employees and left the makeup room. The heels of her stilettos tapped loudly against the floor as she walked down the hall to her client's room.

For almost two years, Shirley had been working at Asian Sensation Enterprises, a company designed for wealthy men who desired to explore their sexuality and fantasies with Asian women. She enjoyed her job a lot because it gave her the chance to have sex with the hottest men in the world.

Through word of mouth, her alter ego, Mistress Charisma,

had created a good reputation in the company. Out of twenty employees, she was the most requested, and it was very competitive to become a client of hers.

Once Shirley reached her destination, she took a moment to flatten her skirt and put herself into a Mistress Charisma state of mind. When she entered the room, it was dim with a few candles flickering. A tall male figure stepped forward, but she couldn't see his face.

"Mistress Charisma, it's so nice to finally be graced with your presence," the man said.

"Likewise. What's your name?"

"Please call me Brody."

"Brody?" Her voice squeaked as she said the name.

Moving closer to him, she finally caught a little light on his face. Her heart started to pitter-patter faster when she realized exactly who he was.

"Yes, I'm Brody. I've heard so much about you, Mistress Charisma. A few of my business partners have been clients of yours in the past. They all rave about how great a fuck you are and that you're hotter than Lucy Liu, Kelly Hu, and Nicole Scherzinger combined."

"Really?"

"Yes," he whispered.

Shirley shivered when Brody's cold hands touched her elbows. Looking up into his eyes, she reverted back to her high school years . . .

"Nerdy Shirley, Nerdy Shirley, look at how nerdy Shirley is," *the Manthis High School football team chanted as they surrounded Shirley.*

"Does your mommy buy your clothes or does she make them

at the sweatshop in China?" Brody Orsino teased as he flicked off the baseball cap she was wearing.

Tears threatened to flood out of her eyes, but she fought hard to keep them in. She hated that out of all the students in the school, she had to be the one teased by the whole football team.

"I didn't know flower-print shirts were in style. Look at this shit, why the fuck would someone wear this?" Brody taunted.

"Not even my grandma would wear that crap," Brody's teammate Jeff said.

"Ju-ju-ju-just leave me alone!" Shirley stuttered as she tried to walk away, but they all blocked her.

"Oh, wow, she speaks. Did you guys hear her speak? I didn't know she could speak English. Ready, boys?" Brody asked as he looked at his teammates.

Shirley closed her eyes as the spurts of Silly String struck her body. The sounds of deep laughter surrounded her, and all she could do was fall to her knees. She'd never felt so humiliated in her life. That day earned her a new nickname. Not only was she Nerdy Shirley, but she was branded Silly String Shirl.

Every day in high school, Shirley was the butt of everyone's jokes. The worst teasing came from Brody Orsino and his football teammates. They never got in trouble for harassing her because they were treated like royalty.

When Shirley graduated high school she was so thrilled. She made sure to attend a college that was hundreds of miles away from Manthis so that she would never see any of her classmates, especially Brody Orsino, ever again.

Yet here she was, staring into his eyes, eight years after he'd tortured her in high school. From what she could see, he hadn't changed much. He still looked like the young jock he was back in high school, and he still had an arrogant aura.

His warm breath brushed her face as he leaned closer to her. Snapping back into her Mistress Charisma role, she quickly dodged his lips and walked away from him.

"Where you going, baby?"

Ignoring his question, she asked, "What exactly brings you here, Brody?"

"I'll be honest. I want some hard-core fucking."

"Everybody wants that."

"Look, Mistress Charisma, I didn't come here for a freaking interview. I need some pussy right now."

"Oh, yeah? Well then . . ." Mistress Charisma reached for her riding crop, stashed beneath the bed.

Walking toward Brody, she grabbed his hair and pulled his head down to her height. She dragged her tongue along the side of his neck, making him moan. He responded by grabbing her ass and pushing his crotch against her. She was actually impressed with his level of arousal. He was definitely packing major heat in his pants.

"Na-uh," she warned, and with the flick of her wrist Mistress Charisma slapped the riding crop on Brody's ass.

"Ow!" he exclaimed as he jumped up in surprise.

"Don't touch me," Mistress Charisma said firmly.

"Fuck this, I didn't come all this way for this shit," Brody huffed as he began to walk away.

Mistress Charisma kept her cool, and before he could even take two steps, she placed her hand on his cock.

"Did you really think all I did to your friends was fuck them?" she asked.

"Yeah."

"I guess they didn't elaborate on exactly what my specialty is. Sex is more than fucking, Mr. Brody Orsino."

Brody's facial expression changed when Mistress Charisma got down onto her knees.

"Now that's what I'm talking about," he said.

"I love to fuck against walls, do you?" Mistress Charisma asked while petting his cock through his pants.

"I'd fuck in a filthy Dumpster if I had to," he grunted, and quickly reached for his zipper.

"Take off your clothes and follow me," Mistress Charisma said as she walked to her favorite wall.

Leaning against it, she lifted her skirt and slid her hand between her legs. She gently fiddled her clit with her manicured fingers. She couldn't wait to start her time with Brody. It made her smile knowing now she had power over him. She never thought she would ever run into him again.

As Brody walked toward her bare naked, her eyes widened when she caught a glimpse of his hard cock standing proudly at attention. She had seen a lot of cock in her life, but, damn, this one was a big pole of a cock that would make porn stars jealous.

"Want to give it a taste? It's lonely and could use a mouth to keep it company," Brody said as he caught her staring at his cock.

"First come closer," she beckoned.

Removing her hand from her pussy, Mistress Charisma scraped her wet fingers across his nose. Brody grabbed her hand and diligently suckled her sweet juices off her fingers. He then let go of her hand, and just as she expected, he pressed his palm onto the wall.

With a simple click, his hand was secured against the wall.

His facial expression changed when he realized his hand was stuck.

"What's wrong, Brody?" she asked while tweaking his nipple.

"My hand, it won't move," he said as he tried to yank his hand off the wall.

"Really? Here, let me help you, give me your other hand."

Once she got ahold of Brody's other hand, instead of helping him she secured the other shackle to his wrist. He was so absorbed with the thought of fucking her that he'd failed to notice she had shackles hanging from the wall.

"What the hell? Now both my hands are stuck," he said as he struggled to break free.

Slipping away from Brody, Mistress Charisma walked over to the light switch and flicked it on. She had to admit, he had a wonderful physique. He obviously took good care of his body and went to the gym religiously. As she scratched her nails down his back, his muscles flexed beautifully.

"Tell me if the name Nerdy Shirley sounds familiar to you," she said.

"What?!"

"Nerdy Shirley, do you remember calling someone Nerdy Shirley?"

"Back in high school, there was some stupid chick I called that. Why are you asking about her?" he asked as he frantically moved his hands, wanting to escape.

"Oh."

Shirley felt her blood pressure escalating, but it quickly went down when Mistress Charisma took over her. It was time to have some fun. Reaching for his cock, she stroked him roughly. He stopped struggling against the restraints and allowed the pleasure to go through his body.

"I know Shirley, actually. She told me all about how much of an asshole you are," Mistress Charisma said as she squeezed his cock hard.

"Fuck! That hurts!" Brody groaned in agony.

"It's a small world, Brody. I never thought I'd ever see you again."

"This is fucking nuts. Just let me go. I'll go find another whore somewhere else."

Tired of hearing Brody's voice, Mistress Charisma dropped his cock and went over to her toy chest. She grabbed a gag and stuffed it into his mouth. He unsuccessfully tried to scream and shout for help.

After watching him struggle for a few moments, she slipped out of her blouse and smashed her bare breasts onto his muscular back. Her dark nipples immediately hardened once they slid against his skin.

"I have a confession to make, Brody," she whispered while dragging her nails along his thighs. "I'm Shirley."

Brody mumbled against the gag and turned his head to the side, wanting to get a better look at her.

"You really ruined my high school life. However, now that I think about it, without you, I wouldn't be the person I am right now. I think it's so wonderful how you would insult an Asian woman like me years ago and would make fun of my mom working in a sweatshop and be here now paying to get fucked by me. I guess I have to thank you properly for giving me so much inspiration."

Moving her hands to his buttocks, she spread his cheeks apart and knelt down to look at his puckered asshole. She gently traced her tongue on his opening. He tried to resist, so she took hold of his cock to calm him down. As the seconds passed, she managed to insert some of her tongue into his succulent ass. She felt him relax and he began to moan in pleasure.

"See, it's not so bad," she murmured.

She could sense Brody was close to ejaculating so she began to furiously rim his asshole. His cock was pressed up against the wall so he started to hump it. To add to his pleasure, she firmly held his balls. It was too much for him. Within minutes, he growled and spewed the wall with his white cum.

"Mmmmm, yes," she moaned as she licked the cum off the wall.

Once all traces of cum were gone, she stood up and removed the gag from Brody's mouth. He was panting as he stared into her eyes. She could see the pleasure, the confusion, and the excitement floating around in his eyes.

"You can't be Nerdy Shirley. There's no fucking way you're her," he breathed.

"Why do you say that?"

"Because there's no fucking way a nerd could make me cum that hard."

"Believe what you want then." She walked away. She went to the minibar and poured herself a glass of red wine.

"It was just innocent fun, nothing to be taken seriously," Brody explained.

"I cried so much over what you all did to me. I hated school and I always thought about killing myself."

"I'm sorry."

"No, you're not, so don't even bother."

An awkward silence fell upon them. Grabbing the keys for the shackles, she unlocked him from the wall. Brody's arms fell down and he relished his freedom.

"I hope you had fun, Brody," she said as she gathered her clothing from the floor.

"Wait! That's it?"

"I can't go on anymore."

"Look, high school was so many years ago. I don't remember much of it. It was a different time. I must admit, I'm very amazed at how much you've transformed. From what I can remember in high school, you were just an easy target, and I knew deep down inside you secretly loved the attention. Now, you're so hot and one of the most beautiful women I've ever seen in my life. I look into your eyes right now and I see a woman who loves herself and is confident with everything."

"Really?" she asked, blushing from his words.

"Yes," he said, closing the gap between them.

"Or are you saying all that just so you can fuck my pussy?"

"That, too." He smirked.

Shirley thought for a moment, then glanced at Brody's huge cock. It looked like it was calling her name. Her pussy twitched and ached for a fucking.

"Go lie on the bed then," she commanded.

Brody did as he was told and lay down on the king-size bed. Shirley climbed on top of him and sat on his washboard stomach. She lazily traced patterns around his chest. Leaning down, she stuck out her tongue and licked his nipples. She then moved her tongue upward and locked her lips with his.

They madly kissed each other, and Mistress Charisma moaned into the kiss when Brody's hand brushed the outside of her pussy. She let out a loud moan when his middle finger slid inside her.

"Oh, Brody, that feels so good," she cried out in pleasure as she rotated her pussy around his finger.

Mistress Charisma's pussy was now soaking wet from Brody's touch. Craving his tongue, she removed his finger. She shifted her position so that her pussy could hover over his lips. He eagerly pulled her down onto his mouth and feverishly lapped the juices oozing out of her. Her whole body was in euphoria as he licked her at lightning speed.

"Fuck, don't stop!" Charisma exclaimed as she grabbed his head and rode his face. A surge of pleasure ran through her as she came, and she squeezed her thighs around his head.

After catching her breath, she took her pussy off his face and smiled when she saw her pussy juice smeared all over his skin.

"Now it's your turn to cum," she said as she guided his thick cock into her pussy and slowly began to ride him.

This was surreal to her. She was having sex with a man she loathed to death years ago. Looking down, it gave her a rush of adrenaline and a feeling of great power to see him beneath her. Taking hold of his wrists, she lifted them to the bedposts, and with the rope that was already there, she tied his wrists to them. He didn't resist; in fact, it made him thrust much harder into her.

"Your pussy is so fucking good," he panted.

"Oh, oh, oh, oh!" was all she could muster for a reply.

Faster and faster their motions went. Having Brody tied up actually made him more enthusiastic. He was fucking her so hard that she thought she would be sent up through the ceiling.

She was swirling in a world of pleasure, and before she knew it her pussy tightened around his cock. A loud moan came out of her mouth as her orgasm hit her. No client of hers had ever made her cum that hard before.

Seconds after she came, Brody followed by shooting his

sperm into her. The added fluid gushing into her body prolonged her ecstasy.

"I'm definitely coming back. Maybe next time we can role-play? I'll be the football jock and you'll be the naughty Asian tutor," Brody suggested, which caused Shirley to laugh.

"Maybe," she said playfully.

Brody ended up staying longer, and Shirley really gave him the full Mistress Charisma treatment.

The Seduction of Nguyễn Lang Ha

J. F. GUMP AND LISA DANFORD

ॐ

DURING THE LAST FIVE days, Nguyễn Lang Ha had driven over twelve hundred miles and made ten sales calls. Not sales calls in the usual sense, but more like customer relations. Her father had grown up in Vietnam and had brought the Asian way of doing business with him when he came to America. He believed that by making friends with his clients they would help him succeed. Lang had continued her father's tradition after he became too old for the road.

Her parents were among the lucky few who had escaped Vietnam during Operation Frequent Wind. They had launched their import and distribution business with a small loan from the U.S. government, then busted their asses to make it work. Lang was fiercely proud and humbly honored to carry on in the wake of their success, so she never argued about the exhausting trips. Sales always improved after her customer visits, so she supposed there was something to be said for her father's way of doing business.

During the last two years, she had actually started looking forward to the trips. She and her husband were childless, and once he'd learned of his infertility, he had quickly become impotent. The doctors said it was psychological, but the problem remained. His attraction to alcohol only made it worse. They hadn't made love in months. In desperation, Lang had purchased a vibrator and used it often, especially when she was away from home where no one could hear her moans of much needed relief.

For reasons she didn't understand, her need for sexual release had become increasingly urgent since turning thirty. She ached for a silken, hard penis to completely quell her inner itch, but the opportunity never seemed to arise. Men often looked at her, but none ever approached. Perhaps it was because she was Asian, or maybe she somehow gave off signals that she was unapproachable. It didn't help that her breasts were quite small, at least according to American standards. She glanced in the rearview mirror. With her glossy black hair, almond eyes, and slightly flared nose, she looked like every other Vietnamese she'd ever seen. Maybe she was just plain ugly, despite what her father had always said.

As she neared her hotel, she noticed an Applebee's across the street. It took but a second to convince herself that she deserved a drink after the grueling week. She headed straight to the bar and grill.

She ordered a rum and Coke, took a deep breath, and waited for the day's tension to float away. She had barely settled into her seat when a man strolled in and sat a few stools away. She glanced briefly in his direction, then turned back to her drink. The man was young, probably in his midtwenties, certainly younger than her. His hair and complexion were dark. He could have passed for Asian, except his eyes lacked the classic epicanthic slant. Her second guess was Latino, which seemed to fit.

His clothes spoke of exquisite taste. He appeared neither fat nor lean, but solid, like someone who exercised frequently. And he was handsome, in a rough, bad-boy sort of way. But she expected that he would ignore her just like every other man she'd ever encountered while traveling. Besides, men were nothing but animals who only wanted to use a woman's body for a few minutes before going to sleep. At this point in her life, she had no need for a man, especially her husband with his mostly useless penis. Her vibrator didn't stop until she climaxed, and it never drank so much it couldn't perform. That automatically made it better than a man. Her thoughts rambled on in an attempt to convince herself that she was better off alone and sexually frustrated.

Just as she finished her drink, another appeared on the bar. "I didn't order this," she whispered to the bartender.

"It's from him." He pointed toward the dark stranger. "He paid for your first one, too."

Lang stared over at the man. He was watching a sports show on the television. She wished he would look in her direction so she could at least nod her acknowledgment, but he kept his head turned away.

She shrugged and sighed. "Tell him I said thanks."

The bartender walked to where the man sat, talked for a second, then went to serve another customer. The man looked over and smiled. By reflex, Lang smiled back. A moment later he stood and walked confidently in her direction.

"Thank you for accepting the drink," he said. "I was hoping for the chance to tell you what a beautiful woman you are."

Lang blushed at his compliment; her heart performed mini-flip-flops. She tried to think of something clever to say, but nothing came.

"Where are you from?" he continued.

"Chicago," Lang said, recovering her voice.

The man laughed. "I meant your ancestors, but Chicago is close enough."

His smile was alluringly sexy, vivid white contrasting against amber skin. Her blush faded as she began to relax. "My family is from Vietnam. I've been there, but I've never lived there."

"Vietnam. I thought so. You remind me of a Vietnamese girl I fell in love with when I was seventeen. She moved away a year later, and that was the end of that. I never completely got over it." He paused reflectively and said, "Sorry for my bad manners."

Lang blinked. "What bad manners? You mean because you had a crush on an Asian girl?"

"No, only because I said it to you. My father told me never to talk about past romances in the presence of a beautiful woman."

"Your father is a very smart man." Previous fantasies of having an affair returned to Lang's thoughts, launching soft butterflies in her chest. "Would you like to sit down?"

He smiled. "I thought you'd never ask. You work near here?"

"I'm here on business. My family owns an import company, and I'm the road warrior. I'm staying at the hotel across the street for tonight and driving home tomorrow." She didn't know what made her blurt out where she was lodging. She took a sip from her drink to cover her returning blush. "What about you?"

"Actually, I'm here on business, too. *And* I'm staying at the same hotel as you. So that makes us like neighbors . . ."

As the evening wore on, he kept Lang's drinks refreshed. Before long, their conversation turned flirtatious and laced with sexual innuendos. She noticed when he pressed his leg against hers, but she didn't pull away. He paid attention to her like no other man ever had. She felt attractive, relaxed, and was having fun for the first time in a long while. The time passed too quickly.

They were just finishing drink number four when he glanced at his watch. "Wow, it's almost nine o'clock. There's a movie I want to catch on HBO before turning in."

Lang felt a pang of disappointment. She had been expecting him to suggest an extended night together. She thought about proposing it, but her Buddhist upbringing wouldn't let her be so brazen. "Maybe we can do this again sometime. I really had fun talking to you. Are you here for the weekend?"

"Unfortunately, no. I'm off to Pittsburgh tomorrow." He paused before adding, "Hey, why don't you come watch the movie with me? I have some really smooth Scotch in my room, and I would love your company for a while longer. If the movie sucks, we'll just talk some more. What do you say?"

That was what she had been hoping for, but now the idea frightened her. She'd never been with any man except her husband. She knew she should just go to her room and let the vibrator douse her fire, but the thought of the stranger possibly making love to her ignited a fuse that had lain dormant inside her for years. "Just a movie?" she asked, hoping to sound innocent.

"I'm only asking for company," he whispered. "Hotel rooms are lonely and boring."

As if another woman had taken control of her body, she said, "What's your room number?"

Lang's hands shook as she maneuvered her car from the restaurant parking lot to the hotel across the street. As she took a quick shower, she made up her mind: family and Asian values be damned; she was going to fuck the dark stranger with the expensive clothes—the stranger who'd once loved a Vietnamese girl. *I'm a grown woman,* she thought. *A woman with desires denied for far too long.*

Not bothering with bra or panties, she pulled on a ribbed, white tank top and slipped into a pair of black silk pants that were loose yet clingy enough to compliment her figure. Trying to hurry, she opted for a pair of heeled, toeless clogs that made her taller and were easy to slip off. She dried and brushed her hair, sparingly applied makeup, and spritzed on a light mist of perfume. Her heart pounded as she walked to his room.

His door was ajar. She stepped inside, shutting it behind her. "How's the movie?"

He stood immediately. His jeans and muscle shirt made him look sporty—and somehow so touchable. His hair was damp, and his smile did its magic.

"Pretty dull, really," he said. "Maybe it'll get better." The gleam in his eyes said more than words ever could. "Here, have a seat while I get you a drink." He led her to the small sofa, then went to pour her a Scotch on the rocks.

Lang had watched the entire movie just last week. "I've seen this before. It doesn't get any better, trust me. Let's see what else is on."

She scanned through CNN, BBC, and MTV. When a scene of

two people making love filled the screen, she stopped. The woman was Asian, maybe Chinese. The man was black and handsome. She had heard about the dimensions of black men, but always thought it was nothing but rumors. His penis was at least twice the size of her husband's; she was momentarily mesmerized. She could almost imagine the black man was fucking her and not the girl in the movie, although she seriously doubted his massive cock could penetrate her.

The stranger returned to where she sat and handed her the Scotch. "Here you go, sexy lady." He glanced at the TV screen. "Whoa . . . what are you watching?"

"I've never seen anything like this before." Embarrassed, she switched the channel.

He watched her for a second, then picked up the remote and turned off the TV, leaving nothing but the soft glow of lamplight. In the silence he slipped off his clothes. She watched as his cock grew from semi-erect to a lethal weapon.

"You know we're going to have sex, don't you?"

She wondered how she could *not* know. Now was definitely the time to leave if she was going to, but she didn't want to. Not at all. "You forgot to ask me." She blushed profusely as she set her drink aside.

"You want it as much as I want you."

His erection twitched as if beckoning her, a bead of moisture appearing at the head. She *did* want it as much as he did, probably more, but she said nothing. She hoped he wouldn't cum too quickly.

"You have beautiful lips," he said, his voice husky.

He pulled her upright, held her waist, and kissed her with shameless passion. He slid his hands to her breasts and held them firm; his thumbs stroked her nipples sensuously. Her wetness awakened as she swelled with desire. Her nipples tightened and strained against her tank top. He backed away just long enough to strip her shirt over her head and toss it aside. Pulling her close, he cupped her small, tight ass in his hands and pressed his throbbing erection against her bare stomach.

He sat on the edge of the bed and pulled her to stand close in front of him. He teased her left breast with his hand as he filled his mouth with her right. He sucked hungrily, swirling his tongue expertly across her swollen nipple and areola, teasing with just the right pressure until Lang thought she would explode with torturous pleasure. Something about the way he held and touched her made her breasts feel full, ample. He made her feel wondrously sexy, and any self-consciousness about her small breasts faded into nonexistence.

He nibbled her nipple gently while sliding his left hand into her pants. Softly his fingers slid up and down the wetness of her outer lips, then into the wetter, warmer, enflamed folds of her inner vulva. When his fingers found her clitoris, it set her on fire like she had never been in her life. Hot spasms of desire intensified her moans. She breathed as if she were on a treadmill running full speed. She pushed her crotch against his hand and pressed her breast almost painfully against his open mouth.

She wanted the dark Latino desperately and she wanted him now; hard, fast, and vicious. As if sensing her thoughts, he stripped off her pants and eased her gently onto the bed.

For a moment he stood still, absorbing her with his eyes. Enjoying his obvious voyeurism, she eased seductively farther up on the bed. On hands and knees, he followed, catching her legs and pulling them apart as she reached the pillow. He stretched his body atop her, buried his hands in her long, silky hair, and kissed her hard, probing her mouth with his tongue until her lips

felt like a sex organ she had never known she had. His hot, pro-
tuberant erection lay unyielding between them.

"I'm hungry to taste you," he whispered as he began a long
teasing trip toward heaven. He nibbled at her ears and neck before again licking and sucking and kissing her sensitive breasts.
She nearly screamed at the pleasure he was giving her. Having
never been touched and wanted like this, she wondered how she
had lived without it. And why.

His breathing quickened and his moaning competed with
hers. He licked his way to her navel, probed it briefly, then
swirled his tongue lower, much lower. He lifted her legs up and
farther apart and went down. His tongue began its delightful
torture at the base of her crotch, then moved up slowly between
her thighs, stopping just outside where she most wanted it. Alternating from side to side, using the top of his tongue, he drove
her to sexual madness. She grasped both sides of his head, placed
his tongue directly between her legs, and guided him as he licked
and swirled upward. His mouth found her clit, causing her hips
to lunge uncontrollably as she groaned and moaned and mumbled nonsensically.

Within a minute her moaning soared to a scream and she
climaxed against his tongue; her entire body radiated with painfully intense pleasure. He completed the fury of her spasms by
keeping steady pressure and strokes against her convulsive
thrashing until the last of the continuous orgasm left her fighting
for air. Releasing his head, she dropped her arms limply to her
sides.

He remained in position for a moment, keeping his tongue
pressed against her clit while inserting his forefinger inside her,
moving it slowly in and out. She felt the last vestiges of her contractions thunder sweetly within as her pussy involuntarily

grasped his finger; she purred low moans of unbelievable satisfaction.

When her quivering abated, he returned to her side and said, "Don't let anybody *ever* tell you you're not sexy as hell. You look good, feel good, smell good, and taste good. You fucking blow my mind."

He held her in his arms, landing soft kisses across her face and down her neck. His erection had not softened. After the pleasure he had just given her, she could not deny him anything, nor did she want to.

"I want you inside me *now*," she whispered, and rolled him to his back, straddling his body. She grasped his penis and slid the head against her outer wetness before dipping it into her velvet sheath. She felt him respond, push slightly, and her desire rose from a smoldering kindle to a merciless inferno. Her inner walls burned in anticipation of complete fulfillment. Despite her profuse wetness, he made no progress past a couple of centimeters. Though she longed for all of him, she realized she was afraid of his size. If he wasn't a gentleman, he could hurt her badly.

"Relax," he whispered, "I'll be very gentle." He cupped his hands under her buttocks, lifting her slightly and kissing her passionately. She took deep breaths, let her muscles relax, and pressed down against him. He continued to push into her with short, thrusting movements as she pulled him into her harder, utterly turned on now and uncaring of discomfort. She bucked too forcefully and the head of his penis plunged inside, exploding needles of exquisite pain within her.

She cried out and he froze, holding his position, waiting for her response. Her pain was nothing compared to the pleasure. She relaxed and pushed down again. Another inch slipped inside and there was no pain. She smiled with satisfaction and said, "I want all of you."

Slowly, gently, he slid his way deeper and deeper inside her. He moaned with animal desire as he violated the depths of her willing vagina until she took him completely, inch by exquisite inch. His immensity filled and stretched her; his increasingly urgent movements applied the perfect friction to sate her long-denied hunger. She fed on him, sucking and milking him with her muscles, showing him it was okay to be less gentle now, savoring his penetration as his girth stretched her to the point of never-before-felt pleasure, touching places no man had reached.

His first strokes were slow and deliberate, yet urgently demanding. Then, as if sensing she was nearing another climax, he grabbed her ass and rolled her underneath him. He increased the speed and depth of his thrusts, pounding and throttling inside her while they clutched and grasped at each other like feral beasts. Now she grabbed his ass and kneaded his flesh. Her arousal surged higher from feeling his muscles thrusting and pumping heatedly into her, his skin slippery with sweat.

Suddenly he stiffened, trembled, and grunted wildly. His facial muscles tightened and his eyes squeezed shut as if he were in pain. His penis swelled and pulsed to an even greater fullness as he plunged into her until their pelvic bones ground together. Then he exploded inside her. She felt every throbbing convulsion of his ejaculation, stretching her with hot spurts of electric tendrils, leaving her breathless, astonished, and moaning. Her body screamed with indefinable sensations that intensified repeatedly as his powerful contractions extended her pleasure. It seemed like hours before their shared orgasm ended. Both gasping for air, they remained together a few minutes before he finally softened and slipped away. While they recovered their breath, they held and touched each other like familiar lovers.

"Until today," he whispered, "I never made love with an Asian woman. I've often thought how it would be, but it was better than I ever imagined, much better. It would be *so* easy to fall for you." He pulled her close and she kissed him in return.

"I should really leave now," she whispered, unsure what to do or say.

"I know. But please, let me have you just one more time before you go."

She smiled at his desire. "Yes," she said, and began her own journey down his chest. "But first there is something I need you to teach me."

Later, when their passions were drained, Lang slipped back into her clothes and gave him a quick kiss, not really wanting to leave, but keeping herself in motion. As she reached the door, he stopped her.

"I'm Lorenzo, pleased to meet you," he said, grinning. He grabbed her hand and shook it.

Lang laughed, realizing they hadn't known each other's names. "Just call me Lang. And the pleasure has most certainly been mine." She winked as a warm blush touched her cheeks.

"I want to see you again. You're truly the most incredible woman I've ever known." He held her hand, his voice hoarse and deep. "When is your next trip to . . . anywhere?"

"I'll be in Pittsburgh tomorrow. I'm in no hurry to get home." She smiled, stood on her tiptoes, and kissed him softly on the lips.

As she walked back to her room, she knew she would see him often. He made her feel like a complete woman. And his phone numbers were in her pocket.

The Wicked Wahine— a Tall Tale

BETTI MUSTANG

ॐ

ONCE UPON A TIME, on the little Hawaiian island of Maui, a curious Caucasian tourist entered what appeared to be a dark and run-down bar in the middle of Waikapu town. The crackling, pink neon light above the door said THE WICKED WAHINE.

As soon as his loafers crossed the threshold, an odd chill ran through his body—a strange tingling sensation that ran from his toes to his head and then back down, lodging itself in his groin.

By nature an observant kind of guy, his senses immediately picked up a few things: The small room was empty except for four young, beautiful Asian girls standing around the bar, and a haggard old woman chain-smoking thin, black cigarettes behind the counter. A strange mixture of seafood, days-old grease, smoke, sweat, and sharp perfume filled the air. The women squawked at each other in a language that his ears found abrasive, yet somehow captivating. The music that filled the room was generic pop without the vocals. For some reason it reminded him of cheap plastic. Karaoke?

He stood just inside the doorway trying to process what his senses were relaying to him. His gut reaction was that he should do a 180 and hightail his white ass back to the resort, to the "matrix" of his vacation—staged luaus, palm trees, watered-down mai tais, and lots of chlorine.

His dick had other plans though, and so did the women.

So, against his better judgment, he cleared his throat, officially entered the Wicked Wahine, and slid into what appeared to be an old diner booth—red and cushiony vinyl.

He felt awkward—the bar didn't give off the vibe of a place of business. He felt more like he was sitting in a stranger's living room—stared at and uninvited. He needed a drink. Fuck mai tais. Vodka—straight. Heineken chaser. Three of each. Please. Now.

The old woman from behind the bar shuffled up to his booth. She wore a faded Hawaiian-print muumuu and royal-blue flip-flops. The melody of Tiffany's "I Think We're Alone Now" (without Tiffany) played out of scratchy speakers. The old woman carried a golden plastic cup filled with ice water in one hand and a pack of cigarettes in the other. Her lips were dry, and the deep, vertical wrinkles above her top lip came from decades of pursing themselves around a . . . smoke?

He suddenly felt a little disoriented. Where exactly was he anyway? Waikapu—he vaguely remembered reading something about this town online somewhere when he was planning his vacation. He got the feeling that whatever he had read wasn't positive. He just couldn't . . . quite remember. *Waikapu*—didn't it translate to "forbidden water" or something?

She set the cup in front of him with a clack and a splash.

"You like wash clothes?" she asked him in a raspy voice. Her

English was broken. Maybe he misunderstood her. Before he could figure out a polite way to ask her to repeat herself, she broke into a phlegmy cackle, her rheumy eyes watering.

He wanted to leave. He didn't. When all else fails, request alcohol.

"Vodka?" Everyone knows that word, right?

She gave him a rough pat on the shoulder as if she appreciated that he proved to be so amusing.

"Ne, ne . . . first you get girl first," she said as she wiped the tears of laughter from her leathery face.

She called out unintelligible names in her foreign language and shuffled back behind the bar.

Things got strange fast.

One, two, three, four girls slid into the booth next to him.

He was to call them (the women that he would remember years from tonight as "those freaky Asian succubus-whores") Tammi, Sherilyn, Tina, and Mimi. Of course, these weren't their real names, but then again at the Wicked Wahine, real names didn't really matter.

"You buy me drinky?"

"Ne, he buy *me* drinky!"

"You buy me drinky, yes?"

The women bickered and hissed in their foreign language. He was instantly reminded of beautiful bettas—fighting fish that were exotic, flamboyant, colorful, and deadly.

Fascinated, he became vaguely aware in the background of the faint pitter-patter of raindrops beginning to fall on the aluminum roof overhead.

Slap! Out of nowhere, the old woman put a quick stop to the symphony of alien tongue by shuffling up and striking her dry, open palm onto the tabletop.

His water spilled. The girls watched it rush, then trickle—dripping onto the filthy, slick carpet—the way one watches droplets of blood fall from a pricked finger.

Slap! The old woman did it again. All eyes fell on her.

"Rain!" she hissed, pointing her burning cigarette to the ceiling. "Rain!"

The women murmured excitedly. He felt, with a tad of relief, like he had disappeared. He was invisible to them. He was aware that their attention and harshly whispered dialogue focused on the girl who called herself Tina. Black-haired, kohl-rimmed-almond-eyed, slim-waisted, fleshy-lipped, mounds-of-white-titties-popping-out-of-a-hot-pink-Lycra-halter-top Tina.

She did not look pleased. The rain began to fall harder.

The murmuring in the dark room grew in intensity.

Tina shook her head violently and crossed pale and delicate arms under her bosom. Her jaw suddenly seemed bigger, more masculine. She set it in a firm, tight line that radiated the word *no* with stubborn finality.

It rained harder.

"*Saw-dool-law, saw-dool-law!*" the old woman shouted. She waved her bony arms toward Tina—cigarette smoke hung in the air like floating runes. "*Jee-gum ee-yah!*"

Hurry up, hurry up. The time is now.

He watched as Tina flared her nostrils. The image of a she-dragon flew across the borders of his rational mind. She muttered something that he thought sounded extremely unfriendly to the old woman, who simply shrugged and cackle-coughed in return.

Tina turned toward him. As she squinted her heavily outlined almond eyes at him in a glare, the she-dragon reappeared. It circled his brain and blew long, searing blades of fire through his consciousness.

He instantly felt what you feel when you realize that you've had a little too much—the sixth shot, the third hit, the fifth drag.

It didn't occur to him that he should still be sober.

Without warning or prelude Tina roughly pulled the elastic fabric of her top down under her right breast—her plump, ivory titty did a little upward *boing* before it settled into the makeshift shelf of the Lycra.

He blinked twice and cleared his throat.

"Drleenk," she commanded him.

He didn't understand what she meant, and besides, the sight of her cherry red, pert-as-a-little-mushroom nipple pointing right at him was rather distracting.

He sat very still, looking foolish, staring at her tit.

"Drleenk, drleenk!" she commanded again. She cupped her breast in a death grip that was oddly accented by mother-of-pearl-colored, acrylic fingernails and jiggled it. "Drleenk!"

The more she jiggled, the more his crotch tingled.

The old woman pulled his ear violently, making him lurch forward, placing the lashes of his left eye less than an inch away from her breast.

"Dr-ink! Dr-ink!" the old woman enunciated in an exasperated tone. "Now! Her teat, drink her teat!"

Tina, evidently sick of waiting for him to get the picture, rolled her eyes toward the ceiling, grabbed him by the chin, and shoved her hard, rosy nipple into his mouth.

The old woman nodded her approval, which made the wrinkled folds of her neck fold in and out like an iguana's. She shuffled over to the jukebox, pulled two quarters from the rusted coffee can sitting on top, plunked them in, hit a button, then hit REPEAT.

Drum machine, synthesizer, the pseudoraspy voice of George Michael's "I Want Your Sex" over scratchy speakers.

Tammi, Sherilyn, and Mimi clapped and cooed their approval.

In another space and time he would have found the scene as ludicrous as it truly was—but not tonight.

He tentatively flicked his tongue over Tina's nipple. Her skin smelled like coconuts. He flicked his tongue again and was rewarded with a drop of creamy liquid. On flick of the tongue number five he realized exactly what the pearly fluid tasted like: piña colada poured with Captain Morgan's Private Stock—spicy and rich on his taste buds.

Tina colada served fresh from a titty, he thought, *ingenious and delicious.*

Simultaneously the room shrank in around him (he was oddly reminded of a Space Bag infomercial), and he became aware that at some point in the past forty-five seconds, his penis had become unnaturally hard.

I have been poisoned. I have been poisoned while on vacation by strange women. The thoughts in his head seemed watered-down and dull—his realization unimportant.

It had been thirty-seven long years since he had been force-fed a boob, and by God did he miss it.

He worked the drug from her breast like a thief until it flowed rich, sweet, and intoxicating. He took it down his throat like a baby bird takes food into its gullet; or like a porn star guzzling cock.

Tammi, Sherilyn, and Mimi began to strip off their clothes—

a denim skirt here, a purple demi-bra there . . . long legs, short legs, a round, vanilla-ice-cream bottom popping high in the air as tight, black jeans were stripped off . . . nipples, nipples, nipples, six different nipples . . . cunts . . . three cunts—two with tufts of soft black pubic hair, and one shaved as bald as a newborn lovebird.

He watched the naked women begin to touch and lick and suck and poke at one another with the same distracted curiosity that a nursing babe has while watching the colors and shapes in a mobile spin above its mother's head.

The rain poured down.

Mimi (the one with the hairless pussy) came up for a breather from between Tammi's long, sweat-slicked legs. Tammi's whimpers of protest were muffled and lost in Sherilyn's hairy little cunt.

The vibration of Tammi's voice, or perhaps simply just her whimpers, caused Sherilyn's purple nipples to harden into sharp points. In return, she rode Tammi's face faster. Her powerful thighs flexed as she dipped her chubby pussy down, like inking a quill, over and over onto Tammi's waiting tongue.

George Michael, one would assume, still wanted his sex.

Mimi patted the dripping lips of her mouth dry with a bar towel, flung her straight, knee-length, blue-black hair over her shoulder, and sauntered toward the tourist.

The look in her black eyes was playful, her grip dead serious, as she grabbed for his iron-hard penis beneath his khakis.

She wedged her long, thin pointer-finger into his mouth (which was still firmly attached to Tina's boob) and plucked sharply at its corner.

The reluctant detachment of mouth from boob sounded like a rubber boot pulling out of mud.

Tina colada dribbled down his chin.

Tina immediately snapped her top back into place, cracked her neck from left to right, smoothed her skirt, slid from the booth, and relocated to a rusted fold-up chair in the corner.

She conjured a nail file out of thin air and began to whittle at her fingers.

Mimi unzipped his fly and skillfully freed his throbbing penis. It was roughly twelve inches long.

His eyes met his dick bulge for bulge in the "bigger than they had ever been" department. He didn't have time to contemplate how his normally average-size member had grown to pony-cock proportions in a matter of seven and a half minutes of bad pop song because Mimi frowned.

What kind of woman frowns at a foot-long penis? he thought.

She made an irritated *hmph* sound and spun toward Tina.

"He too small," she said in a breathy, childlike voice that was so very Minnie Mouse meets Marilyn Monroe.

The sound made his scrotum ache in a pleasant way.

Tina gave a nonchalant shrug and kept filing. "So make big."

Mimi pursed her lips in a second of thought, then turned her attention back to him. She expertly spun some of her silky hair into a knot on top of her head, the remaining length of it trailing to her waist, and took a deep breath.

The action reminded him of a potter pushing up her sleeves, or a doctor snapping his gloves—a simple ritual to prepare herself for whatever it was that she *did*.

She began to blow.

The air from her pursed lips felt warm and alive.

Deep breath; the rain came down in torrents.

"Huffwhoooooooooooooooooooooooooooo."

She blew again.

He looked down at his humming dick and was astonished to see that with each gust of air that she pushed from her lungs he seemed to grow another inch.

Fourteen, fifteen, sixteen . . .

Tammi wiggled over and slipped his khakis off while Sherilyn came up behind him and ran her hands over his shoulders and down his chest—nails teasing nipples over his polo shirt.

Tammi tugged at his shoes and socks, then rolled her pointy nipples between his toes.

Twenty-one, twenty-two . . .

Mimi kept blowing.

His dick was thirty-seven inches of quivering pink flesh by the time the blowing stopped and the festivities began.

The girls began to dance and sing:

Giant dick, giant dick, no let in
Girl never know where it been
Lick it, suck it, juice it give
Save it, swallow it, long we live

The tourist was just beginning to think that their strange song reminded him of the Three Little Pigs when Tammi turned her back to him and swung a mile-long leg over the base of his cock. Arching her back into an exaggerated curve, she nestled her warm, wet, sticky pussy down onto his shaft.

Get ass and *Fuck pussy* were two of the few phrases that he was currently capable of processing.

He gripped her hips and slid her, face forward, toward the tip of his cock.

He pulled her back until her round butt was flush against his pubic hair.

He pushed her forward again—her pussy glided down his shaft, her thighs squeezed.

Sherilyn faced Tammi and straddled his cock—when he pulled Tammi back she would push her ass out behind her, pussy lips spreading and swallowing the upper half of his head. When he pushed Tammi forward, Sherilyn would thrust her powerful hips forward and grind her mound against the other woman's.

Again and again, over and over, until all three of them were covered in sweat—the only sounds coming from their throats were growls, gasping, and the occasional "Aiyee."

When he thought that no sensation on earth could possibly be more pleasurable than two naked Asian women riding your three-foot-long dick, it got better.

Mimi undid her hair and spun it around her wrist until she held a feather-duster-like spray of it in her hand. She knelt in front of him and began to lick at his head, steamy, pink tongue slipping and darting and caressing him, while she stroked the underside of his cock with hair that felt like silk.

Fuck was now the only word that he was capable of processing.

His eyes rolled around the room. Every cell in his body buzzed and vibrated with a supernatural frequency.

His eyes found Tina in the corner. She was still filing her nails, but now she had her feet propped up and her knees spread wide. Her skirt was hiked to her hips, panties pushed aside. The old woman fucked her hard with a curved, black dildo.

He watched as Tina's cunt took the ominous-looking sex toy. He groaned as he saw the wetness drip out of her cunt and pool onto her seat.

She yawned.

Tammi and Sherilyn cried out in orgasm. The rain slapped at the roof with the sound of a hundred thousand metal pellets hitting their target. George Michael got louder and louder—a crescendo of pleasure and sound and water and . . .

He exploded. It felt as though his body would shrivel in on itself as the most intense climax that any man has ever experienced hit him. His body shot off the bench as gallon after gallon of semen launched like a group of missiles from his cock.

The rain stopped.

The women were drenched in his sticky, hot, living cum. They licked it from one another's body and poured what they could into dark glass bottles.

He struggled to remain conscious as he watched Tina stand and take one of the filled bottles from the girls. She knelt before the old woman, kissing her craggily old toes, and held the bottle up in what looked like an offering.

The old woman grasped it in trembling hands. While gently uncorking it, she began to chant:

Yook-chae eui mool,
Young-hin eui mool,
Keum Ji dwen mool.

Water of your flesh, water of your soul, forbidden water.

The old woman repeated her chant three times, then took his cum down her throat like one would swallow a shot of bourbon.

She clutched her stomach and fell to her knees. A transformation was taking place. A beautiful, blinding transformation.

The last thing that he remembered seeing before he passed

out into a sea of blackness was Tina's eyes soften and her teeth flash behind a smile.

She had a beautiful smile.

The sun burned right through the tourist's eyelids. Dehydrated, he felt extremely dehydrated. He opened crusty eyes and found himself sprawled in a small, overgrown lot behind a ramshackle building.

Where in the hell am I? he thought.

He struggled to his feet—his head pounded, and his loafers were missing.

He stumbled to the front of the building and read the splintery sign that hung above the door.

WAIKAPU WASHERETTE was painted in neon-pink, flaking letters.

An uneasy feeling washed over him. He tapped his forehead with his palm to try to jar the memory that was causing anxiety to well up in him from his brain.

He jumped when the door to the washerette creaked open and a beautiful young Asian girl with black eyes and a playful smile opened the door. She was the most beautiful creature he had ever seen.

She threw his loafers at his feet.

He stood there, stunned and confused.

She took a long drag off a thin, black cigarette and eyed his filthy khakis.

"You like wash clothes?" she asked in a voice that was too raspy for her flawless body.

Vivid flashbacks of the Wicked Wahine slammed into him like a linebacker.

He remembered. He remembered it all.

His mouth opened and closed without forming words. The flashbacks had left him as mute as a guppy.

She gave him a rough pat on the shoulder as if she appreciated that he proved to be so amusing.

He shivered.

An old woman came up behind him carrying a load of laundry. She muttered incoherently as she bumped her way past him into the building.

The beautiful girl nodded an acknowledgment to the old woman and slammed the door in his face. He could hear her laugh travel throughout the washerette.

In a panic, he unzipped his fly to validate that his penis was still there—that everything was normal and alright—to prove to himself that he was just temporarily insane.

Last night was just a weird hallucination that is lingering, he told himself. *I have a normal-size dick and had an allergic reaction to the alcohol, that's all.*

He pulled out his cock and had a moment of immense relief when he saw that, yes, everything was okay.

He looked closer and began to feel dizzy. Very, very dizzy. The whole world spun around him.

His flaccid penis was covered in thousands of silver stretch marks.

He heard the cackling laugh behind the washerette door become hysterical.

He zipped up his pants.

Inside, a girl named Tina and the beautiful girl who threw him his shoes began to make love . . .

The old woman knelt beside them and prayed for rain.

Geisha Girl

KISSA STARLING

ʊ

1

"I TOLD YOU WHEN I was sixteen and I'm telling you again, Mother—I'm a lesbian. I'm attracted to girls, get it? Not boys." It was exasperating to go over this again and again. It was 2008, not 1940.

Takumi was the daughter of a female advertising agent. Such a position was unusual for a woman in a country as conventional as Japan. Traditional Japanese women were thought to be stale if they didn't marry by the age of twenty-five—Takumi was twenty-four and had a birthday coming up quick. Her mother simply did not understand her.

"I blame myself for this. You didn't have a father around, and now you don't know how to relate to men."

"That isn't it, Mother. I just relate better to women. I like the way their bodies curve, the sweet smell of their hair, and the way they moan when—"

"Enough! You're not normal, Takumi. You will go to a teahouse in Kyoto. It is decided." Takumi's mother was one Japanese woman who broke the standard mold. She'd gotten pregnant at thirty, never married, and still had a successful and thriving career. She'd flipped when she found the adult movie in the disc player that morning.

"I can't believe you. Just because *Takumi* means 'artisan' in Japanese doesn't mean that I can become a traditional geisha, Mother. I wasn't meant to become a person of the arts. I prefer other things. You can't send me to one of those places. It's like prison."

"You won't be working with some slimy businessman in today's society. If you learn the old ways, you'll be able to entice a very wealthy man to marry you. That, my daughter, is your only hope. You're going and that's final!"

Takumi had thought her mother would understand. "I guess you're more old-world than either of us realized!"

Neither of them spoke another word.

2

TAKUMI'S MOTHER SENT HER off to a teahouse in Kyoto despite the begging and pleading. Takumi found, after several months, that she enjoyed the teahouse very much. She'd become an excellent player of the *shakuhachi,* which her newfound friends referred to as her "singing bamboo flute."

"Play it again, Takumi. I have such a hard time with this instrument." Sometimes she helped the other girls practice. Sendai was a simple-minded girl named after the city in which she was born.

Her rich aunt had sent her to the *okiya* hoping she could learn the tea ceremony, but years of practice had proved fruitless. She would never become a geisha or even assist one. Her aunt paid a monthly stipend for her to stay with the girls she'd come to love.

"You have so much more patience than Madam Oy." Comments such as those made Takumi smile and enjoy her penance even more. She still didn't want to be here, but the friends she'd acquired made life better than she could have hoped for.

All of the teachers admired her performances of the classical Japanese dance. They tried to enter her in competitions in town, but Madam Oy thought they were cheap and frivolous.

A few select patrons would ask for her. "Who is this lovely young girl, Madam Oy?" they would say. "I wish for her to assist in the tea ceremony this evening."

These requests became so regular that the human encounter referred to as a tea ceremony became second nature for Takumi. She liked it best when the ceremonies were held in the garden.

"Don't forget that you are merely a *hanto*, Takumi. I am the *teishu*."

Madam Oy never wanted her girls to shimmer more than her. All the guests were aware that she was the house master, and they treated her as such. Takumi led the guests to the dewy ground so they could "rid themselves of the dust of the world."

After purifying her hands and mouth with a ladle of fresh water, Madam Oy would walk wordlessly through the gate and bow to her guests. Takumi stepped in behind her to guide the guests from the coarse physical world to the spiritual tea world. All present entered the garden through a sliding door that forced them to bow their heads down.

Takumi's eyes admired the Buddhist picture scroll hanging on the wall of the tearoom. The kettle and hearth took a few seconds of her attention next. She felt like it was her duty to guide the patrons who didn't know their role in the ceremony. Madam Oy saw this as one of Takumi's faults.

Madam Oy sat first and greeted each guest as he/she sat down. Sandalwood incense was dropped into the fire. Takumi had prepared all three courses for the meal and added fresh cedar chopsticks to the serving tray. White rice filled the small ceramic bowls.

Sake was served first to the guests and then to Madam Oy. Each guest took a turn serving her. This gave each person a chance to be the host, which is the most honored position. After the meal the guests departed so that the host could prepare the tea.

Takumi whispered to those gathered, once they'd departed from the tearoom, "Madam Oy will strike a gong five times to signal our return to the tearoom. I do hope you all are having fun." The group smiled and nodded their heads, afraid to speak too loudly and spoil the moment.

Gooooooooong, goooooong . . . the sounds reverberated throughout the gardens and stunned the guests at first. *Goooooooong, goooooooooong, goooooong.* Five echoing vibrations brought the guests silently into the tearoom.

The last steps of the ritual of cleaning and preparing the tea are witnessed by the guests. Madam Oy poured three scoops of tea into a bowl for each person. The steamy fragrance drifted up and tantalized the noses of the guests.

The guests know their time in the tearoom is almost at an end when they are offered thin tea. This tea rinses their palate and prepares them for leaving the spiritual tea world. The cushions and hand warmers were indications of relaxation. Several minutes passed before the guests rose to leave.

"Thank you so much, Madam Oy. The tea was quite good,

and your art for the ceremony was comparable to none. We shall certainly return." The principal guest spoke and left first. The other guests complimented her profusely.

"Another beautiful and fulfilling tea ceremony, Madam Oy," said Takumi.

"Yes, my child. You have become quite adept at making my guests feel comfortable, and for that I thank you. Your studies are coming along nicely."

3

SOME CLIENTS THOUGHT SHE was an *oiran,* or Japanese prostitute, but that wasn't the case at all. It took talent to entertain the kind of men that she came in contact with.

It was unusual for an apprentice geisha to live, and work under, a madam who owned a teahouse. Takumi's mother knew the owner well; in fact she'd grown up with her. It would take many years to be a geisha. The three years Takumi had spent at the teahouse were a fraction of the time she would need to perfect her skills.

For now Takumi was having more fun than she had ever had in her entire life. She was surrounded by beautiful women day in and day out. She helped them dress. She played music for them. Some nights she climbed out onto the roof and dreamed of becoming one of them. She would look up at the stars and wonder when she would find her own true love. Little did she know that she had already met the one destined to be her soul mate.

Aiko, meaning "love child" in Japanese, was the name of Takumi's roommate at the teahouse. She took no classes and didn't know the ways of the geisha. She'd been given to the madam, by her family, to repay a debt. She earned her keep by cleaning up after the parties, tea ceremonies, and many regulars who frequented the establishment.

She'd been a great help to Takumi in the beginning. She guided her where she needed to go and helped her stay out of trouble. Aiko was also a great listener. She quickly became the one Takumi could turn to no matter what her problem.

Takumi loved hearing Aiko talk about her family back home. One night, when neither of them could sleep, Aiko shared the story of how she came to live at the teahouse.

"My brother used to frequent teahouses just like this one every evening. He liked listening to the stories the geisha told. He observed the fan dances, the tea ceremonies, and reveled in the attention. The consideration he loved most of all. I come from a poor family, and my brother just wasn't meant to be a fishmonger's son. He was so drawn to the excitement and the lure of sexual promise."

"Most of them are, Aiko. According to my mother, men are good for only one thing."

Aiko smiled and continued her tale. "Tadako liked to throw his money around, what little he had of it. He started selling opium to support his socializing. Before we knew it, he was running a tab at every teahouse in this area. He disgraced our family but my parents could not shun him. He was the firstborn son. They held such store in him.

"Your madam offered to help. She paid his debts and asked for nothing in return. It was whispered around the village that she and my father were once together. I volunteered to come here. It was the only way to save the family honor and stop the gossips. I did not want my mother to be shamed. My brother goes out on the fishing boat every morning now and seems resigned to his destiny. He has even started seeing a local village girl."

It surprised Takumi that Aiko didn't sound bitter; in fact, the love in her voice could be heard when she spoke about her family.

"I'm so sorry, little Aiko. It's not right that you were meant to take the burden of an entire family. You should be free to live and love as you wish."

"Do not worry, Takumi. I am where I need to be, where I want to be more than anyplace else. I was not so sure about my decision before you came. You have become my best friend and I cherish you. Let's get you ready. I'll be right back."

Takumi realized how much Aiko had come to mean to her. As soon as Aiko returned, Takumi was calling her name.

"Aiko, I need my face paint. Have you seen it? Please help me, Aiko. I can't be late. Chika will kill me if I am not there to help with her kimono."

Aiko rushed into the room from the outside. "I am here, Takumi. Here is your face paint, right where you left it, behind your silly fan."

Aiko smiled as she handed the face paint to Takumi. She gently put each of her hands on a shoulder and guided her to the dressing table.

"I will put it on for you. Calm yourself, you are the best apprentice geisha here."

Takumi was often praised by those she spent time with and was used to it.

"It is harder on you, Takumi, since you do not live with your mentor geisha. The owner of this teahouse is not a geisha. You have no one to learn from day in and day out. I heard Madam say that she was surprised at how well you are progressing."

Takumi relaxed as her friend spoke to her. The circular motion of fingertips on her cheeks and neck was calming as well.

Takumi stretched her head back and relaxed as the stress left her body. Aiko was right. She was doing everything she was supposed to do, everything she could do.

Aiko covered Takumi's full lips with red lipstick and drew black accents around her eyes and eyebrows. Aiko also put a touch of red around the eyes. It was unusual for Aiko to be helping with the preparations to go out, but the madam had a teahouse to run and Takumi's mentor geisha lived elsewhere. She preferred it this way. Aiko was good at what she did and seemed to be getting better every day.

Looking in the mirror confirmed Takumi's thoughts. Aiko took pride in her work. Aiko started rubbing the white paste on Takumi's chest. It felt so good. Little Aiko always knew what Takumi needed. The paste was made even with several strokes of a bamboo brush. The soft bristles heightened Takumi's senses and caused her breasts to tighten. Her nipples poked out and enlarged. Aiko could see everything since Takumi was not yet dressed. Aiko whisked the brush over the engorged nipples. Takumi gasped.

Aiko rolled back the bench that Takumi was sitting on and looked into her eyes. "Do not move. Your makeup will mess up. We won't have time to repair it, Takumi."

"Of course I won't move. I'll just rest my eyes for a few moments until it is time to dress. Please come back in about fifteen minutes."

Takumi let her eyes close and her mind drifted away. She heard the door close softly as Aiko departed.

Takumi's mind rolled back to the day she had told her mother she was a lesbian. She still had the same wants and desires. Staying here had not changed that. If anything, it had enhanced her needs and wishes.

Her mother didn't know that she'd never actually been with another female. She wanted it so badly. She dreamed of being held in another woman's arms. She dreamed of kissing and touching and loving. It was ironic that she was here being trained as a geisha for men.

She saw more of the female form here than she ever would have back home. Alas, she had no hope of finding fulfillment here. These women were looking for a *danna,* someone to support them. Takumi was looking for no such thing.

Thinking of all of the female forms she had been privy to got Takumi excited. Her head tilted back slightly as she cupped her breasts in her hands and pushed them together. Her index fingers stretched out to twirl around her nipples. All of the blood in her body rushed into the tan mounds of flesh between her fingers. Her breasts felt heavy as she manipulated them. She loved grinding them together. She wanted so badly to take her nipple into her mouth and suck it hard. She loved flicking her small nipples with the tip of her tongue until they grew stiff. Her makeup made that task impossible.

Her fingertips ran down, beneath her breasts, to her hips. She drew circles with her palms around her stomach and belly button. She sucked on one finger, then circled her belly button once again.

Her thumbs flipped up, as she bent forward, to brush her nipples. Bending her hands back the other way, she traveled slowly over the flesh of her hips and the tops of her thighs. Mmmmmm, every nerve ending in her body was alert. Her thighs parted slightly and she ran her fingernails up and down her knees.

Soft moans escaped her lips. Her right hand cupped her curly, dark mound. The moisture beneath her palm only excited her more. Her pinkie finger and thumb entered her flesh at the same time. Her thumb was circling her clit as her pinkie darted in and out of her tunnel.

Too excited to slow down, Takumi made a rod with her four fingers and dipped them straight into her. Clear, slick dampness enclosed each of her fingers. She dipped up the succulence and lapped at it with her tongue. Oh, how she wished it were the wetness of another girl.

Another delving between her legs produced enough liquid to smear all over her nipples and in the valley between her breasts. She thought again of how she wanted to suck the drying mustiness from her skin. Takumi pulled her legs back and pointed her feet into the air.

She opened her eyes, for the first time, to gaze at herself in the mirror. Watching her image only made her that much more excited. She fixed her eyes upon the mirror . . . and saw Aiko, standing right behind her.

Her mouth fell open and she gaped at Aiko.

Before she could speak, Aiko rubbed the tops of her shoulders and reassured her in a soothing voice, "You are so beautiful, Takumi. Let me lick your luscious juices from your nipples. Let me dart my tongue deeply into your most inner parts. Let me make love to you. I wish to be your first."

Takumi was astounded. She was also tense from the inevitable syrupy release that was soon to come. Her eyes rose up and looked into her friend's eyes.

"Please, I would like that."

Aiko removed the straps on her dress and it fell to the floor. She rubbed her own breasts together as Takumi watched in the mirror. Aiko bent her head forward and took her nipple into her delicate mouth.

Takumi ran the palm of her hand back and forth between her damp center and her own bursting breasts. Aiko was lighter-skinned than her, which made her nipples a creamy pink. Oh, how Takumi wished to taste those nipples between the folds of her tongue.

Aiko leisurely sucked her own nipple as she came around to stand in front of Takumi, who was still seated.

"Remember, Takumi, you cannot move, your makeup will be ruined."

Aiko sat across Takumi's knees and settled her mouth in front of the ashy, brown nipple. Takumi couldn't believe what was happening. Her very first sexual experience was going to be with a woman whom she already cared about. Nothing could be more perfect.

Aiko's teeth scraped just slightly across the tan flesh of Takumi's right breast as she pulled a nipple into her mouth. Takumi clenched her pelvic muscles and felt a tingling ripple engulf her entire body. She reached for Aiko, but her hands were moved away.

"Takumi, you must remember your makeup."

Aiko gently took Takumi's hands and clasped them together beneath the bench as she pushed her into a horizontal position. She reached for a black, silk kimono belt and tied it firmly around Takumi's hands.

"Now you shall not be tempted to ruin all of my hard work."

Takumi felt more alive and aroused somehow knowing that she had no control whatsoever. She closed her eyes and delighted in the feel of the long, moist muscle making its way down past her ribs and into her belly button.

"Please, Aiko, let me feel your tongue between my legs. Lap at my juices and then kiss me."

Her lover did not disappoint her. Her tongue stood out straighter and harder than any penis ever could have. It dove into the center of her being and caused her whole body to gasp as she rose up off the bench. Takumi knew that if her hands hadn't been tied, holding her body to the bench, she would be on the ceiling at this very moment.

Takumi's hips swayed to the rhythm of her lover's lips. She felt her backside being pinched as every liquid in her entire body gushed out between her thighs. Stars, lightning, fireworks, nuclear explosions . . . nothing could describe the moment when she experienced her first real orgasm. It was nothing like when she masturbated; oh, God, it was so much more!

Just as she started to settle down, Aiko used her fingers to press Takumi's lower lips together. One of her left fingers poked in toward Takumi's clit as her right palm massaged her soft, curly mound. The sensation was so intense that her breath stayed inside her body for at least a minute.

Aiko bit softly into Takumi's inner thigh. Her rubbing became more rapid. The friction built higher and higher. The final release was an explosion of mountainous proportions. Takumi came three more times before Aiko untied her. Takumi couldn't imagine a man ever making her feel this mixture of romance and lust combined.

4

IT WAS TIME TO dress and Takumi had only one hour to finish and make her way to Chika's *okiya*. Aiko assisted her by putting a colorful orange kimono on her sated body. The seamstress had embroidered it with green, yellow, and brown leaves. Fall was

coming to an end and this kimono was a perfect way to symbol-
ize that.

Takumi placed the styled, black wig on her head that Madam
had bought for her. On the way out the door she stepped into her
flat-soled sandals and went on her way.

She stepped hurriedly knowing that Chika would be waiting.
Chika had once been a singsong girl in Shanghai. Takumi hoped
to hear one day about how she had come to be a geisha. The
rumor was that her sponsor's wife ordered her out of town and
gave her a substantial amount of money to go. Chika was re-
vered by most patrons. She was booked up for months in advance and was a regular at Madam's teahouse. Takumi knew
that Madam owed a great deal to Chika. Her weekly appearances at the teahouse meant more money.

As Takumi suspected, Chika was waiting by the door.

"Hurry, Takumi, we don't have much time."

They actually had several hours, but it would take most of
that time to prepare Chika's makeup, hair, and dress. Chika
never wore wigs like some of the other girls. She always had her
own hair braided before entertaining. It was getting harder and
harder to find a hairdresser who was qualified and did not mind
traveling to the *okiya*.

Takumi did none of the actual preparations for Chika; she
didn't know the ways well enough. Chika demanded that she be
there, beginning to end, regardless. Takumi sat in a corner as
Chika was getting her hair braided.

The feel of Aiko's hands on Takumi's waist had been breath-
taking. The mouth that had suckled Takumi's nipple was soft
and gentle. The tongue that entered her hole had been magnificent. The way Aiko held on to her clit with her teeth was unbear-

ably erotic. The orgasm that exploded from Takumi had been volatile.

Takumi couldn't stop thinking of her time with Aiko. It had been way too short. She was looking forward to more private time with her new lover.

The snap of Chika's fingers brought Takumi back to reality. She brought a hand mirror, as requested, and glided back over to the corner. The next few hours were spent dancing with Chika, pouring tea, and smiling at unsuspecting patrons. None of them knew who she was inside. None of them knew what she wanted.

She made it through the endless entertaining only because she was so well trained. She could flip the sleeve of her kimono to show her wrist without batting an eye. She could dance and play instruments while she dreamed of lying with Aiko once more.

At the end of the evening Chika asked where her mind had been, but Takumi just smiled and feigned exhaustion. Chika sent her home to rest and went inside to retire. Takumi knew that Chika was not merely being nice; she was meeting a friend down by the water. Takumi wished her luck and happiness. She thought everyone should have someone to love.

Madam offered to help Takumi undress, but Aiko appeared and Madam went off to chat with a patron. Takumi, with the assistance of Aiko, undressed slowly and carefully. Aiko folded the kimono and placed the wig and sandals where they went.

Takumi understood that they had the entire evening ahead of them, but what about tomorrow? What about next week? Next month? Aiko shushed her questioning look by putting her finger upon Takumi's lips and lightly kissing her cheek.

"I love you, Takumi. I always have and I always will."

Looking into Aiko's eyes gave Takumi strength. She knew for

certain that Aiko did love her. Takumi loved her also. They'd started out as friends and now they were lovers. She was so glad that Aiko had made the first move.

"Come with me, my love. I want to show you something."

The two girls slipped out of the *okiya* in nightclothes.

"What if we're caught, Aiko? Surely Madam will beat the both of us."

"We aren't going far. Hold my hand and stay close to me."

They only snuck past a few houses before Aiko stood still. She looked all around her, then tiptoed toward an old building. Many years ago it had been some sort of religious building.

"This is it. Remember, don't let go of my hand."

She led Takumi up the stone steps and opened the old wooden doors that squeaked from nonuse.

"We'll stay here tonight."

"Stay? Here? We can't. Madam will kill us when she finds out we left the *okiya*. We have to get back. My mother will kill me. I can't dishonor her."

"Trust me."

It was hard but Takumi agreed to trust her friend and lover.

"We have to shut and latch these doors."

The two girls huddled together and fell asleep on a rough, splintered bench close to the main entrance.

5

THE SUN HAD NOT come up when Takumi awoke. "Aiko, we slept too long. We must hurry and get home before Madam wakes up. Please, Aiko, hurry."

"Takumi, there's no need to rush. Unlatch the wooden doors and pull them open."

There was one short moment of dread, but Takumi had no choice but to obey. She'd put all of her faith in her dear friend and didn't want to lose that special feeling.

Her entire body struggled against the doors. She didn't remember their being so strong and sturdy the night before. By the time they were fully open and latched to the inside walls, the sun had risen.

"What . . . what is that? I don't understand, Aiko. I see the clouds with the beautiful sunshine sending rays around the edges. That's all I see. Where are the streets and the *okiya*s that litter every space of our town?"

Aiko smiled. "This is our special place, Takumi. My grandmother told me stories about this magical building when I was little. I wasn't sure until this very moment that the legends were true."

"What legends? I'm so confused."

"The legend of love, Takumi. It is said that any two people who stop over here to sleep will wake up to a fantasyland. It only works if the couple are truly in love. We can stay here as long as we like. Time means nothing here. If we played with one another for ten years and went back, it would still be the same night that we left. In fact, mere minutes would have passed."

"You mean it's up to us? How long we live and love . . . we have control over it all?"

"Yes, love, that's it exactly. Who would have thought something like this existed in modern-day Japan?"

"Not me, but I love it, and most especially—I love you."

The two women pressed their lips together. The kiss was soft at first but soon became much more demanding.

They dreamed separately but the events were the same, the

two of them together, forever—a future where they lived and breathed the fragrance of a lover.

The women fell asleep and woke to an orange and pink sunrise.

"Time to get back, Takumi. We both have commitments today."

"If I had my druthers, we'd stay here forever and never return."

"Takumi? Where is that girl? Takumi? Aiko, please go find Takumi. She has a visitor she needs to prepare for."

"Yes, Madam. Should I tell her who is calling?"

"I've set up an appointment with a prospective *danna*. Tell her she has about three hours, so she should start getting ready now. You help her."

"On my way, Madam."

Aiko hurried down the hall as fast as she could without getting yelled at. Takumi was practicing her fan dance outside when she found her.

"Takumi, we have to get you ready for a client. We must hurry. It sounds like he may be an impatient man. Madam usually gives us all morning to prepare you, but she says you only have three hours and . . . and . . ."

The words that had previously fallen from Aiko's mouth had turned to tears. Wracking sobs erupted from her chest, and soon Aiko was in such a state that Takumi was worried. "Aiko, what's wrong? I'll be ready, don't worry. You're an amazing makeup artist. There's no better in all of Japan."

"It's, it's not that, Takumi. Madam Oy has advertised you as a full-fledged geisha. There is a prospective *danna* on his way now. He is coming all the way from Tokyo. I heard one of the other girls talking about him. He's very old and likes young girl geishas." Aiko continued weeping into her hands.

"I've been out with prospective *danna*s before, Aiko. I always manage to turn them away from me. Why would this man be any different?"

"I can't explain it, Takumi. I have a feeling that both of our lives are about to change, and not for the better. Go away with me. We can go to the old building and stay. I don't want you going out with this particular man. Please, Takumi."

Takumi pondered the insane request. It puzzled her that Aiko would ask such a thing of her. "I'd like for you to help me prepare, Aiko."

"I won't do it, Takumi. Find someone else to whore you up for the pleasure of the old goat—I refuse."

Takumi watched, flabbergasted, as Aiko ran down the hall and out the side door of the *okiya*.

Sendai was the only girl in the whole *okiya* who wasn't busy, so Takumi had her assist with preparations. She had to put her makeup on, fix her hair, and try to knot the kimono with literally no help. There was no way she'd be ready in three hours.

Takumi had Sendai hand her the lotions and powders she needed to get started. It didn't help that both girls needed glasses and didn't wear them. Geishas were thought to be the epitome of the perfect Japanese female. How would that translate into eyeglasses?

The lotion that should have gone on her legs got rubbed all over her face. The powder that should have set her cream makeup went all over the floor when Sendai sneezed. Takumi's hair was down, the kimono had a spot on it, and her lips appeared to be twice their normal size. She obviously didn't know how to out-line and fill in.

The door opened, without so much as a knock, and Madam Oy walked in. "Why aren't you ready, Takumi? Mr. Takanobu Nagumo is waiting downstairs for you. I've told him how well you perform the fan dance, it's his favorite."

Takumi looked up with fear in her eyes. There was no good explanation for the way she looked.

"Oh my God, child. You appear horrendous to me and cer-tainly will to Mr. Nagumo. What in the world will I do?" The old woman paced the room silently, her cane tapping the floor every time she lifted her left foot.

"You must do the dance anyway. Use your skills to hide your face and finish as fast as you can. Leave your hair down. We will have to hope and pray that this *danna* will not take offense to you. Get dressed and be downstairs in five minutes."

Madam Oy left without another word. The slamming of the old wooden door added a finality to Takumi's situation. "Help me get dressed, Sendai. I'll show her."

6

WHEN TAKUMI MADE HER entrance downstairs, Mr. Nagumo was sitting waiting for her. Madam Oy started to wheeze when she saw that Takumi was wearing a white bathrobe with a purple-painted dragon on the back. She wore no shoes, her hair was wrapped in a lavender towel, and the huge umbrella she held hid all of her face.

She snuck a peek at Mr. Nagumo before she began. His re-ceding hair was black, what was left of it. He wore expensive clothing and shoes and she could smell his cologne from across the room. His belly hung over his custom-made leather belt. There was no kindness in his eyes. His lips drew together in a thin line of determination. *What was this man here for?*

The dance started out as it always did with structured hand movements up and down. Her legs both bent at precisely the same angle when she moved. She lowered the umbrella onto the floor and picked up a black, silk fan. Tiny steps were taken as she stared at the garden scene that adorned the fan.

Takumi shook her head and let the towel fall down. She touched the closed fan to her hair and smiled. In one slow moment she had whipped the fan open and was following its motion with her head. The music was soft vocals that seemed to tell a tale of love lost.

With her arms connected she simulated the waves of the ocean. Her still-wet hair swished against her upper arms as she moved. The fan was laid down and her palms came to rest upon one another. In one fluid motion she knelt on the floor. Cupped hands rested beneath her chin, then rose into the air as she lowered herself onto the floor. Her eyes were closed to the stares that surrounded her.

The unusual position, with her legs bent under her, caused her robe to flop open and reveal her bare, virginal pussy. She had used black makeup to draw whiskers, a nose, and ears there— Mr. Nagumo was privy to geisha kitty.

Takumi made no effort to rise when the dance was over. Madam Oy fainted and no one moved to revive her. Quiet overtook the room for several minutes.

Clap, clap, clap. The round of applause piqued Takumi's curiosity, so she sat up and opened her eyes. Mr. Nagumo was clapping. A smile was on his face. He'd gotten up from his chair and was right at that moment heading toward her.

"Well done, you little minx. Very well done indeed. I've never met a geisha who would dance as you just have. You're exactly what I'm looking for. I'll be back tomorrow night. We'll be going out. You may want to wear a kimono, but clothing is always optional with me." He was still laughing when he exited through the front room of the teahouse.

Takumi got up as fast as she possibly could and ran out of the teahouse and back to the main part of the *okiya*. Tears of rage covered her face. White makeup poured off her face. She threw off the robe and dropped onto her bed immediately after tearing through her bedroom door.

It took at least an hour, but her fury did diminish with time. *I can't believe he liked that. What kind of* danna *wants a geisha who would shame herself like that?*

"Uh, mmm, Takumi."

She hadn't realized someone else was in the room with her. Aiko sat on the edge of the second bed with her hands folded in her lap. "I heard what you did, how he reacted. We must leave tonight. There's no more time, Takumi. Please."

"I have brought shame upon Madam Oy, upon my geisha sisters, upon my own mother, and worst of all I have shamed myself. You were right, Aiko. This man is looking for a plaything, nothing more. I'm doomed."

"No, please don't say that. More importantly, don't think that. We were meant to be together, and together we will be! Enough self-pity. Let's leave right now."

The young girls held hands as they crept from the *okiya*. They hoped that the falling darkness would cover their tracks. They stepped outside, shut the door, and leaned down to put on their shoes—and Madam Oy materialized from inside the *okiya*.

"Going somewhere, girls? You wouldn't steal from me, would you? Both of you are my personal property, don't forget that."

She grabbed the girls by the hair and dragged them back inside screaming. After they were dragged through the house, they were locked in separate closets with no light. "You won't be released until tomorrow. Mr. Nagumo has agreed to become your *danna*, Takumi.

"I'll have one of the girls pack your things. He wants you to live with him. I've already called your mother and explained what a golden opportunity this is—she was thrilled for you." Loud, heavy footsteps could be heard as Madam Oy walked away.

"Aiko, can you hear me?"

"Yes, I can hear you. Why wouldn't you listen to me, Takumi? Now you'll be moving to Tokyo with the old pervert and I'm destined to reside in this horrible house, loveless, for the rest of my days. You should have listened to me."

"I'm so sorry, Aiko. You're right of course. I had no way of knowing this time would be different than all of the last times."

"You had every way of knowing—you had me."

"I promise I'll listen to you from now on. Aiko? Please, talk to me."

All of Takumi's pleading was met with silence. Aiko might as well be on the other side of the earth. Takumi had torn down her lover's trust. She'd painted her pussy to look like a kitty, what was she thinking?

I wasn't thinking, that's the problem. I haven't had to think for myself, ever. My mother thought for me at home. Madam Oy thinks for me here. If I get shipped off to Tokyo, Mr. Pervert will do all of my thinking for me I'm sure. It's time I figured out what I want and go after it.

"I love you, Aiko. I love the way your hair smells after you've walked in the rain. I love the way you smile when I bring you sweets from the kitchen. I love the tenderness you show when you help me prepare for a night out in the teahouse. How hard that must have been for you each time. I'd never thought of it before. You never complained, not even once. I want to spend the rest of my life with you. Not here, not in an *okiya*. I want to get a small hut and live with you by the ocean. I want to make love to you on the sand as the sun sets on the horizon."

Her grand statement was met with quiet.

"We were meant to be together. You know it as well as I do. We're soul mates, you and I. You're the only reason fate saw fit to send me to this terrible place. Say something. Say you hate me. Say you never want to touch me, laugh with me, or walk hand in hand again. I can't stand the stillness, Aiko. Please . . ."

The closet in which Takumi had been placed opened up. Mr. Nagumo stood before her, hand stretched out. "Come with me, my child. I have a driver waiting. Your things are already in my trunk."

Takumi withdrew from his touch and scooted back into the recess of the wooden corner. "I won't go with you. I don't even like men!"

A strange look came into the old man's eyes. "You have never been with a man?"

"No, and I don't plan to be either. I lick pussy. I kiss soft, full lips. I won't be of any use to you."

"Hmm, Madam Oy was being truthful then. I had my doubts. You were such a slut tease during the fan dance. I'll teach you what happens when young girls show their bodies to men."

Takumi prayed as she'd never prayed before. *Please, God, don't let this happen. I'm a good person. I love Aiko. Don't take me away from her.*

God didn't seem to be listening. An old, wrinkled arm extended into the opening and grabbed her. He didn't even slow down to get a good grip. He pulled her all the way to the front door, then threw her outside on the ground. A tall, stocky man dressed all in black picked her up and carried her to the vehicle.

"Let me down. Aikoooooooooo!" Takumi beat her fists against the burly giant, but it had no effect. The driver threw her into the backseat and locked all the doors. Mr. Nagumo slid onto the leather seat from the opposite door.

"Wave good-bye, little one. Your time here is done."

Takumi shifted as close to the back window as she could. All of it was fading away with distance. She kept watching, waiting for something that never came. Finally she sat on the seat keeping the distance between her and Mr. Nagumo as wide as humanly possible. Her arms crossed and her knees pulled up to her chest. It wasn't the most comfortable position, but it was the best she could do to fend him off for the moment.

7

AT SOME POINT TAKUMI fell asleep. She awoke with a film of dried tears on her cheeks. "Open your eyes, child. We're here."

A large home stood before them on a hill. The driver took a dirt drive up to the main entrance. Two servants were standing by the front door ready to greet this monster of a man home.

The giant came around to open the door. She become conscious of the fact that her new *danna* had tons of money.

Mr. Nagumo took hold of her wrist and pulled her out of the car on his side. "You will smile when you meet my servants." It was a command, not a request.

It was all Takumi could do to walk without tripping. She didn't even attempt to fake a smile. One servant was a man and one was a woman. It made sense that Mr. Nagumo handed her off to the woman. "Please show her to the guest room. Stay with her at all times. Do not let her out of the house for any reason. She's been ill and I want to make sure she acclimates her system before she goes running off. I'm sure you understand."

"Yes, sir. Of course, sir."

Mae had been in Mr. Nagumo's employ for several years. She knew he was a dirty old man. He'd practically raped her one night in the kitchen. Luckily she'd grown too old for his tastes. Her arm draped around Takumi's shoulders as she guided her to the third-floor guest room.

"What's your name, child?"

"I'm not a child. I'm twenty-seven years old."

"Really? Well then. You do look much younger. But please tell me your name. I'm Mae. I do all the cooking and cleaning around here. It isn't paradise but it isn't an alley in Bangkok either."

"My name is Takumi. I was living in the house of Madam Oy learning to become a geisha when Mr. Nagumo found me. Is he as perverted and sick as he looks?"

"Yes, dear. I'm afraid he is."

"I thought so. Could you help me out of here?"

Mae wrung her hands nervously. "Quiet. Don't let anyone hear you talk about leaving. He'll have all of our heads if he even suspects something like that is going on. The last time he fired everyone save me and Paul. We were lucky to keep our positions, and we didn't even know the young lass was leaving. Paul's English. They don't do this sort of thing back where he lives."

"Wait a minute, Mae. What do you mean by the last time? He's taken girls before? Was she a geisha also?"

"No, not exactly. I shouldn't be speaking of this. You have clean clothing in the wardrobe and fresh fruit in the bowl by the bed. I suggest you get some rest."

"Please, Mae. Don't leave me here alone. What if Mr. Nagumo comes?"

"I'm sorry, Takumi. I can't."

Mae closed the door when she left, and Takumi could hear a key flicking the lock into place. Living with Madam Oy hadn't been great, but this was a real-life prison. She couldn't go outside or talk to anyone. *I wonder what Aiko is doing right now?* The best thing to do was just lie down and go to sleep. She could be with Aiko in her dreams. No one could take that away from her.

I can see Aiko. Her tiny figure is standing at the top of the stairs in front of our old building. Her arms are out straight, beckoning me to them. There's a sad look on her face. "Why are you sad, darling?" I want to ask her, but the words won't form in my mouth.

I run toward her, but the more I run, the larger the chasm between us grows. "What's happening?" I call to her, but she doesn't answer. "I miss you." I see her mouth moving but no sounds come out. "I miss you more."

Suddenly she points emphatically behind me. I turn and run right into Mr. Nagumo. Why is it that he can hear me, touch me,

and probably smell my fear? "I don't want to go with you. Leave
me here!"

Takumi felt the sweat on her skin. Her eyes were puffy from crying, and she found it hard to open them. Who cared anyway?
She might as well lie in bed the rest of her life if this was to be
her destiny. Thoughts of suicide crossed her mind. *Was life even*
worth living?

8

MAE ENTERED THE ROOM and shoved the floor-length cur-
tains aside. "Time to rise, ma'am. The master expects for you to
join him for breakfast this morning. He's requested that you
wear something blue, his favorite color."

"I dress for no one. Tell him to get stuffed."

"Please, don't be like that. I think this will be a safe meeting
for you. He only wishes to talk—for now. Here, I've picked
something for you to wear."

Mae held out a simple blue dress, and Takumi pulled it over
her head. "Fine."

She walked down two flights of stairs to reach the dining
area of the home. A huge buffet had been prepared for just the
two of them. *What a waste.*

"Takumi, so glad you've joined me. We need to discuss a few
things. Please sit across from me. That will be your regular
seat."

Her defiant manner wouldn't allow her to do as he asked.
She sat in the armchair right next to him and gave him an inso-
lent glare. "What do you want with me?"

"I own you now, Takumi. I understand you had a life before you came here, and that's fine, but now you are here to serve me and do as I wish. The first thing I wish is for you to sit across the table from me."

How far should I push my independence?

Mae pleaded with her eyes from across the room and gave Takumi a reassuring nod. Takumi stood and walked to the requested chair.

"Thank you. Now, for the other rules of the house. You will not leave the grounds without a chaperone. You will be at my every beck and call. If you need or desire something, please ask. I do a lot of entertaining, and it is likely that you will be asked to join in the party festivities. You will find that I can be most accommodating when I get what I want."

Takumi turned up her lip and looked away.

"I expect you to look into my eyes when I speak to you. Some gentlemen think women should look down, but I know that the eyes are the windows to the soul. They never lie. This way I shall always know what you are thinking. Your eyes will speak louder than your words."

Her eyes rose to meet his. She spoke not a word.

"Do you agree to abide by these rules, Takumi? The alternative is to be locked up in your room for the rest of your days. You will still do as I ask, of course, but you will forgo the before-mentioned perks of the house."

"I will do as you ask until the day I escape this wretched hell of a mansion you call home."

"Hmm, so glad you brought up the escape option. If you try to leave my perimeter, I will have you shackled to the wall in the dungeon and brought up only for parties. It's your choice of course, but with me you get only one chance."

"May I leave now?"

"You may eat now. When you're finished, you are welcome to spend the remainder of the day on your own recognizance. Don't make me regret giving you this leeway, Takumi."

"Of course not, sir."

The food tasted bland in her mouth. She ate only because she had to. Freedom had been so close. She'd had everything a person could possibly want only a few days earlier—a devoted lover, a place to live, and the promise of a happily-ever-after future. Now she had a tyrannical master who had bought and paid for her services. She lived hundreds of miles from everyone she'd ever known. Life sucked.

9

TAKUMI SPENT THE DAY exploring the grounds, gardens, and escape routes. She had no intention of staying here any longer than she had to. One constant was in her mind: Mr. Nagumo had her body, but he would never have her heart or her soul.

Since she had a while before lunch she retired to her suite for some alone time. Thoughts of Aiko whirled through her brain. Images of their building filled her mind while she fell into a deep slumber.

"Aiko? Is that you?" A person stood before her in a long, white dress. The person's back was turned to her, making it difficult to identify who it was. She stood before the double doors of the building with the sun pooling around her outline. Takumi's eyes couldn't adjust to the brightness.

Suddenly the figure turned and walked toward her. Features became recognizable as the person came closer. "Aiko, it is you!"

Takumi ran to close the distance between them. She wrapped her arms around shoulders covered in white, gauzy material and laid her head down. Aiko didn't speak. She didn't lift her hand to pat Takumi's back. She didn't open her eyes to gaze upon her long-lost lover.

"What's wrong with you, Aiko? What have they done?"

Whispers drifted into the air although Aiko's lips never separated. "They have bartered for my servitude, Takumi. Tomorrow I go to live with another madam in another city. Madam Oy has chosen to retire. She complained about the price she brought for me. I've been quite useless since your move. Please come to me. Together we are everything. Alone we are nothing."

The figure turned to leave the building that they had both come to love.

"No, don't leave me, Aiko. I will get back to you. I will find you. Don't let yourself be taken off. Go to the building, Aiko. Go there and wait for me. I vow to meet you there one day. If it kills me, I will escape this horrid man I've been sold to. Don't give up on me!"

The spirit raised a finger into the air and gave a nod as she exited down the old stone steps. Takumi couldn't tell if Aiko had given her a positive or negative response. She would hope for the best. Escape was her only option. Tears poured down her cheeks.

"I'll be there soon, my love."

Takumi woke with dried goop all over her skin and in the corner of her eyes. Her heart felt a stab of forewarning. *I must run to-*

night. The rest of the morning and afternoon would be spent calculating a plan of flight. No land or prison could contain her love.

"Sleep well, ma'am?" Takumi hadn't realized that Mae was standing over her until she opened her eyes.

"I slept fine, thank you."

"Something troubling is brewing in those eyes of yours, young lady. What are you planning to do and when are you planning to do it?"

Takumi looked down at her hands and fiddled with the blanket covering her legs. "I don't know what you're talking about, Mae."

"Takumi. Please, I won't share your thoughts or intentions with that ogre of a man that I must serve. I, too, stay here against my will. It has become commonplace for me, but the thought of leaving is a distant hope in all of my nightly dreams."

"I had no idea, Mae." Takumi thought for only a few moments before revealing her plan. "I'm leaving tonight."

"Tonight, ma'am? Mr. Nagumo has a special party planned for tomorrow tonight. Did he not tell you? He plans to out you to his business friends and family. He flaunts girls like others flaunt money. He is truly an evil human being. I detest him. It eats away at you to hate someone so much, but I can't help myself."

Takumi saw a weird look pass over Mae's face when she mentioned Mr. Nagumo.

"Did he used to flaunt you also, Mae?"

The shock that registered on the woman's face verified Takumi's suspicions. That's why she still lived here. She was as much a prisoner as the young geisha herself. A thought flashed through Takumi's mind: *I must take her with me.*

"I want you to come with me when I escape. You must. This is no life for the likes of you, for anyone for that matter."

"Takumi, you don't understand. He will catch us. He will catch us leaving his lands and bring us back. I saw what happens to girls who attempt that—you don't want it for yourself."

"What is the worst he can do? I would risk anything to be free of him."

"The last girl, Denee, was English. Her family sold her to him to get rid of a massive debt. Her brother came for her one night. He disagreed with the way her family had cast her off for monetary gain."

"How sweet. How far did they get, Mae?"

"They never made it out of the house. She was thrown into a cage in the dungeon, and he, well, he was never seen again. The poor girl quit eating and starved herself to death. Some men like that emaciated look, and he used that to his advantage. When she became too weak to speak, he sold her off to such a man. I heard that she died soon after."

"Don't the authorities come looking for some of these missing people?"

"He sells to them also, Takumi. There's no hope to be found in this situation. Please, promise me you won't attempt it."

"I can't make you that promise, Mae. In fact, I wish you would promise to come with me. There's no honor in staying. There's no hope that things will improve. At least this way you have an inkling of salvation on the horizon."

"I'm sorry, ma'am. I don't have it in me after all these years. I'm tired. It's a sad, lonely life to be sure, but it's the life chosen for me to live."

"I don't understand your thinking, but I'll respect your wishes, my friend."

Takumi formulated her plan in her mind over lunch and into the early afternoon. Mr. Nagumo gave her many strange looks throughout the time she spent with him.

"How are you enjoying your stay here, girl?"

"It is fine, sir. I'll come to be used to it, I expect."

"A very good attitude indeed. Some come here with thoughts of returning home, but those must be squashed immediately. You belong to me now. My property is quite valuable to me. I fight for what's mine."

A sinister glare greeted her when she looked up into his burly face.

"Of course, sir. I wouldn't dream of trying to leave you or the good life you've made for me here."

Seemingly satisfied, Mr. Nagumo looked down into his dish and continued to tear into the food before him. He didn't speak another word during the meal.

Takumi wandered the household looking and listening for a sign. Aiko had said she was coming for her. Surely she would announce her presence with some sort of sign. By dinnertime Takumi became withdrawn and sullen. Aiko should have been here by now.

"Is something wrong, girl?" Mr. Nagumo had no patience for those around him.

"No, sir. I don't seem to be rested up from our long trip quite yet. May I be excused to my suite?"

The old ogre didn't even answer verbally but waved her away from the table with the back of his hand. Takumi slipped a steak knife into her sleeve, stood up to push her chair in, and left the dining room.

She walked up the stairs as if they were a carpet leading to a death sentence. *I can't do this again and again. I can't live with this hideous creature who calls himself a man. If Aiko doesn't show up in some form tonight, I will end it myself. Better to be dead than mating with a monster!*

Mae assisted Takumi with her nightgown and stoked the fire on her way out. Mae didn't speak of the escape out loud but she pleaded for normalcy when she looked at the young geisha. Takumi didn't have the words to tell her the plan had changed.

Aiko's plan must have been thwarted. It was the only explanation. This would be Takumi's last night of sleep. At dawn she would hike to the top of the hill behind the mansion and watch the sun rise. When the rays were shooting through the air with hope and the day was at its pinnacle, Takumi would stab herself through the heart.

"I want you to look over my mother. She never understood me, but she did the best she could with what she was given. Please let Aiko move on and lead a happy life. Mae needs to get away from this prison household. Give her the courage to attempt her own escape. I'd ask you to forgive Mr. Nagumo and Madam Oy, but that is something I can't do myself. Please do forgive me for what I must do in the morning. It's my only way out, the only way to preserve what is truly mine—my body and soul."

Takumi unfolded her hands and folded them under her head. The knife she put beneath her pillow. *Maybe it will cut the pain of losing my true love in half.* She was asleep within minutes.

10

THE OLD BUILDING *was before her. Takumi looked down and she was standing in the street looking up at the magical doors. If only she could reach those doors. Aiko must be waiting*

for her there. Try as she might her feet would not move. The
doors opened and Aiko stood before her. Madam Oy was hold-
ing her by her unraveled hair.

"Help me, Takumi. We must be together. I love you. Don't
let them take that away from us!"

"I'm coming, Aiko. I do love you. More than the moon and
the stars in the sky. Wish it and it will come true. You are so close
to the magic—it must work for you. Try it, Aiko."

Takumi woke with a gasp. Had she really seen Aiko? She often
dreamed of events before they happened. This time it felt like she
was witnessing an event from the past. The dense night was lifting. The sun would soon rise. She could not waver. Second
chances never came easily. This might be the last time she could
get away—be it to escape physically or mentally, she would escape. Knife in hand she crept down the stairs and out a side door
to the gardens.

She saw no reason to change what she was wearing. The bil-
lowy, sheer fabric that made up her nightgown swayed in the
morning breeze as she plodded up the grassy hillside. No one
was about this early. The sweet smell of fresh-bloomed flowers
rose to her nostrils. Mr. Nagumo did have a magnificent garden.
He used the blossoms to decorate for his many parties.

Takumi reached down and picked one pale pink flower. It
was called a wineberry in these parts. Mr. Nagumo paid lots of
money to get exactly what he wanted. This flower needed lots of
care, and he paid someone to do that for him. He did nothing
himself except rule over his massive domain.

This flower would be his last gift to Takumi. She slipped it
behind her ear and continued her ascent. Once she was at the

highest point of the hill, Takumi sat down, eager to watch her last sunrise. The cool morning air chilled her, but she made no effort to warm herself. It seemed silly knowing what she was about to do.

Below her the first rays of sun shot through the sky. The light took on her favorite color and mimicked the pink of the petals that adorned her hair. A ball of pale pink fire rose on the horizon. She must prepare herself.

Takumi stood, legs straight and stiff, and slid the knife from inside her sleeve. Both hands encircled the handle of the ordinary, black steak knife. Her arms lifted into the air and her wrists rotated toward her body. She had it positioned to the exact point of entry. This is how she intended to view the last minutes of nature's spectacular wakening, in suicide mode.

It wasn't like her to lie to herself or try to make things pretty. She wasn't a pretender. This was her only way out and she was taking it. Before her the last of the fiery ball rose above the land. Bursts of sunshine pervaded her inner being. It was time.

Takumi lifted her arms out straight in front of her and plunged the knife to her heart. Two events happened simultaneously. Her legs, which she didn't realize had locked up on her, gave out and made her fall to the mossy ground. And she heard a voice call out to her that she had never thought she'd hear again—Aiko's.

"Ta-kum-i. . . ."

The knife had plunged deep into her body. Luckily for her, falling to the ground had messed up her mark. The knife stuck out between her shoulder and neck. The pain was intense but so was the joy of hearing her lover's voice.

"Oh my goodness, Takumi. What have you done?" Aiko leaned over her with concern and tears in her eyes.

"It was you or death, my love."

"You idiot! I'm here now. How will you run with this wound, Takumi?"

"I'll run, girl. I'll run like the wind, just help me get up."

The pair knew that removing the utensil would cause a great flow of blood so they left it in as they fled. They ran hand in hand to the edge of the Nagumo property and laughed as they did so.

Mae stood at a window and watched the pair flee in their quest for freedom. She envied the both of them. *It's too late for me, but I'll do what I can to help the both of them.*

"Mae, where is Takumi? I'm ready for breakfast early this morning. Get that girl down here."

"Of course, sir. I'll bring her right back."

Mae spent so long upstairs that Mr. Nagumo came to the end of the staircase and yelled up to her. "Mae, what's taking you so long?"

"Sir, Takumi is feeling quite ill. Would you care to come up here and speak to her?"

"Ill? Of course I don't want to speak to her. You know I detest germs. Make her stay in bed all day and tend to her. She must be better by tomorrow. I'm having a party and I plan to introduce her talents to my many male guests. Make sure she's ready."

"Of course, sir. She'll be ready."

The day of respite allowed Takumi and Aiko to travel to their building. Neither knew how they'd made it so quickly. It seemed that every road had a willing driver who would let them tag along. It was as if they were meant to reach the building.

Hand in hand they walked up the steps of the magical respite. Each of them opened a door and slipped inside, closing and locking the gigantic structure behind them. The two doors interlocked on the inside.

"Are we done, Aiko? Is all of the bad stuff behind us? Will we really and truly be together forever?"

"Yes, Takumi. As long as we vow to stay here and never leave."

The two women interlocked their pinkie fingers. "I vow it."

Chocolate Cream

TRACEE A. HANNA

ᵱ

ARE YOU THE GOOD girl or the nice guy—you know, the one who always makes the right choices and never rocks the boat? Well, I am. . . . I was raised in a traditional South Korean society where, even on television, couples did not kiss in public unless it was a serious relationship that was leading to marriage. I am such a goody-goody that it took a year of dating and a marriage proposal for me to finally lose my virginity. That was five years ago, after I finished college, and although that relationship has ended, not much has changed.

I am a Korean-African-American, dimpled darling, a hot, single suburbanite, in my midtwenties, with a great body and hair down to my waist. I was born in Old Songtan City, now known as the Shinjang section of the Songtan area of Pyongtael City, which is located right outside the American air force base in Osan, South Korea. I am the product of a love affair that my mother had with an American soldier. My parents died in a freak boating accident seven weeks after I was born, the day before they were to marry, leaving me to my elderly South Korean grandparents. *Harabujy,* my honorable grandfather, died when I was only three years old, and *Harmuny,* my devoted grandmother, died the year after. I was raised in shame and poverty— being of mixed race and the child of an unwed South Korean lady was a major social encumbrance. My life seemed bleak until I moved to the United States when I was eighteen, which is when I obtained dual citizenship, with the help of my loving African-American grandparents.

I hated being poor, therefore I was determined to make something of my life and make my African-American family proud of me—I will forever be grateful to them. Unfortunately, I have allowed my corporate and financial ambitions to control my life. I have successfully traded in the companionship, sex, and the multiple orgasms of a personal love life for the praise, promotions, and financial rewards of the corporate world.

I have secretly been jealous of the women who are bold and liberated enough to go with the flow, take life as it comes, and welcome life's sweet taboos. I have yearned ever since I was in college to be one of those wild and free females who have amazing sex lives. I would frequently fantasize about indulging in just one moment of reckless abandon. I have always wanted to know what it felt like to take a walk on the wild side. So finally one night I did. . . .

The story that I am about to tell you concerns my one night of being bad; last night. I can never tell my family or friends this story simply because they would never understand, plus they would never believe me. But, I have to tell someone. Who better than a complete stranger? Who better than you?

Every Friday after work I go to my local ice cream parlor to get my Friday-night treat, chocolate Yukimi Daifuku ice cream. In my busy life I don't have time for any other indulgences. I don't go to bars, nightclubs, or even out to dinner. I go to the office, to the gym, and back to my house. What's worse? I haven't been out on a date in over a year. And what's even sadder still? Until yesterday night I had been celibate for so much longer than that. However, last night changed all of that. I lost utter control of my senses and inhibitions for one moment. I allowed my inner diva to rear her sexy, saucy head. I guess what they say, timing is everything, is so very true. If I had not stopped to break past the rice crust of my ice cream ball and take just one teeny tiny nibble before exiting the store, I would not have run into the sexiest man that I have ever laid my eyes on. I was standing in front of the entrance licking my spoon when the door swung open.

"Excuse me. I am sorry," I said as I looked up, already smiling a guilty smile. "I just had to—"

"Take a taste." He finished my sentence. His sexy baritone voice caught my attention.

"Yes, exactly." I smiled; my voice was just above a whisper.

We both felt the spark between us—a primal chemistry. It was as if our eyes were speaking the words that we could just not say, having met only seconds ago. I thought to myself . . . *Oh my, he is lovely. Oh, wow! Tall, dark, sexy, and he has dimples, just like me. He is definitely fuckable, even if only for one night.* Just to think, if those were my underexperienced thoughts, I can only imagine what his must have been. But I can tell you this, the expression in his gaze made my libido soar.

"Geoffrey." He introduced himself in a word.

Geoffrey was a well-built, masculine man with loads of sex appeal and distinct features. He was an all-American manly man, not some pretty boy or metrosexual. He was the kind that I would not mind walking two steps behind; to hell with being liberated, I would take my place.

"Tessa." I followed his lead.

"Tessa?"

"Yes, I am named after my father's mother."

"Wait for me, please?" His voice was so laden with passion and promise that I had to agree.

"Alright," I purred.

I do not know what I was thinking at that moment or if I was even thinking at all, because I just stood there and waited for him as he bought a pack of cigarettes and some gum. He took me by the hand and led me to the ladies' restroom. As we walked, I looked up at him, my uncertainty clearly written all over my face. He took notice right away.

"Do you want me?" he asked candidly.

"Yes!" I answered unequivocally.

"Alright then. Come on in here with me." He read the chart on the door. "It was just cleaned by Janis less than fifteen minutes ago. So, let's indulge ourselves."

I followed him into the bathroom. We entered unnoticed. He locked the door behind us and turned to me. I was so excited— filled with anticipation and concupiscence. We looked into each other's eyes, pausing for just one moment. He grabbed me and kissed me hard. He pulled back, looking intently into my eyes as he tugged my shirt up over my head and dropped it to the floor. Geoffrey unhooked my red satin bra as he kissed my neck. He slowly pulled down the straps as he trailed kisses down to my collarbone. He gently freed my breasts, deftly discarding my bra as he kissed his way to my nipples and suckled my tits, sending waves of pleasure through my body. All I wanted was to grip the back of his head and press him to me—but all I could do was clench my fists and ride out the deluge of sensations that were flooding my body and breath. Geoffrey kissed his way down my stomach. He knelt in front of me—pulling my pants down as he went. I stepped out of my slacks and kicked them to the side. He sank his teeth into my pussy through the red satin of my thong— making me gasp with delight and cream soak my panties. I pulled his shirt over his head, exposing his muscular chest, stomach, and back. He had just enough hair on his chest and stomach to be wonderfully alluring. He gripped the front of my thong in his fist, then looked up at me.

"Snatch it off!" I commanded. No one had ever done that to me before; however, it had long been a fantasy of mine. I smiled a wicked smile as I awaited for him to follow my instructions. He tightened his grip and ripped my thong right off my body. "That's it, big boy!" I exclaimed. He reached his arms through my legs—palming my ass cheeks—and hoisted me up onto his shoulders. "Oh my!" I could not help but cry out. I loved the way he was handling me. He was definitely a take-charge kind of guy: strong, bold, and confident.

"Your pussy smells so good, so sweet. I just want to taste it." He licked from my clitoris to my anus and back again like a kitten nipping at its milk. "M-mm-hmm, oh yeah, just as I hoped." He hungrily ate my pussy. "What is that scent?" he asked in between slurps.

"Dansim, the rose of Sharon," I sputtered—I could barely speak clearly as I was so enjoying the oral pleasures.

"I am going to eat your pussy like you need it to be eaten, like it's never been eaten before." He plunged his whole face in between my legs, lapping his tongue deep inside my salacious canal. "M-mm-m-mm," he purred as he swished and swirled his tongue around my nether lips, making sure to lick every millimeter of my pussy. "You've got some sweet juices, baby. Go on ahead and eat your ice cream while I eat you."

I was amazed, completely awestruck. "M-mm!" I found myself licking my chocolate ice cream in the same rhythm that he was licking my cunt. His tongue was so wet, so supple, so velvety smooth. It felt so good sliding around my clit and in and out of my pussy. "*Ye! . . . Yes!*" The pleasure of his oral manipulations coupled with the sweet, rich chocolate decadence of my ice cream was just mind-blowing. To taste and feel such sweet sensations at the same time was truly titillating. I was trying my best to ride out the waves of pleasure as long as I could, but the intensity persistently built to the point where my breath kept catching in my throat. I was going to cum all over his face at any moment. I was quickly losing control. My body began to buck wildly, making my pussy slam against his face repeatedly. My ice cream fell to the floor. "*Anijo!*" No! He took notice right away. He loved my total loss of restraint. He stood up, taking me with him. I reached up and palmed the ceiling for support as my body spontaneously gyrated and quaked. "*Ne jaji na hal at ra!*" I cried out for him to suck my vulva. The very moment that I began to cum he slid his middle finger into my ass, which heightened my pleasure. He sucked on my clitoris, taking long, deliberate suckles, nursing every ounce of cum from me. It was all that I could do just to hold on. He gave my pussy one final kiss before sliding his finger out of my body and lowering me to the floor.

"Nice!"

"That was truly incredible," I said as I looked into his eyes. "*Kamsahamnida.*" I thanked him as I hugged him and kissed him on his cheek. "Thank you very much." I gathered up my clothes and shoes from the floor. "Good-bye."

I was on my way to a stall to get dressed. He grabbed me by my arm as I was walking past him.

"That's all you want from me?"

"Yes."

"Are you sure?" He released me.

"Oh, yes, I am sure." I took a step away from him. "By the way, I come here every Friday to get ice cream. Hopefully I will see you again."

"Until we meet again then." He smiled a mischievous smile as he reached his hand into his pants. "This is what you are missing." He showed me his cock, which was hard as steel. "But you don't want that now, do you?"

Yes, I do! was the first thing that popped into my mind. *Nice! Very nice indeed. Girl, you had better go and get that dick, you know that you want to . . . besides, it's too late to be shy now.* Yet I was frozen in place. I literally could not move. He placed his penis back into his pants, slid his feet into his shoes, and retrieved his shirt from the floor. Just as he placed his hand on the door, I called out to him.

"Geoffrey, wait."

"Yes?" he responded good-naturedly as he turned to face me again.

"There is something else that I want from you."

"Name it."

"Better yet, let me show you. Come on back over here." As he approached, I threw my clothes to the floor and knelt on them. The moment that he stopped in front of me, I pulled his pants and boxers off him. I didn't hesitate, I grabbed his rock-hard cock with both of my hands, took a second to look up at him, and smiled as I licked the head, making sure it was nice and wet before taking it past my lips. "Come on now, move with me.

Fuck me in my mouth," I demanded. He gripped the back of my head and slowly started gyrating his hips as I sucked and stroked his magnificent dick. "M-mm-hmm, m-mm-hmm!" I purred. The skin on his cock was silky soft. He had a slight salty taste to him, like the perfect snack. "M-mm-mm-m!" I vibrated my lips up and down his shaft as I sucked and kissed his dick. I watched him watching me, which excited me even more. "Ooh, yeah!" I let every ounce of my exhilaration show as I licked his penis from tip to base, then tickled his testicles with the tip of my tongue, teasing him as I stroked his cock with both hands.

"Come up here!" he demanded. "Come on over here and show me how well you can ride my dick."

He pulled me up and took me over to the stall. He sat on the commode. I straddled him—slowly taking in his cock inch by inch. I started off with an unhurried circular grind and increased my stride with alacrity—changing to a bucking bounce—as I built toward my orgasm. I reared back and rode his cock like I was on a Black Angus bull, until my legs felt like jelly, until I was so wet from my own juices that my pussy lips started to smack. He gripped my ass and then stood up—picking me up as he went. His cock penetrated my body a little bit farther. I wrapped my legs around him. It felt so good, so right. He stood there in the middle of the floor fucking me. I was pummeled off his cock like a ball off a bolo bat. And just to think it wasn't over yet.

"Oh, God, you are strong!" I exclaimed in amazement. "I have never been fucked like this before."

"You like that?"

"Oh, yes . . . oh, yes, I do!"

"Okay, little lady, the night would not be complete if I didn't hit it from the back. I want to fuck you up against this wall." His voice was laden with concupiscence. Geoffrey spun me around and placed my hands on the wall. He gripped my hips and thrust the entire length of his dick into my pussy in one powerful lunge. I could not help but cry out from the thrilling shock. He was a robust lover. His stride was strong and true. I came for him over and over, to the point that my cum was spilling down my legs and onto the floor. His drive was dominating me, my pleasure, my senses, my every move. Geoffrey was all that I could want. He was all that I ever needed in a lover but never had. He slapped my ass and pulled my hair, adding to our already overzealous passions. He plunged harder and faster, causing me to cry out. He was fucking the hell out of my pussy. Our licentiousness amazed me. Each thrust drove me even farther over the edge in a staggering cornucopia of pleasure and pain. All that could be heard was our pleasure-filled moans as we both strove for the same goal.

"I am going to cum inside of you!"

"Come on, baby. Cum for me."

He wrapped his arms around my torso, holding me perfectly still as his semen shot into my body. He collapsed on my back, pressing me against the wall.

"Same time next Friday?" Geoffrey asked, as he breathed heavily on the back of my head.

"Oh, hell, yes!" I agreed enthusiastically. "Tessa Lim."

"Geoffrey Anderson." He kissed me one last time. "Hello, pretty lady."

"*Annyeonghaseyo. Manna boeeo ban gapseumnida.*" I smiled gracefully before I translated, "Hello. Nice to meet you."

So now you know my sexy little secret. Can you blame me? I am so looking forward to next Friday.

The Land of the Rising Sun

LOTUS FALCON

ॐ

1

I WAS ON MY way to Japan from Washington, D.C., by way of San Francisco, and I was ecstatic. I recently received an educational grant and was traveling with a study group to learn about Japan's educational system. It was my goal to fill myself with all the sights, sounds, and culture I could obtain in three weeks. The plane ride was uneventful, especially since I had the good fortune of being sandwiched between two elephant women. I kept taking regular bathroom breaks just so I could get the feeling back in my arms. The elephant women tag-teamed me and cut off the circulation to my arms every time I tried to use the armrests.

On my way to the bathroom I eyeballed a cutie that had been eyeballing me when we were boarding the plane. I didn't pay him too much attention at first, but now that I had some time to kill, I decided I might as well kill it with "homeboy." It seems as though he was on his way to the bathroom at the same time I was trying to take a leak.

When we couldn't decide who should go in first, we did the next best thing and went in together. I have been in tight places before, but nothing is tighter than a bathroom on an airplane. I really did have to pee and didn't have any shame in pulling my skirt up and dropping my draws. I don't think he thought I was going to pee at first, but I let it rip, like the falls at Niagara. Since his mouth was hanging open like he'd never seen anybody pee before, I thought I would give him a special little treat by taking some toilet paper and wiping off my pussy.

2

I WIPED IT JUST the way my mama taught me when I was a little girl: from the front to the back. I cleaned my pussy so good it was clean enough to eat. I started from the top, first licking my finger to separate my pussy lips. Since it was so tight in the bathroom, I wanted to make sure homeboy didn't miss a stroke, so I pushed his head down and made him watch me so close he could smell my punany!

The more I wet my pussy with my fingers, the more it started to pop and whistle. I had no intention of fingering myself, but I guess one thing led into another once I got into a good groove. I worked the fingers on my right hand around the hood of my clit, which was starting to swell from the teasing.

The more I rubbed my pussy, the better it felt. I almost forgot I was on a plane. I didn't ask for any audience participation, but homeboy started giving me stage directions from the peanut gallery. He told me to pull the hood back over my clit as far as it would go, so he could see how big it could get. Since I'd never had a request like that before, I wanted to see how big it got myself, so the more I worked it, the more he started blowing on it, until it popped out just like a "baby dick." I had to turn to face the mirror and admire it myself, because I had no idea a clit could get so big.

My pussy was on fire and needed a tongue bath, and homeboy was only too happy to oblige. He positioned himself so as to get a suctionlike grip around my clit, like one of those rubber things on the bottom of a bathroom mat. The turbulence coming from the plane only heightened an already great mouth fuck.

3

I WANTED TO SPEED things up before we got caught, so I hoisted my leg up on the sink and started humping his face as if I was trying to bury him in the pussy. Being the "squirter" that I am, when my time came, homeboy got caught up in the mix without any warning. Pussy juice was dripping from his eyes, his nose, and all around his mouth. It was funny. He never saw it coming!

There was a knock at the door and I'm sure a long line had started to form outside the bathroom. I grabbed a corner of his shirt, wiped my pussy off, pulled down my skirt, and got out of Dodge. By that time homeboy had to really take a leak, so I squeezed between him and the door as he began to drain the lizard. As I was leaving, the woman in front of me looked me up and down before turning the doorknob. Looking over my shoulder, I casually smirked at her and said, "You may want to wait a minute. Someone is still in there!"

We finally landed in San Francisco, where we waited for the

jumbo jet, flight #837, heading for Japan. We landed at the Narita International Airport in Tokyo safe and sound, even though I had turned a putrid shade of green from the altitude.

There's a fourteen-hour difference in time between Tokyo and my hometown, Washington, D.C., and without doubt I was a long way from "the hood." Before taking the shuttle bus to my hotel, I needed to relieve myself and had a challenge finding the bathroom. I made the mistake of asking a Japanese employee where the "bathroom" was and was told that there were no "bathrooms" at the airport.

4

NOW I ALREADY KNEW about those Japanese bathrooms that had the toilets that were flat on the ground and you had to squat to take a leak and balance yourself at the same time, but I didn't expect not to find someplace to relieve myself. Dag, was that too much to ask? After a little more investigation I discovered I was asking for the wrong thing. The Japanese consider the *bathroom* a room that you bathe in. I should have asked for the *toilet.* By that time my pee was somewhere up to my neck, getting ready to flow through my ears at any moment.

When I finally found the *toilet,* I couldn't believe how state-of-the-art it was. It was all chrome and shiny with glass fixtures everywhere. All kinds of gadgets were on the toilet, and I couldn't figure out how to flush it. As I was messing around with all the buttons, I realized it was a bidet and not just any old toilet. There were buttons to wash your ass, buttons to dry your ass, and even a button that would mask the sound of taking a dump and breaking wind. What really blew my mind was the button that heated the seat so your ass wouldn't catch a cold. Now that was a shithouse fit for a queen!

As I turned on the button to wash my ass, I realized how warm the water was and how accurate the nozzle's aim was, so with a little manipulation I adjusted it so that it pointed right at my pussy. I straddled the toilet and turned it up as much as I could stand it. The warm water hitting my pussy sent piercing streams all up in me. I was able to hump the water as it came toward me.

The feeling gave me a different kind of buzz that felt good and painful at the same time. Picking up my rhythm, I rubbed my clit a little until it popped up enough to meet the stream of water. I didn't want to look as though I had just peed on myself so I finished myself off on the cold, rounded decorative side of the bidet, which looked like a big ceramic dick. I love Japan! The Japanese think of everything!

5

I CHECKED IN AT the New Otani Hotel in Tokyo just overnight until we could take another plane to Hiroshima. As soon as I stepped foot in my room, I headed straight for the *toilet,* and to my surprise I had my very own bidet. I pretty much knew where I was going to be spending a lot of my free time!

After making enough cultural faux pas for one day, I prepared myself for the plane ride to Fukuyama, Hiroshima, where I would meet my Japanese host family. They would probably be right on time, like most Japanese. Unfortunately, that would be a challenge for me, because all I knew was CP time! All five of my Japanese family members came to greet me. They kept looking at me saying, "Beautiful, beautiful," and immediately I knew I was going to love these people. There was Masaki, the fifty-year-old father; Meiko, his forty-four-year-old wife; and Kazue, Masaki's seventy-six-year-old mother. There was also a sixteen-year-old daughter, Sawa, and a thirteen-year-old son, Itasuki. They all gave me the warmest reception, and instantly I knew I was home! My home stay was just for two nights, but I realized that I was a long way from "my hood."

I knew I should have picked up a Japanese dictionary when I was in Tokyo, because the only one who could halfway speak English was Masaki, and his English wasn't all that good. He was taking English lessons on the weekend, and he wasn't skilled at comprehending spoken English. He spoke better than he gave himself credit for and was relieved that I could halfway understand him.

6

ON THE FIRST NIGHT a lot of Japanese talk was going on, and all I could do was smile and pretend not to think they were talking about me. For all I knew they could have been calling me a "black American bitch," but by the way they kept smiling at me I doubt it could have been anything negative. We spent the evening trying on different family kimonos and drinking green tea, and various family members were trying to teach me how to make origami cranes.

The next day Masaki took me to a temple that had little scrolls carefully placed in the trees, and he told me to get a fortune out of the tree. Masaki read it, then told me it was good. He took a lot of pictures of me in the temple and tried to explain the significance of the artifacts, but had difficulty finding the

English words he needed to use. Masaki was trying to explain something to me and started speaking Japanese a mile a minute. He kept looking at me wanting me to answer, and I didn't have the slightest idea what he was talking about, so, not to be culturally disrespectful, I shook my head yes every other time he paused for a reply. I figured he was asking me what I wanted for dinner, either "octopus or squid," like he had asked me the night before.

Later that evening many neighbors came over for my last night, and we ate octopus and seaweed until it was coming out of our pores. I drank sake until my 20/20 vision had downgraded to 20/40. The sake was beginning to blur my eyes and wake up my coochie. It was all good though, because everyone was having a good time.

7

WHEN THE COMPANY FINALLY left, Masaki came to me and started that Japanese babble again, and I nodded my head again like I did at the temple. Out of respect he bowed, then began talking with Kazue and Meiko. They smiled at me, bowed, and immediately left the room.

Kazue went to prepare my bathwater. In Japan everyone uses the same water. It's tradition that guests bathe first, and I thought to myself, *Thank goodness I am company!* The thought of getting into someone else's nasty, dirty bathwater was not appealing. That sounded like a good way to get all kinds of unwanted pussy infections. In the bathroom, a sink was outside the actual room that housed the hot tub. The water was a beautiful green that smelled like pine, which was supposed to be good for the body.

Kazue showed me how to scoop the water out to rinse myself off, before getting into the hot tub. The tub was not for bathing, I was told. It was for soaking and relaxing. A timer was set for one minute of soaking. After soaking in the green water, I was supposed to set the timer again to soak one minute in the ice-cold-water basin. After Kazue left, I knew I wasn't going to do the ice-cold water, so I wasn't even going to trip about it. I just pretended to get in it, splashing my hand around in the water to make it sound like I was actually rinsing off.

A huge picture window faced the back of the house, which was surrounded by trees. I was pretty sure someone was looking at me. Hell, as big as the window was, I wouldn't be surprised if all of Japan was watching me. The tub was so narrow I had to almost wash up in a fetal position. So I climbed out of the tub and straddled my legs over the sides of it and took the sea sponge and started to trickle green pine water down my pussy. The water gave my pussy a little buzz like it was some kind of Japanese magic potion. The more I rubbed my clit with that sponge, the more my nipples hardened and the more my pussy started to light up. The movement in the bushes began to appear obvious, and I figured it was now showtime.

8

I TURNED MYSELF OVER and lay across the tub so that my legs were hoisted high in the air so that my pussy could be seen from the back. Without trying to fall headfirst in the tub, I opened my legs as far as I could and reminded myself of one of those contortionists from the UniverSoul Circus. I worked my pussy, alternating from the back to the front, until the cum from my pussy mixed with the pine in the water. The combination of the cool night air and the hot pussy juices gave me aftershocks that caused me to turn over and finish myself off by rubbing my clit until I came again. With the little strength I had left, I slid back into the tub and enjoyed the rest of my therapeutic bath.

When I was ready to get out of the water, Masaki's wife, Meiko, escorted me to my room and started drying me off. I thought she was just going to dry my back, but she dried between my toes, in my ass, and under my pussy. In another time and place I would probably have thought she was trying to jump my bones, but she caressed me in a way that relaxed me and put me in a meditative state. I figured my paranoia was probably just the sake settling in.

Meiko then started to rub me down with some pine-smelling oil that was warm to the touch. She used some hand massager as she rubbed it on me, then she parted my legs to rub it on my pussy. My clit responded in the most inappropriate way. Noticing what she had done, she placed a silk pillow behind me to elevate my hips and pulled out some pink, Japanese-looking "bullet." She parted my legs gently and used her fingers to pull back the hood of my clit, exposing my swollen knot.

9

SHE USED SOME TYPE of clamp to hold the hood in place so it would not obstruct what she was doing and also had a stream of cold air blowing on it with the other hand. With her thumb she began massaging my clit until I started mumbling some American obscenities, like "Oh, shit," "Work that pussy," or something ghetto like that. Good thing she didn't understand what I was talking about. After acting like a pussy-whipped fool, she started buzzing me with that little pink bullet, and I never saw it coming. By the time she finished with me, it felt like I had undergone some sort of electric shock therapy.

My pussy felt better than it had ever felt in my life, and I knew my pussy lips must have been smiling! I could hardly walk, but gimpy-legged as I was, I managed to hobble over to some sort of chair that had the oddest shape. Seeing that I could hardly stand up, Meiko helped me to the chair. Without even letting me catch my breath, she strapped me to the chair with leather straps and metal clamps. My head and neck were positioned toward the floor. The middle of the chair had my exposed pussy elevated upward. My legs were straddled to the sides, reminding me of those stirrups the doctor uses when you get a Pap smear. If I didn't know better, I would have sworn I was in some kind of "fucking chair." I knew Japanese technology was advanced, but a "fucking chair," how fucking great was that?!

The whole time Meiko was drying me off, Masaki and Kazue were watching. Kazue took Masaki's silk robe off to expose his pink, erect dick, and with two hands he pulled back his foreskin (making the head of his dick look like a cherry Blow Pop), while Meiko lubricated it with some green stuff. I couldn't get up if I wanted to because the chair had me on lockdown. Meiko applied the same green stuff to my pussy, and when she finished, she bowed to Masaki and he bowed to her, then she took her place beside Kazue. It just hit me that this was what Masaki must have been babbling about back at the temple. Oh, well, I figured, we might not have been able to speak each other's language, but we were about to break down all barriers and communicate in that universal language of sex.

10

MASAKI ENTERED ME SLOWLY as he stood over me with his hands on his hips, looking like one of those ancient samurai warriors. Handrails and straps were built into the chair, making it easy for him to keep pumping me without coming up for air or losing balance. The way my pussy was elevated, he could go deep inside me without me having to raise my legs. The shape of the chair made it easy for him to rock it slightly, making his dick go in and out of me on every other stroke. He kept mumbling some Japanese jargon, which probably was on the lines of "Whose pussy is this!" or more likely "I'm getting ready to cum!" Just as I was thinking that, he pulled his dick out of my pussy and positioned himself behind me and came all over me, making sure he deposited most of his cum on my face.

On cue, Meiko wiped his limp dick off like it was made of gold, and Kazue helped him with his robe, and he exited the room after taking a long bow in my direction. Together Meiko and Kazue bathed me in the green pine water, laid me on the futon, massaged me with some warm oil, and left me alone for a while to recuperate. When I joined the family in the living room, Meiko was preparing our meal, Sawa and Itasuki were juggling, and Kazue showed me some of her beautiful flower arrangements.

11

LATER THAT EVENING WE all drank green tea and ate rabbit cakes (not real rabbit), and for my last night in the Land of the Rising Sun, Masaki and Meiko presented me with an exquisite black lacquer music box that had a hand-painted picture of a *sazanka* on it. In Masaki's broken English he explained that *sazanka* was a flower that blooms in the winter, even in the snow. It was the strongest of flowers, which maintained its beauty even in the worst weather. I liked the sound of that and decided Sazanka would be my new Japanese name. I was given many more gifts that evening, and as I celebrated my last night with my Japanese family, we all seemed to be speaking the same language!

The Flow of Qi

MICHELLE J. ROBINSON

"Shit!" Monday morning, 9:45 a.m., and Tony still wasn't here. Susan had been here since eight in the morning. This was the third time in six months that he had been late—time to hire another assistant.

Tony walked in at ten, mumbling something about the subway.

"Tony, get Jessica on the phone," Susan said abruptly.

Some people might have found it a wee bit heartless to have their assistant call the office manager to institute their own dismissal, but Susan wasn't most people. She had made it crystal clear to Tony that he was to be at his desk *on time,* ready to start work at precisely 9:30 a.m. each day—not 9:31, not 9:45, but precisely 9:30 a.m. She had also made it clear from day one what would happen if that requirement was not met. Sure, he was a good assistant, but New York City was littered with good secretaries. She wanted—*no,* she demanded—the complete package. Her law practice was an around-the-clock business. As she saw it, any assistant she had was lucky she didn't ask him or her to come in before 9:30 a.m. Therefore, she expected Tony or anyone else she employed to be there on time. As far as she was concerned, the minute he walked in at 10:00 a.m. was the moment he tendered his resignation.

After Tony got Jessica Williams on the phone, Susan slammed her office door.

"I'll just cut to the chase," Susan said abruptly. "Tony was half an hour late today. I believe I made it very clear to everyone concerned that any assistant working for me needs to be on time—every morning. Did I not?"

"Yes, Ms. Perkins, but Tony is one of our best employees. He does a great job, stays late, and all of the clients and partners think he's great."

"Point one—he works directly with me, and my review of his work is adequate, at best. Somehow we've become a society that rewards mediocrity. He does his job and gets paid rather handsomely for doing so, nothing more. Point two—he is *not* always on time or you and I would not be having this conversation, would we? He has been late three times in six months. Point three—he does not work for the clients, nor does he work for the other partners. He works for *me.* The partners in this firm have given me a certain level of autonomy, not out of the kindness of their hearts, but because I bill over four hundred hours every month and have established a reputation as an attorney who wins her cases. I want Tony out of here, and I want him replaced with an assistant who understands my requirements. Do you understand that, Jessica?"

Susan laughed to herself when she thought of the other reason she was able to call the shots around here. Susan had made it a point to keep her eyes and ears open from day one. Because she was a woman, the partners at the firm had greatly underestimated her. When they finally figured out what they were dealing with, it was too late. Susan knew all their dirty little secrets. She knew who was stealing, who was gay, who was fucking their secretary, whose sexual tastes bordered on the unusual, and who wanted her to disappear. But, Susan was smart and compiled an arsenal of proof, just in case she needed it. She also made herself invaluable, ingratiating herself with as many clients as she could come into contact with as well as compiling her own rather extensive and elite client list. Susan had clients from virtually every sector of the planet, from athletes to actors to leaders in government. She had become one of the most sought-after attorneys in New York City, and not even those who despised her most could challenge that she was damn good at her job.

"Yes, Ms. Perkins, I understand. I'll start interviewing potential candidates right away."

Susan watched Tony pack up his belongings and decided that since she didn't have an assistant for the rest of the day, she would go have a martini and unwind.

Susan got bored quickly, worked around the clock, and therefore had little time for bullshit—that's why she liked Pleasure Principle. The club had been started by Janet Myers. Susan and Janet had been partners at Mullens & Schneider. After several years there, Janet became disenchanted. She was sick to death of the old boys' network, and the law no longer excited her. The difference between Janet and Susan was, Janet was uncomfortable trying to fit into the mold society had created for women in business, while Susan had decided she would create her own mold and everyone else would have to find a way to fit.

One night Susan and Janet had had a drink with a prospective client at a local gentlemen's club. Susan and Janet were both attractive women, and Susan presumed that this client was in a position to kill two birds with one stone: he could sit and watch the sexy, scantily clothed women onstage bump, grind, and remove their clothing while he imagined what both Janet and Susan looked like under their gabardine suits. That night Susan was wearing a black, single-breasted Barneys suit, with a white silk blouse underneath, which she had left unbuttoned enough to reveal her ample 38D cleavage. The skirt stopped right above her knees and showed off her wonderfully shapely legs. The formfitting waist of the jacket accentuated her curvy hips, and instead of the ponytail she usually sported, her long brown hair cascaded past her shoulders, lending her a dual air, as conservative wild woman. Instead of a flesh-toned lipstick or gloss, she was wearing bright red, a stunning complement to her mocha complexion. Susan liked playing cat and mouse as much as the next guy, but she would never under any circumstances be the mouse, and if that was what this client had in mind, he would be sorely disappointed.

Janet's blue shirt was buttoned up to her neck, and she had chosen a suit that camouflaged all of her assets. You could never tell that Janet was five feet eleven inches, 135 pounds, with an impressive set of hooters and an ass as round as a basketball. Her legs went on for days, but the long, pleated skirt she was wearing hid all evidence of that. What she couldn't hide was that shock of red hair and beautiful freckles. Janet was a natural beauty who required little embellishment, and even with a suit of clothing like a potato sack, she couldn't hope to hide that beautiful face of hers.

Susan was hooked from the moment she entered the gentlemen's club. She was always fascinated with the sheer power of sex, and this place was a glowing representation of its influence.

Despite her earlier reservations, it only took Janet half an hour at the club to figure out what a fucking gold mine the place was. Always the businesswoman, she started her wheels turning. The bar was turning over money hand over fist. The women were scantily clothed, and the combination of libido and alcohol helped money to flow. Janet had been looking for a business venture that would work, and this seemed like a moneymaking idea, something that hadn't already been done. It could be risky, but it could also be exactly what she was looking for. So-called gentlemen's clubs were all over New York City, but she had never in her life heard of a "ladies' club." Within five years she had started a chain of clubs all over New York City. Her first, her baby, was Pleasure Principle. One year after all the kinks had been ironed out, she opened Epic, and two years after that, Dionysus, Eros, and the Lollipop Lounge.

Janet had tried to get Susan to come in as her partner, but Susan liked things just fine the way they were. Pleasure Principle was Susan's home away from home, and as with anything that gave her pleasure, she protected it. She was Janet's attorney, and despite the local bureaucrats' desire to shut the places down, Susan made sure they didn't.

Susan walked in, sat down at the VIP table expressly reserved for her, and surveyed the room. Sam, a muscular black dancer with an extremely large dick, came over to the table. Susan palmed his taut ass and stroked his butt cheeks. He was wearing a white G-string, which made his dick look even larger than it was. She had fucked him before, and he was well-endowed. She had only fucked him once, though, because he didn't take instructions well and he talked too goddamn much. She couldn't stand it when a man felt the need to talk through the entire thing. This was probably all well and good for someone looking for love, but she wasn't caught up in illusions of some great romance. She wanted to get fucked, licked, and sucked and usually had little time to get that done. She didn't have time for whispered words of love and admiration; she was on a clock.

Susan ordered a dry martini and thought of asking Sam whether Wiley was working tonight, then thought better of it. The dancers were artful at "cock-blocking." They knew Susan paid well, and each vied for the coveted role of stud for the night. Tonight, she wanted her pussy eaten. Wiley was the man for the job. One night he ate her out so good, she went home and masturbated to the feeling his tongue had left implanted on her pussy walls.

As she sipped her martini, Marvin Gaye's soul-stirring tune "Sexual Healing" began to play, and Wiley made his way onto the stage. He wasn't a big man, about five feet nine inches tall and about 165 pounds, but he looked like Mickey Rourke. She had masturbated many a night to 9½ *Weeks* and *Wild Orchid*. Wiley executed an artful bump-and-grind routine, leaving Susan's pussy dripping wet. Her cunt was doing involuntary Kegels and she was glad she hadn't worn any panties. No use in wasting time. She wanted whoever would be dining on her feast tonight to get straight to it. Susan winked at Wiley and he quickly got her meaning. After his show he came over to where she was sitting.

"Hey, Susan, how's it goin'? Can I get you anything?"

"How's that nice long tongue of yours?"

Susan would have liked nothing better than to jump on the table, spread-eagle, and let Wiley go to town, but the last thing she wanted was for this place to get shut down. So, they proceeded to a "private room," classified as a place for private drinks and conversation for legal purposes—its true and primary function being a "fuck den"—and there wasn't a room Susan hadn't christened. In one of the rooms Susan had convinced Janet to install a chair similar to a dentist's, but with stirrups, like at the gynecologist's office, and harnesses. No expense was spared having it made, designed to Susan's exact specifications. It had a massage feature and could tilt 360 degrees. Susan shut and locked the door and welcomed sweet release. She positioned her legs in the stirrups and scooted down to the end of the chair. Her pussy was wide-open and her juices trickled onto the chair below in anticipation.

"Lick every drop of cum that comes out of my pussy—I'm going to give you some very easy instructions, and all you need to do is follow them. Okay, Wiley?"

"Okay," he responded.

"You see that stool over there in the corner? Bring it over here and sit down, right in front of me."

Wiley wheeled over the spinning stool, and when he sat down, he was exactly eye level with her pussy. He knew he had his "work" cut out for him, because the cushion on the chair was already thoroughly saturated. He began licking first from her ass crack where her cunt juices had dripped, then licked up to where her pussy began. The more he licked, the wetter she got. He began to think this tongue bath would never be complete. For every lashing his tongue gave, there was yet another cascading wave of liquid pleasure. He licked and she came. He sucked and she came. Eventually Wiley realized no amount of licking was going to dry this multi-orgasmic pussy banquet before him, so he plunged his tongue deep into her pussy, exploring her tunnel like his mouth had a cock extension. Her phallic haven made his dick just as hard as the men he fucked in his spare time. In many ways she reminded him of a man. She was beautiful and shapely, but her every other characteristic was like a man's. She demanded excellence in every facet of her life and accepted nothing less. He admired her, even as one of her "humble servants."

"No, no," Susan said. "Lick my clit. Yes. . . . Like that . . . with the tip of your tongue. Oh, fuck . . . yes!"

She grabbed a handful of Wiley's chestnut-colored hair and urgently pushed his tongue even deeper into her cunt. He gave her *exactly* what she wanted, a long, slow mouth fuck, and he gobbled up every drop of cum that gushed from her, licking with the flat of his tongue for maximum coverage. His mouth could feel her swollen pussy lips, and he hoped the services she required went beyond her usual request for a tongue bath. She must have been reading his mind, because suddenly she answered his silent question.

"Wiley, can you fuck?"

"Only you can be the judge of that."

"I think not, Wiley. A man knows if he can fuck or not, even if he doesn't want to admit it to himself. So, can you or can't you?"

"I will fuck you so good your pussy will conform to the shape of my dick."

"Damn, I like a man with confidence. Let's get to it!"

Susan had Wiley sit in the chair. She mounted his pulsating erection so that her back was facing his chest and wrapped her pussy walls around him, devouring his cock with hard, demanding thrusts, sliding up and down his shaft, as their fucking built in intensity. Each time Susan slid her pussy down to the very end of his dick, she contracted her muscles so tight she thought she could almost feel the lines of his veins protruding through the skin of his now extremely taut member; when she reached the tip, she started all over again. She loved the way this dick filled her pussy up, but more than that she loved the effect of her strokes on him. He looked ready to pay her for her services rather than the other way around. Her techniques in fucking made her feel masterful; and she was. As Susan ground her pelvis into his now quivering form, she could sense that Wiley was about to shoot an impressive load into the Trojan he was wearing. If there was one thing Susan liked even more than having her pussy eaten out, it was getting fucked in the ass, so before Wiley could shoot his load, Susan dismounted his dick, encouraged him to rise from the chair, and told him exactly what she wanted.

"No, lover, we're not done yet. I want you to give it to me up the ass."

He bent Susan over the seat of the chair and slowly eased his cock into her anxiously awaiting butt hole. Susan gasped as soon as the head of his cock was inside her. He increased the speed with which he ass-fucked Susan, causing her to counter each of his powerful thrusts. He fucked her ass so good Susan dripped great gobs of pussy juices onto the floor. The room was a combination of pungent odors, her cum, his sweat, the mixture of cock against ass—all of which made Susan hornier than she already was. As Wiley's breathing became labored, Susan knew her fun was about to come to an end. With one gigantic thrust Wiley exploded, his hand flat on her back. He was so spent, he would probably have fallen over if he hadn't been holding Susan's back for leverage. He gripped the condom he was wearing and slowly eased out of Susan's now satiated asshole.

Any money she paid Wiley for his services tonight would be well worth it. On a scale of one to ten he had been at least a nine. *Uhm,* Susan thought, *I might need to put him on staff.*

Susan and Wiley put their clothing back on, did a double check in the mirror, and prepared to exit into the main area of the club. Susan handed Wiley ten crisp $100 bills before caressing his cock through his pants.

"That is a first-class tool you've got. If I were you, I would have that pussy-pleaser insured with Lloyd's of London," Susan said.

He was a living, breathing jackhammer to satisfy her not-easily-satisfied hungers, free from drama. Thank goodness for Pleasure Principle. It was like shopping for a sweater. You could get whatever you wanted for the right price; all that and no uncomfortable attachments.

Janet had made a good number of client contacts in Hong Kong, and she convinced Susan that it would probably make good business sense to branch out and take their business "on the road." Susan knew the real reason Janet wanted to "branch out" was because the love of her life, an art specialist at Christie's New York, had recently been offered a promotion and transfer to Christie's Hong Kong. Susan agreed to go and check things out, never one to forgo an opportunity to expand her horizons, although it occurred to her that Hong Kong was not the place. Besides, if nothing else, she could see some really great art.

The sixteen-hour flight to Hong Kong left Susan feeling no less horny than usual. She had an insatiable appetite, and being a visitor to a strange place, she suddenly missed Pleasure Principle more than usual. She was reminded of Janet's insistence that she not fuck her man; and Susan had promised herself she wouldn't. Even she had some principles.

Kyung, Janet's art specialist/lover, had suggested she take a taxi to the Christie's salesroom, since it was right near the Grand Hyatt where she would be staying. But Susan desperately wanted to ride the metro (the Hong Kong subway system or MTR). So per Kyung's instructions, she rode the Tsuen Wan Line from the airport to Wan Chai Station, not far from the Christie's salesroom, where Kyung would be waiting to take her to dinner. Boarding the train, Susan was acutely aware of the massive overcrowding and how any crowds on any given day on the New York City subway system paled in comparison to this. However, she boarded the train prepared to fully enjoy her first experience on the MTR. The pushing and shoving was commonplace, and everyone was packed in like sardines. Just as Susan thought the ride was becoming unbearable, she felt the most masculine, powerful hands caress their way up her thighs.

"Uhm," she gasped, more audibly than she would have liked.

"You are Susan?" the voice attached to those warm hands asked.

The only person who knew she was in Hong Kong was Kyung. But he was Janet's man and she had promised to keep her hands—and everything else—off. But damn, this felt good!

As his hand traveled to places farther south, Susan spread her legs wide enough to grant him entry, surprised that no one around them seemed to notice. As her juices quickly lubricated his artful explorations, she could feel his hard dick beckoning to her. As though mentally in sync, he turned her toward the door, hoisted her skirt above her hips, and entered her now quivering pussy. The rattling and jerking of the train and the numerous passengers shoved in around them provided all the movement they needed. His dick was guided by force in and out of her pussy, leaving her head spinning with wanting more.

"Do you feel it? This is our qi, our spirit, the electricity that flows between us and all around us."

"Yes," Susan whispered, so as not to alert her surrounding passengers to what they were doing, although some seemed to notice anyway.

As the train began to grind to a halt entering the next stop, her stop, Wan Chai Station, this beautiful, driving force inside her seemed intent on coming at the exact moment that she arrived at her destination, but not before he introduced himself quietly in her ear.

"Susan, I am Cho. My brother Kyung sent me to welcome you to Hong Kong and all the many riches it has to offer."

The Big Bang Theory

ZANE

ॐ

WHEN I ENTERED THE club True Meaning, the DJ was working his ass off and remixing "Tambourine" by Eve. That was a booty-shaking song if I had ever heard one. Women were lined from wall to wall in tight clothes, showing off their assets, whether they were hitting on everything or nothing at all. I had never been one to have all my shit hanging out. If a man was lucky enough to get to the point of finding out what I had underneath my clothes, that was a privilege, not a right.

I worked out five times a week at the twenty-four-hour World Gym in Largo, Maryland. I was cut from head to toe and I knew that I was a sexy bitch. Yes, I said *bitch,* because I did not take shit off anyone, especially shitty-ass men out there. That was one of the reasons why I worked out so much. From childhood, I had always set out to prove that I could do anything a man could do, only better. I worked out like a man; I played sports like a man. Most important, I raced cars like a man.

I loved cars. When I was a teenager, I would always tell my mother, "Look at that sexy thing there." She assumed that I was talking about the young men driving the cars, but I meant the cars themselves. By the time I turned twenty, I had six cars in my garage and driveway. I went to mechanics school and learned how to repair them and rebuild them. I had a 1980 Trans Am, a 1993 Mustang, two high-performance trucks, a 1970 GTO, and a 1991 Chevy Nova. I was the shit and I knew it.

I raced at the track, for the most part. But street racing was what really got my adrenaline rushing. The only problem was that all the other women were punks. I was the only bitch who raced the men. They could not stand me because I would whip their asses every weekend. In fact, as I entered True Meaning, I was cheesing because I had won yet another one earlier that night at the track.

Quincy was this brother I had grown up with in Bowie, Maryland. He was cool but determined to get into my drawers, and that shit was not happening. I had done his older brother once, more out of curiosity than anything. Other women claimed he was the ultimate in bed. His ass could not even handle me. It was a true disappointment. So when Quincy started insisting that we hook up, I finally had to tell him that his brother had a pencil dick and I bet that trait ran in their family. His brother, Robert, didn't really have a pencil dick. I only said that to see if Quincy would try to find out. Men are so strange. They will try to scope out other dudes' wang-wangs to see if they measure up. After about three months, Quincy told me that his brother was hung like a mule, just like him. I made a scene with him and asked if he found that out when his brother was ramming it up his ass. Everyone laughed; except Quincy. We were at the track and he challenged me to a race. I love challenges. We raced around the track at 140 mph and I won by a frog's hair, but I won.

Quincy was the first man I spotted as I walked into the club. I could not miss him gritting on me. I gritted right back. Sitting next to him at the bar were Hakaru and Chiyo, two Asians who were cousins. I had to give it to them, they looked good, but they were still assholes. Always primping, always bragging about their rides. Hakaru had once told me that his name meant "one who measures, plans, thinks things through." That name fitted him perfectly because he was one conniving, deceptive mother-fucker. Chiyo's name meant "thousand lifetimes, thousand years." That name fit him as well because he had what my grand-mother used to call "an old soul." She used to look at certain kids, even babies, and say that they had been here before.

I walked right up to them at the bar and started bragging. "How'd you all like that shit earlier tonight? How I wiped up the track with all of you?"

"Larissa, you ain't wipe shit," Quincy came back at me. "You need to go wipe that ass though. I smell something foul."

Chiyo and Hakaru chuckled, and all three of them clanked their beer steins together.

"Quincy, you're just mad because I wouldn't let you tap this ass," I said. "Everyone knows you've been trying to get me in bed for years."

Quincy turned his nose up at me. "I was just treating you like the obvious trick that you are. I can get pussy when I can't get sleep. Good pussy."

He was getting on my last fucking nerve. "Oh, really, and they don't mind that pencil dick of yours?"

The other men laughed, and Quincy didn't like that at all. "Look, I don't have no damn pencil dick. Neither does my brother. You're just mad because he fucked you once and kicked you to the curb."

I sat down and waved the bartender over. "That's his version. Men are a trip. They have a one-night stand and think it was them, but what about the fact that the women never call their asses again either?"

I ordered a beer with a whiskey chaser and proceeded to get drunk. I talked mad shit to the three of them for the next hour. Then I got so tipsy that I ended up slow-dragging with Chiyo to "Bed" by J. Holiday. I don't even remember how we got on the dance floor, but there I was, grinding into him. His dick was hard and I was pleasantly surprised. At the end of the song, I pulled away from him in disgust and said, "Don't ever touch me again, trick!"

Chiyo laughed and went back to the bar. I got angry and started talking even more trash.

"You know what? I'm so sick of all three of you. Let's settle this, right now."

Hakaru glanced at me. "What do you mean?"

"I'm challenging all of you to a street race," I stuttered, struggling to find my tongue.

Quincy said, "Larissa, you're drunk. Take your ass home."

Chiyo looked me up and down. "Maybe I should drive her home. She's drunk."

I knew what the body-check look meant. "Hell naw, you're not taking me home. You practically dry-fucked me on the dance floor."

They all fell out laughing.

"Whatever! I'm going up the point and I'm going to wait," I

said. "Anyone who doesn't show up is a straight punk. I'll see you scared motherfuckers when I see you."

I left the three of them sitting there with silly expressions on their faces. When I got into my GTO and revved it up, I grinned because I knew at least one of them would take me up on the challenge. I loved challenges.

The point was really a long, deserted stretch in Aberdeen, Maryland. People used it for street racing all the time. As for the cops, half of the time they were the main ones watching and cheering people on. Many of them bragged about what they had at home in their garages. Fact of the matter is, a lot of people become cops because they want to be in high-speed chases, and they love to show off their driving skills as much as the next racing enthusiast.

Surprisingly, no one was out there when I arrived. Then again, it was nearly three in the morning and most street racing ended by midnight or one, on a typical Friday or Saturday. I sat in my car, jamming to my iPod until one of those punks showed up. Less than fifteen minutes later, I spotted three sets of headlights coming over the bend, side by side. "This Woman's Work" by Maxwell was playing, and I was ready to show them what I had. Shit, I was born ready for this race. I closed my eyes and sang the lyrics, taking in deep breaths as I always did before a race. When I opened them again, Chiyo's Nissan 350Z was on my left, Hakaru's Porsche 911 was on my right, and Quincy was beside him in his Dodge Viper.

I glared from one side to the other and we all gave each other "that look." We did not have anyone to wave a flag, as it was usually a hoochie mama who was trying to get laid in one of their backseats. Instead, Hakaru held his left hand up, covered in a leather driving glove, and counted down his fingers from five to one. Then we all hit it. "Come to Me" by Diddy was blasting on my iPod as I floored it. On the track, we went up to 140 mph, but fuck it, I was going all out and planned to hit 180. In case you're wondering, we weren't crazy. All of us had on helmets and racing harnesses.

We took the first hill at about the same time, then I was in the lead. Quincy came up behind me on my bumper but I swerved from side to side to keep him from passing me. Chiyo appeared out of nowhere in his 350Z and almost took off my side-view mirror. That did it! I was not about to lose, not that night. Hakaru was having issues but was catching up fast. I could see him in my rearview mirror. I hit the top gear in my GTO and tried my best to keep all of them off me. There was less than a mile to the end of the point and the "chicken wall." A few teenagers had hit the wall and totaled their cars; one did not make it, but we were all professionals. At least, that was what we were supposed to be.

"Umbrella" by Rihanna came on, and then it happened: the big bang. Chiyo lost control of his car and slammed into Quincy's Viper. The Viper flipped over and brushed over my hood; all I saw was red metal as my windshield blew out, along with one of my tires. I hit my brakes and tried to turn to the left. No sooner had I done that then Hakaru's 911 crashed into my driver's-side door, crushing it into my side. Then there was silence; dead silence.

I lost consciousness for some time, probably minutes that seemed like hours. I heard Chiyo yelling out my name, then someone yanked open my passenger-side door. I felt myself being pulled from the wreckage, and then I was lying on the ground, next to Quincy's Viper. I finally regained my bearings as Hakaru removed my helmet.

Hakaru said, "I think she's going to be okay. Larissa, can you hear me?"

Chiyo yelled out, "Shit! Look at our rides!"

Hakaru took off his jacket and placed it under my head. "Someone call 911."

Quincy, who had seemingly been in a daze, popped back into reality. "Fuck that! We can't call the cops! We aren't supposed to be out here in the first place!"

"But Larissa needs to go to the hospital," Hakaru said. "Plus we all have to put in insurance claims."

I pushed Hakaru away from me. "I'm fine. I'm tougher than all you motherfuckers." I sat up. I had a killer headache, but miraculously, I was fine outside of that. "Besides, asshole, our insurance companies aren't going to pay. We were racing, dummy."

Quincy glared at me. "This is all your fault."

"My fault." I struggled to stand up. "Quincy, how the hell you figure that? Chiyo ran into you, you flipped the fuck over me, and then Hakaru slammed into my door. Tell me when I hit any damn body."

Quincy rolled his eyes at me. "It's your fault, bitch, because your drunk ass had us all come out here."

"Did you just call me a bitch?" I balled my left hand into a fist. "I will punch all your teeth clear out your head, motherfucker!"

Now I had no problem calling myself a bitch, as I explained earlier, but I sure didn't play men calling me a bitch.

"I didn't drive your cars out here. I didn't force you to do shit," I added. "You three high rollers came out here together, like gangbusters, and now our cars are fucked the hell up."

Chiyo said, "Larissa, you were drunk."

"Chiyo, you're the first one that hit someone. What the hell are you smoking? We all sat at that bar drinking and shit."

It was getting cold outside and I started shivering a little. Hakaru came up to me and placed his arm around me. "Let me warm you up. Fuck the cars. Are you sure you don't need to go to the hospital?"

"I'm fine. Just pissed the hell off."

Quincy took out his cell phone. "I'm going to call Robert and tell him to come get us."

I rolled my eyes. "Great. All we need out here is your pencil-dick brother."

"My brother does not have a pencil dick," Quincy stated in disdain as he dialed.

I snickered and pointed to my ass, again implying that he had personal knowledge. "How do you know?"

"Fuck you, Larissa!" Quincy turned his back to me. "Robert, bro, I need you to come get me and Larissa, and Chiyo, and Hakaru. We're out at the point." He paused. "All our cars are toast, man. Larissa's drunk ass had us out here acting a fool."

I broke loose from Hakaru's embrace, ran up behind Quincy, and slapped him upside his fucking head. He dropped his phone, turned around, and grabbed both of my wrists.

"Larissa, you stop that shit right now! You're drunk!"

Chiyo came up beside us. "Quincy, let her go. She'll be cool."

Quincy let my wrists go. I waited two seconds, then punched him in the jaw. Next thing you know, Quincy and I were on the hood of Chiyo's 350Z, tonguing the hell out of each other. It had been a long time coming, the "angry sex" I wanted. I wanted to fuck him to death or die trying. I reached down between his legs and grabbed his dick through his jeans. I already knew that he didn't have a pencil dick. I had admired his hump through pants for many years. I had really wanted to fuck Quincy instead of Robert, in the first place. Shit just went haywire. Quincy was about five feet ten inches with deep chocolate skin; the color reminded me of my favorite candy bar.

"You want some of this pencil dick," Quincy whispered in my ear when we came up for air from kissing. "Huh, *bitch*? You want some pencil dick?"

I slapped him across the cheek. "Shut the hell up." I glanced over at Chiyo and Hakaru, who were both standing there with their mouths hanging open. "What, you plan to watch or join in?"

I pushed Quincy off me and stood up on the hood of the car. Piece by piece, I ripped off my clothes until I was ass-out naked. "I bet all three of you have always wondered what was under these clothes, haven't you?" I turned around and slapped my muscular ass cheeks together. "So, do you like what you see?"

None of them answered at first. Then Hakaru said, "We can't do this. She's drunk. We can't take advantage of her." It seemed like he was trying to convince himself more than the other two.

I motioned at him with my index finger. "Hakaru, come here." He hesitated, then took baby steps toward the car. When he was within reach, I grabbed him by the neck and buried his face in my pussy. "Sniff. Do I smell like liquor? Huh? Do I?"

He took my left ass cheek in his hand and I threw my leg over his shoulder. "Taste it. Lick it all over. Then tell me what it tastes like."

Hakaru, who was tall with a slender build, had these incredible slanted eyes, eyes that now stared up at me in bewilderment. I looked down at him. "I'm not drunk. Trust me, I want this."

Those must have been the magical words because his tongue became a snake and started navigating my love tunnel.

"Damn!" Quincy exclaimed. "I can't believe this shit!"

I gazed at both Quincy and Chiyo as they stood there, watching. Then I pushed my right breast up as far as it would go and flickered my long tongue over the nipple. "Umm, these are mighty tasty, too. Any other taste testers up to the task?"

I pushed Hakaru away slightly so I could lie down on the hood. Actually more like "hoods," because the whole scene was a mass of metal, all four cars linked together. Just like the four of us were about to be. Even though I had raced cars, had fixed cars, and lived and breathed cars, I had never fucked on top of a car. I had sucked many a dick and spread my legs in backseats all over Maryland, but never on top of a car. That was one of my biggest fantasies. Now I was ready to fulfill two of my fantasies in one shot: fucking on top of a car and being gangbanged.

Hakaru barely missed a beat as he went back to lapping at my pussy. Chiyo dove right in and sucked on my titties, pushing them together so he could devour them at the same time.

Quincy came closer and looked lost. "What am I supposed to do?"

I grinned at him. "I want you to feed me some of that pencil dick."

"Oh, I've got your pencil dick," he said, unzipping his jeans and whipping out the most scrumptious thing I had ever seen.

I gripped it like a vise and pulled him onto the cars by his dick and tried to swallow as much of it as I could handle. Quincy ate a lot of salmon, and let's just say, that's good for sisters giving blow jobs, along with fruit. His nine inches plus were pulsating as he slid them in and out of my eager mouth. He tasted like a dream.

I spread my legs wider so Hakaru could get to my clit better. My pussy was hotter than the flames of hell. Chiyo had my nipples so hard, they could've banged most of the dents out of the cars. I continued sucking Quincy off something fierce. I was determined to give him the blow job of his life. I played with his balls, then squeezed them, gently at first and then harder.

After Quincy came, I pushed his dick out of my mouth. "I want to see all the dicks," I demanded. "Right fucking now!"

By the time Robert arrived in his SUV, I had ridden all three of them and was sucking off Chiyo, who was standing on the hood feeding me, while I was slamming my pussy on Hakaru's dick.

Robert jumped out of his truck. "What the hell!"

Quincy was lying there on the mass of metal, looking up at the stars. I had worn his pencil dick out. "Bro, she's off the chain, man. Larissa has lost her damn mind."

Robert shook his head. "Oh, I remember the pussy. It's addictive." I made eye contact with him. "You're such a bad girl."

I let Chiyo's dick slip from my mouth. "I'm just testing out a theory."

"What theory?" Robert asked.

"The Big Bang Theory," I replied. "Get undressed. There's room for one more."

They all laughed as Robert started getting naked. "Like I said, it's addictive."

ABOUT THE CONTRIBUTORS

ANNA BLACK resides in the Midwest, where she enjoys both reading and writing a wide variety of fiction ranging from mysteries to science fiction. She collects tarot cards and enjoys watching her eclectic collection of DVDs. She has published erotic fiction in *The MILF Anthology, Cowboy Lover—Erotic Tales of the Wild West,* and Zane's anthology *Purple Panties.* She is currently working on an erotic mystery.

JOCELYN BRINGAS lives in northern California. Her stories and poems have been featured in anthologies such as Zane's *Caramel Flava* and Alison Tyler's *Got a Minute.* When she's not writing a story, she's either listening to Backstreet Boys music or updating her website: www.flirtingwithobscene.com.

ANNE ELIZABETH debuted in Zane's *Caramel Flava* with her spicy story "Sugar and Butter Poured over Muscle." She has a sweet romantic story, "A Heart's Hunger," in the Highland Press collection *Recipe for Love.* AE is involved in a variety of writing and publishing mediums and has a cameo in Laurell K. Hamilton's Anita Blake Issue #7 comic book. She can often be found at the Dabel Booth at a Comic Con, participating at the Romantic Times Convention, giving workshops in marketing, or writing at an intriguing or favored locale. For the latest news or appearances, check out her websites, anneelizabeth.org and anneeliza beth.net, or send her an email at mail@anneelizabeth.net.

LOTUS FALCON is a native of Washington, D.C., who holds a bachelor of science degree in education and a master's of public administration. She is an educator in a public school system who also leads women's empowerment/sexuality workshops and sells adult toys and products in her spare time. She is currently writing several projects for children and adults and is married with seven children.

IAN FREY lives and writes in Chicago, Illinois, and is a firm believer in the healing powers of both sex and alternative medicine. When not busy writing or dreaming, he can be found on bicycle trails and in local restaurants, where he suggests you try something new at every meal.

S. J. FROST resides on a mini-ranch in Ohio with her wonderful husband and many spoiled pets. She graduated from the University of Toledo with a BA in English/creative writing. To date, her published works include three short stories featured in separate anthologies: "No More Mirages" in the 2007 edition *Best Gay Romance* published by Cleis Press, and "Invoking the Past" in *Best Gay Love Stories: Summer Flings* and "The Sound of Your Voice" in *Ultimate Gay Erotica 2008*, both anthologies by Alyson Books. She also enjoys writing book reviews for the website of TCM Reviews, www.tcm-ca.com/.

JESSE GUMP has spent many years working in the Orient. His publishing credits include a trilogy of three novels: *Even Thai Girls Cry, The Farang Affair,* and *One High Season,* all set in Southeast Asia. Jesse's novels reflect his unique understanding of the Asian culture. LISA DANFORD is a writer of various genres, whose poetry has appeared in many anthologies, including several published by Remus House in the UK. She is also the owner of a popular website focused on helping new writers advance their skills. Jesse provided the basic story while Lisa added a woman's perspective and a lot of spice.

TRACEE A. HANNA, author of the book *A Little Bit of Sinning* and the story "The Masquerade Party," featured in Zane's *Caramel Flava,* was born in St. Louis, Missouri, and currently resides in Arizona. She is the mother of two exquisite daughters. Special thanks to her wonderful friends Lisa R. and Travis C. Visit alittlebitofsinning.tripod.com.

M. LAVONNE JACKSON lives in central Ohio with her husband, Jeff, their two daughters, and their dog, JayVyn. Mrs. Jackson credits her creative talents to her vivid imagination and past life experiences. When not writing, M. LaVonne dedicates her time to local and national charity work, photography, and her family and friends. "May I Ask a Favor of You" is her first published work in the Zane anthology series. M. LaVonne is currently completing her first novel.

FRANCES JONES is an emerging author of erotic short fiction whose work has been published in *Clean Sheets* and *Five Minute Fantasies 2.* She is a member of the Erotica Readers and Writers Association and is working on her first short-story collection.

She lives in San Francisco. For more, visit www.frances
-jones.com.

LARISSA LYONS loves cats, chocolate, and her husband (though
not necessarily in that order!). She's been a clown, a tax auditor,
and a pig castrator >^..^<, but none of those endeavors satisfied
quite like putting pen to paper and seeing her stories in print.
To read more and indulge *your* sensual side—or craving for
chocolate—Larissa invites you to visit her website at www
.larissalyons.com.

RENÉE MANLEY was born and raised in the Philippines and
moved to California in her teens. She writes mostly historical,
literary, and gothic gay fiction. Her stories have appeared in a
number of publications, including *SoMa Literary Review*, Tor-
quere Press, Iris Print, *Suspect Thoughts: A Journal of Subver-
sive Writing,* and *Harrington Gay Men's Literary Quarterly.* She
currently lives in the San Francisco Bay Area with her husband
and three cats.

MITCH taught one of the social studies at a large Southern in-
stitution for almost forty years. In that life he published a large
body of work, served as an editor on a number of disciplinary
and multiple-disciplinary journals, and presented papers at local,
regional, national, and international meetings on four of the
seven continents. He discovered fiction and erotica upon retire-
ment.

BETTI MUSTANG was born and raised in Hawaii. She is a
newspaper editor by day and an Asian succubus by night. When
she's not weaving words into tantalizing spells, she's ghost hunt-

ing or changing diapers—both of which take skill and balls of steel.

LISA G. RILEY's work has been called "character and issue driven; exciting, passionate and thought provoking." The author of several novels and novellas, Ms. Riley resides in Chicago, where she is hard at work on her next project. Please visit Ms. Riley at www.lisagriley.com.

MICHELLE J. ROBINSON is the mother of twelve-year-old identical-twin boys and resides in New York City. She studied journalism at New York University and is planning to attend film school in 2008. Her erotic short story "Mi Destino" is included in the *New York Times* bestseller *Caramel Flava*. Michelle is also a contributing author to the anthology collections *Succulent: Chocolate Flava II* with the story "The Quiet Room" and the forthcoming *Missionary No More: Purple Panties 2* with the story "Hailey's Orgasmic Splendor." She has recently completed work on four novels, *Color Me Grey, Pleasure Principle, Serial Typical,* and *You Created a Monster,* and is currently working on the screenplay adaptation of "Mi Destino." Michelle can be reached at Robinson_201@hotmail.com as well as on www.myspace.com/justef.

KISSA STARLING is new on the erotic-romance scene. She loves putting pen to paper and finds time to write each and every day. Her stories run from sweet to sizzling depending on her mood. When she isn't writing, Kissa is spending time with her family and numerous pets in Georgia. One of her favorite pastimes is reading mail. Feel free to email her at kissa_starling@yahoo .com.

JEAN YOUNG was born in China, but by now she has spent an equal amount of time in the States as in her native land. As a scientist, she is rational and logical, but as a person who loves music, art, and literature, she is full of passion and lust for life. Such affection and enthusiasm led her to publish a couple of short love stories. "The Meaning of *Zhuren*" is her only attempted erotica. This story came from a short relationship she had. Her ex-boyfriend's eccentric and powerful sexual appetite opened a mysterious and forbidden door to her. However, his coldness and aloofness eventually drove her away from his life. This bizarre experience only exists now in her distant memory and in this story.

ZANE is the *New York Times* bestselling author of more than ten titles; the publisher of Strebor Books, an imprint of Atria Books/Simon & Schuster; and executive producer of numerous films and television shows. You can visit her on the Web at www .eroticanoir.com.